WASN'T THE FUTURE
WONDERFUL?

A View of Trends and
Technology from the 1930s
Tim Onosko

WASN'T THE FUTURE WONDERFUL?

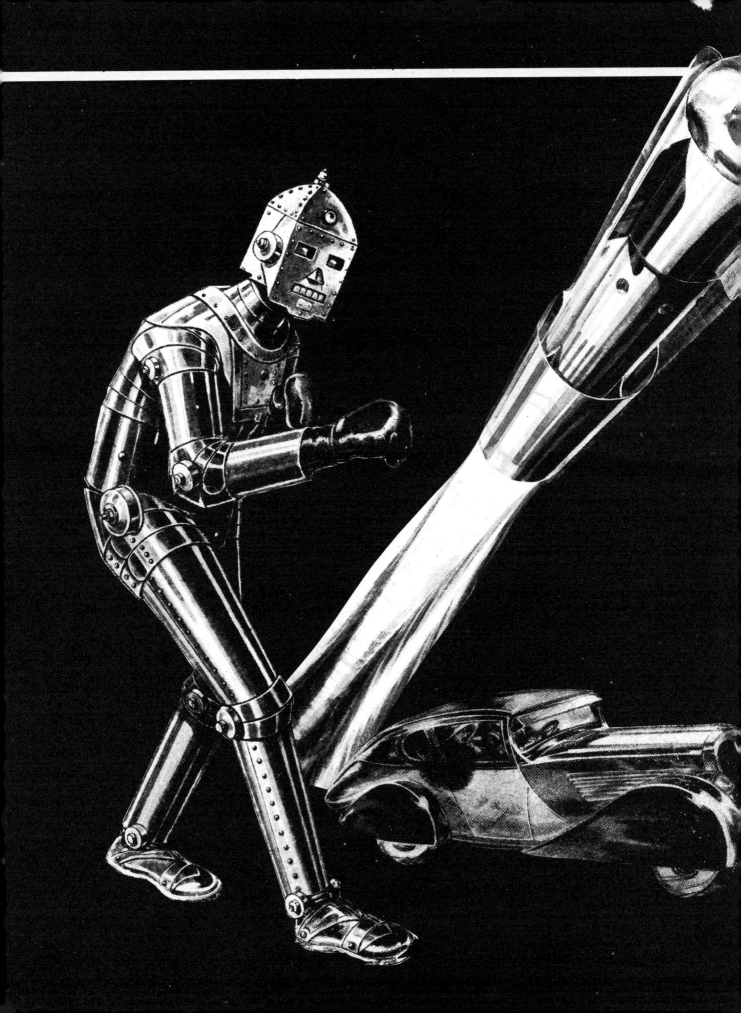

WASN'T THE FUTURE WONDERFUL?

A View of Trends and Technology From the 1930s

Tim
Onosko

A Dutton Paperback E.P. DUTTON · NEW YORK

For information contact:
E.P. Dutton, 2 Park Avenue, New York, N.Y. 10016

Library of Congress Cataloging in Publication Data
Onosko, Tim.
   Wasn't the future wonderful?
    1.   Twentieth century—Forecasts.
2. Technology and civilization. I. Title.
CB425.056 1979   909.82   78-11834
ISBN: 0-525-47551-6

Published simultaneously in Canada by
Clarke, Irwin & Company Limited, Toronto and Vancouver

Designed by Nicola Mazzella

10 9 8 7 6 5 4 3 2 1

First Edition

Introduction

"We enter a new era," wrote designer and architect Norman Bel Geddes in *Horizons* (1932). "Are we ready for the changes that are coming? The houses that we live in tomorrow will not much resemble the houses we live in today. Automobiles, railway trains, theaters, cities, industry itself are undergoing rapid changes."

Bel Geddes was foresighted in noting that "in the perspective of fifty years hence, the historian will detect in the decade 1930–1940 a period of tremendous significance . . . when new aims were being sought and new beginnings were astir. Doubtless he will ponder that, in the midst of a worldwide melancholy owing to an economic depression, a new age dawned with invigorating conceptions and the horizon lifted."

Finally, as if offering an ultimatum, Bel Geddes wrote: "Now is the time, for the world is changing, and the fellows on top when the smoke clears, will be those who changed with it."

Just as evolutionists debate the question of at what point, and for what reason, man became capable of higher thought, historians will continue to ask why the future became a real and attractive commodity during the decade of the 1930s. The world's fairs of 1933 and 1939 are most often cited as the events that turned public attention to the new visual styles and technologies of the decade, but Bel Geddes' book was written prior to the first of these. It can also be said that the forecasts put forth at the 1939 fair (a milestone to futurists) were little more than a compilation and distillation of those that had appeared for a decade in the pages of Sunday supplements, in the halls of industry, and, more importantly, in the "popular science" magazines, *Popular Mechanics, Popular Science,* and *Modern Mechanix.*

This book offers selections from the visions of that decade and its future, put forth by those magazines—the style, the attitudes of their writers and editors, and the forecasts. It should be obvious, from glancing at the reproduced pages, that this was a past whose imagination was vivid and a future that never happened. In fact, if these visions were not so detailed, it would be easy to dismiss all this as the ravings of crackpots from a desperate age.

Of course, this future was not defined solely by the pages of these magazines. The future movement of the 1930s was composed of many talents—from architects and designers, to engineers and scientists, to politicians. Some of the thoughts of the period are still highly regarded, and others are occasionally reconsidered. The influence of the science fiction authors, whose work found wide public acceptance during the 1930s, cannot be dismissed, nor can the political futurism of the Technocrats, which opened the door for the marriage of sociology and technology.

Looking at the literature of the Depression—particularly the periodicals—it is impossible to find a single source better than these magazines for an overview of that future. The same ideas that appeared in their pages may have been discussed more elaborately or eloquently elsewhere, but these magazines were the public forum and a miniature exposition for the trends of the times.

To put this book in perspective, a bit of background on futurism is helpful. It should be remembered that there were elements of this future that might have made it an interesting one.

A History of the Future

Prior to the nineteenth century, there was relatively little serious speculation regarding the technological future. Early important futures novels, such as Samuel Butler's *Erewhon,* tended to be satirical fantasies about the future of man and his society.

A debate continues among science fiction fans and scholars over the importance of the works of Jules Verne. The relative merits or demerits of Verne's writings, however, cannot detract from the author's importance in the establishment of a popular market for scientific writing. *In the Year 2889,* a Verne novel far less popular than *From the Earth to the Moon* or *Twenty Thousand Leagues Under the Sea,* is important to the concept of past futures. Unlike its predecessors, this book was originally published in an American magazine (the *Forum*) in the English language. It dealt with the future of America, one thousand years from the date of the book's publication.

(Though Edward Bellamy's *Looking Backward* was published a year earlier, that book must be considered primarily political in its theme, rather than futuristic.)

H. G. Wells continued to expand the popularity of science writing with his short stories and novellas, the first of which was *The Time Machine,* published in 1895. (The earliest version of this Wells story, though, appeared in 1888.) Again, there remains a debate over the "scientific" preferability of Wells over Verne, which began with a series of published clashes between the authors themselves.

Present critical opinions seem to give Wells the edge over Verne in the areas of technological speculation and forecasts. Verne, though, is generally given credit for being more adventure-oriented and possessing a sharper sense of wonder. Wells brought popular science fiction into the twentieth century, not just in terms of time, but in tone as well.

Popular Science Monthly was founded in 1872 by Edward L. Youmans, a staff editor for D. Appleton & Co., publishers of *Appleton's Journal.* Youmans originally intended the *Journal* to include features on scientific developments. The magazine's readership, however, preferred its fiction features, like the serial publication of Victor Hugo's *The Man Who Laughs.* When Youmans created *Popular Science,* though, it was "popular" only in the Victorian sense. Its presentation of new topics, such as sociology, electricity, and evolution, were directed toward an audience of educated gentlemen, rather than the masses.

A change in *Popular Science*'s ownership, in the mid-teens of the twentieth century, brought changes to the magazine's format, as well, which made it more faithful to its title. Further changes were prompted by competition from magazines with more enthusiasm for technology, and more imagination.

In 1909, Hugo Gernsback, who left his native Luxembourg in 1884 and came to America to continue his electrical research, began publishing *Modern Electronics,* a periodical that became the first important, popular nonfiction scientific publication and the harbinger of the popular science magazines that would follow.

Though Gernsback's publishing history began with the factual *Modern Electronics,* he soon became more highly regarded for his science fiction publications and frequently intermixed fact with fiction. For instance, after he had established himself as an inventor (with the introduction of a popular, low-cost wireless telegraph), an entrepreneur (he imported and distributed European electrical gadgets), and a magazine publisher, Gernsback began to write science fiction. His first story, *Ralph 124C 41+,* was published in *Modern Electronics.* Despite the relatively low quality of Gernsback's prose, the piece is generally considered to be the first pure example of modern science fiction.

(One earlier, odder blend of fact and fiction was Garrett Serviss's *Edison's Conquest of Mars* (1896), which depicts the inventor as leading a team of scientists to Mars, supposedly to retaliate for the damage done in Wells's *War of the Worlds.*)

In 1913, Gernsback changed the name of his magazine to *Electrical Experimenter;* then, finally, to *Science and Inventions,* in 1920. Both titles regularly interspersed fiction works with fact-based features, and in 1923, Gernsback began publishing an annual "scientific fiction" issue. Later the titles in Gernsback's publishing enterprise included *Wonder Stories, Science Wonder Stories, Air Wonder Stories,* and *Amazing Stories,* all of which were fiction magazines.

Before the focus of his activities had shifted, however, Gernsback established the look and feel of the popular scientific magazines. He realized that the public had gleefully met the technical achievements of the early part of the century and sought more technological news. To illustrate *Electrical Experimenter* and its subsequent versions, Gernsback retained the services of Frank Paul, an architect and technical illustrator whose style became the standard for both the popular scientific and science fiction genres.

Paul's own crossover between Gernsback's fiction and nonfiction publications began the trend of using fiction artists and illustrators to portray fact-based technological forecasts.

Although there are hundreds of other references that can be cited as important to early futurism, this short chain brings the popular aspect of futurism to its first great period of acceptance.

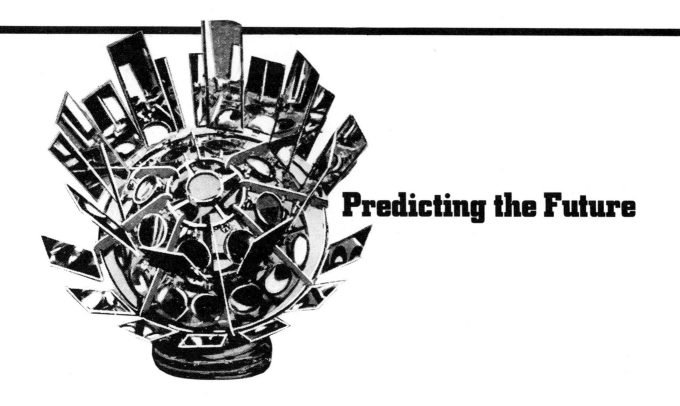

Predicting the Future

Some of the predictions and proposals in this book seem quite absurd today, from a distance of some forty years. But instead of blaming the lack of skill with which they were made, perhaps we should applaud the active imaginations that made them. The desperation of the age must have led to this "try anything" attitude. Arthur Schlesinger, Jr., in *Crisis of the Old Order* characterized this period: "Suspended between past and future, the nation drifted as on dark seas of unreality. It knew only a sense of premonition and change; but the shape of the future was as baffling as the memory of the past."

It is important to keep in mind that these predictions and proposals were positive ones, which reveled in the possibilities for the future, and their failures were innocent ones. This kind of raw enthusiasm over technology is seldom seen today. Futurism is now cautious and serious. Even the editors of today's popular scientific magazines admit that the embarrassments of past predictions have made them more careful about radically new ideas. (Some recent issues of these magazines, however, suggest the same liveliness in coming up with new energy schemes.)

Much more embarrassing, and less innocent in their intent, are the failures of negative predictions about the advance of technology. In *Profiles of the*

Future, a primer for today's futurists, Arthur C. Clarke categorizes these failures as two: Failures of Nerve (which occur when a negative forecast is made, despite all the relevant facts indicating otherwise) and Failures of Imagination (usually the result of not acknowledging the possibility of the existence of facts not yet discovered).

The classics of negative blunders are monumental ones. A 1967 report of the Congressional Research Service of the Library of Congress culled dozens of fine examples from negative forecasting's notorious past. The report, entitled *Erroneous Predictions and Negative Comments Concerning Exploration, Territorial Expansion, Scientific and Technological Development,* included these:

> As far as I can judge, I do not look upon any system of wireless telegraphy as a serious competitor with our cable lines. Some years ago, I said the same thing and nothing has since occurred to alter my views.
>
> —SIR JOHN WOLFE-BARRY,
> *at a meeting of the*
> *stockholders of the*
> *Western Telegraph*
> *Company, 1907*

> Subdivision of the electric light is an absolute *ignus fatuus.*
>
> —ARTHUR PEERCE,
> *Engineer-in-Chief of*
> *the British Post*
> *Office, 1878*

> Jupiter's moons are invisible to the naked eye, and therefore can have no influence on the earth, and therefore would be useless, and therefore do not exist.
>
> —*the pronouncement*
> *of a group of Aris-*
> *totelian contemporaries*
> *of Galileo, made*
> *following his discovery*

That Professor [Robert] Goddard with his "chair" at Clark College and the countenancing of the Smithsonian Institution does not know the relation of action and reaction, and the need to have something better than a vacuum against which to react—to say that would be absurd. Of course, he only seems to lack the knowledge ladled out daily in high schools.

—*the* New York Times
*in a 1921 editorial
criticizing the rocketry
research of Robert H.
Goddard*

The actual building of roads devoted to motor cars is not for the near future, in spite of the many rumors to that effect.

—Harpers Weekly
August 1902

This is the biggest fool thing we have ever done. . . . The bomb will never go off, and I speak as an expert in explosives.

—ADMIRAL WILLIAM
LEAHY, *in conversation
with President Harry
Truman, regarding
the atomic bomb, 1943*

And finally, as a few kind words for the entire field of scientific and mechanical invention:

The advancement of the arts from year to year taxes our credulity and seems to presage the arrival of that period when improvement must end.

—HENRY L. ELLSWORTH,
*U.S. Commissioner
of Patents, 1944*

Despite promises of an autogyro in every garage, mechanized homes, and robots, the positive predictions of the popular scientific magazines seem cheerful by comparison. Several omissions from the magazines can be cited as a bit more serious. Digital technology, for instance, was never mentioned, despite the existence of its principles, proved by Charles Babbage's "analytical engine" project of the early nineteenth century. (The key to automation, during the 1930s, was believed to be the photocell.) The advance of medicine and biological engineering was never mentioned in the magazines, and a familiar topic, aviation, never foresaw jet propulsion.

Today we are caught in a debate between antitechnologists (and "appropriate technologists") and those who welcome and anticipate new technology. Many futurists seem to feel that the antitechnologists are winning. There are no showcases for new technology, like the world's fairs of the 1930s, and the "back-to-the-earth" movements of the 1960s want to convince us that technology is unnecessary.

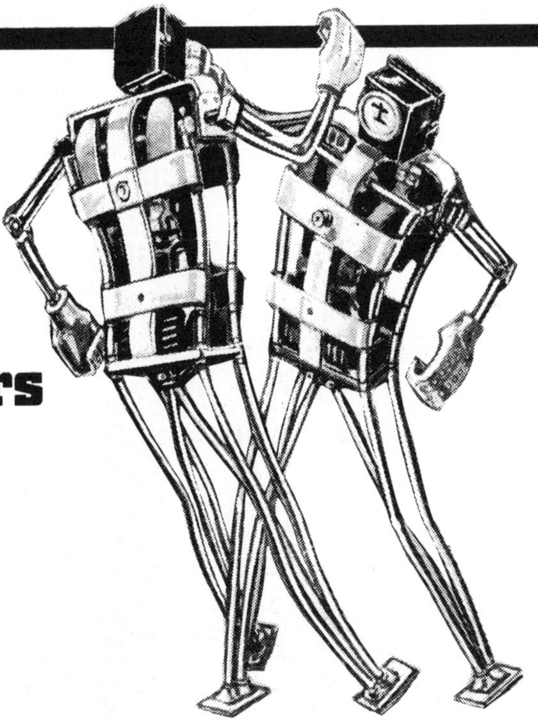

Modern Mechanix and Others

Most of the pages of this book are taken directly from issues of *Modern Mechanix* (née *Mechanics*), as published between 1930 and 1937. The reason for the heavy emphasis of this title over others is simple: *Modern Mechanix* was the most imaginative, liveliest, and best illustrated of its genre. *Popular Science* and *Popular Mechanics* relied more heavily on home-workshop and construction articles. Gernsback's *Science and Inventions* did not have as high-quality editorial matter and was sometimes too reliant on sound engineering principles that stymied its imagination.

With the exception of *Modern Mechanix,* the above magazines used their fanciful cover illustrations as sales gimmicks, rather than as accurate portrayals of what their interior pages were like. *Modern Mechanix* was different: It delivered the future.

The magazine was published by W. H. Fawcett, who achieved notoriety (and great wealth) as the publisher of the humor magazine, *Captain Billy's Whiz Bang.* Fawcett himself was Captain Billy after the commission he reportedly received in the World War I infantry. Likewise, his brother, Captain Roscoe, was a balloonist in the same conflict.

Both men retained their titles, as well as their senses of adventure, after

The Fawcett brothers—Captain Billy, left, and Captain Roscoe, right—with boxer Jack Dempsey. Dempsey is holding a copy of *Screen Play Secrets,* another Fawcett magazine title. (*Photograph courtesy Norman Saunders*)

Cover illustrator Norman Saunders at work on an imaginative "Biplane-Tank" cover for *Modern Mechanix*, 1931. (*Photograph courtesy Norman Saunders*)

the war was over. Captain Billy had a personal reputation as a soldier of fortune; Captain Roscoe was a dilettante on the outer edges of emerging technology. (In early issues of their magazine, the brothers' credentials were strongly and frequently stated.)

Artist Norman Saunders was a staff illustrator and cover designer for *Modern Mechanix*. Other artists who contributed to the magazine's unique appearance included Stewart Rouse (early, pastellike covers), Douglas Rolfe (interiors and aviation art), and George Rozen (whose bold, carefully composed covers were some of the most attractive in the magazine's history).

Saunders began working for the Fawcetts as a free-lance contributor of cartoons for the *Whiz Bang,* which was published in Minneapolis, close to his hometown of Rosseau, Minnesota. At the time (1928), Fawcett was buying illustrations for ten or twenty dollars, and Saunders thought this pay adequate while he was attending the school of the Chicago Art Institute. Soon, however, he became the magazine's full-time art staffer and took a front-row seat to watch the development of *Modern Mechanix.*

Saunders remembers the major editorial influence at the magazine as coming from Weston Farmer, whom he credits with suggesting to the Fawcetts the idea of publishing such a magazine. Although Farmer was probably the most influential member of the staff, he disdained credit and is variously listed as "technical editor," "consulting editor," and "naval architect and light plane designer." This last title could usually be found under a headline on the contents page that proclaimed the magazine was "published by experts" and listed a dozen or more other names with similarly impressive credentials.

Saunders recalls the colorful depictions of new technical developments or proposals: "Westy [Farmer] would get something from the *Sunday Times,* or someplace—an invention or something—and he'd bring it to me without an illustration and we'd work it out. He was an impressive man with the looks of John Gilbert, the film star, and a firm grasp of the technical aspects of things."

Saunders remembers Farmer as sensing the public's infatuation with things technical and fantastic, and credits him with the direction the magazine took as it entered the 1930s. The success of this approach and Captain Billy's interest in a new idea (and making money) led also to a one-shot magazine in 1933.

The Technocrats' Magazine, published by the Fawcetts (without credits for either editor or publisher), is a remarkable piece of exploitation publishing. Technocracy was a radical movement that first caught press attention in 1932 and purported to believe in a master plan to resurrect the economy and society. The Technocrats' plan embraced new technology, and its economic system was based on energy resources and equipment, rather than commodities. (So thorough was their scheme, that one aspect of it would have replaced standard denominations of currency with new units—ergs and dynes!) The Technocrats claimed that the United States could attain a sound and prosperous economy with its labor force working approximately thirteen hours per week per man.

Technocrat leader Howard Scott was recruited to write an introduction to the magazine, explaining Technocracy in broad terms. Around less than a full page of text, the Fawcett staff then assembled the remainder of the publication, using newly created, suitably prophetic text, with photos and illustrations from *Modern Mechanix.* Some of the chapter titles were: "The Bloodless Revolution," "The Price System Doomed?," and "Secret Inventions Which Could Ruin Industry." The staff took Technocracy, which had enjoyed some degree of respectability, and reduced it to the level of another *Modern Mechanix* item.

Weston Farmer immediately sensed the differences between *Modern Me-*

15 CENTS

The Technocrats' Magazine

THIRTY MILLION
OUT OF WORK
IN 1933—
        OR
$20,000 A YEAR
INCOME FOR
EVERY
FAMILY—
    WHICH?

EXPLAINING TECHNOCRACY
A REVOLUTION WITHOUT BLOODSHED

chanix and his competitors. "I wanted to have things in it that interested me," he now says, ". . . round-the-world cruisers and aviation. The future? It was something everybody was talking about and thinking about. I had Jean Picard and his balloons in the magazine, and I bought one of the first articles by Robert Goddard, the rocket man. I bought it and paid twenty-five dollars for it! We were trying to be different than *Popular Mechanics* because they were very staid. And *Popular Science* went down into the classroom for their material."

The fondest recollections, though, are for the time he was with the magazine: "It was a yeasty time for technology. We were only seven or eight years from the proposition of airplanes as weapons of war. Electricity was coming along. Radio was only six years old when we started the magazine. Engineers could project about certain things. I wasn't always right, that's for certain. But it made good drama."

Farmer left the magazine twice before it moved its editorial offices to New York. One temporary leave was halted by the Fawcetts' invitation to publish Farmer's personal favorite project, the "mechanical package magazine." Only a handful of issues of this magazine were actually published. Each one included the critical parts necessary for a simple mechanical project—a steam engine, a telegraph key, or an electric motor. After a financial dispute with the Fawcetts, though, Farmer left permanently and, among other things, went to work with Walt Disney on the development of new mechanical techniques for films.

In 1938, *Modern Mechanix* changed its name to *Mechanix Illustrated* (as it is still known), and its editorial stance changed as well. Editor Robert Hertzberg sensed the changing tastes of its readership, as signaled by the final months of the Depression. Soon after, the masthead included the name of Fawcett's son, Bud, as the new publisher, and the magazine took on a less fanciful, more practical tone that appealed chiefly to young boys. (Example: The 1939 November issue carried a cover photograph of Mickey Rooney with a model airplane, for which plans were included inside.)

At the end of a decade-long love affair with technology and its possibilities, *Modern Mechanix* became more interested in model cars, movie star pilots, and the mechanics of the Ice Capades, and left speculation about the future to others.

WASN'T THE FUTURE WONDERFUL?

Is Man Doomed by the

by BENNETT LINCOLN

View of an automatic telephone installation, a mechanical development which put thousands of "hello girls" out of jobs.

With thousands of men unemployed, many of them because machines have forced them out of their jobs, the old cry that man has created a Machine Age which will destroy him has been taken up again. Which is the true picture—is the Machine a destructive monster, or a means to leisure and wealth? Is our civilization doomed to destruction because of our dependence on machines? Read the opinions of eminent scientists and industrial leaders in this article.

EVER since the invention of the steam engine by James Watt in 1769—a date commonly accepted as marking the beginning of our present Mechanical Age of civilization—there have been two schools of thought regarding the Machine: one maintaining, with varying degrees of vehemence, that machines are works of Satan which will sooner or later engulf and destroy civilization; the other seeing in the mechanical age man's greatest hope for leisure and universal wealth.

As far as numbers go, those whose attitude toward the Machine Age is friendly are in the majority. Few of us, indeed, could conceive of living in an age or a country where there were no automobiles, or where power and light did not flow at the touch of an electric switch. Yet the present era of industrial depression, with millions of men thrown out of work—as some maintain, because machines have taken their places, working swifter and cheaper—has seen a renewal of the outcry against machinery. This protest was familiar to Arkwright, inventor of the spinning jenny, when his machine in 1769 began to put hand manufacturers of fabrics out of business; and familiar, too, to the engineers of the first locomotives who piloted their crude iron horses before the jeering

MACHINE AGE?

Symbol of the Mechanical Age is the Robot, the iron man — Slave or Master?

eyes of skeptics who held that the steam monsters were a violation of the laws of God, man, and common decency.

Well, where are we heading? Will machines, sooner or later, destroy civilization by putting all men out of work and concentrating wealth in the hands of a few? It is only fair to point out that machines create new jobs as well as destroying old ones.

Take the example of the radio. This invention has been with us ten years. During that time half the homes in America have been equipped with receiving sets, and the building of these millions of receivers has employed thousands of men and women. This is the pleasant side of the picture. Now let's look on the other side. The business of manufacturing and selling pianos, and, to a lesser extent, other musical instruments, has confessedly slumped. It is usual to charge this slump to the radio and other forms of mechanical music, which have supplied the need for music in the home. Business fell off alarmingly for talking machine manufacturers until they, too, started turning out radios, either alone or in combination with their standard product.

The obvious answer is that the invention of a new machine may throw out of work men in a particular job, but at the same time the

A play recently presented in New York depicts mankind, as represented in a man and a woman, hopelessly enmeshed in a tangle of machinery which eventually destroys them. This is typical of a current attitude toward the Mechanical Age. A scene from the play is shown above.

Machines of war have become fearfully efficient. This photo of battleships on the Hudson was taken from the mighty dirigible Los Angeles.

Symbolic of the possibilities of destruction inherent in the Mechanical Age is this 70 m.p.h. tank.

machine itself creates new jobs. The automobile, and industries depending on it, employs upwards of 4,000,000 men and women. The automobile put out of business a few thousand proprietors of livery stables, but no one nowadays has the temerity to charge this against the industry.

Let's see what opinions scientists and industrial leaders close to the public pulse have expressed on this consuming subject.

Joseph N. Weber, president of the American Federation of Musicians, is the leader of a campaign in which more than $500,000 was spent last year to stem the advance of "Robot Music". Magazine advertisements reaching thousands of people appealed to the public to oppose itself to the advance of mechanical music in the theatres. But the musical robots came marching down until today there is hardly a theatre in the country which is not equipped for sound effects for talkies.

Behind this campaign lies the distress of thousands of musicians put out of work by the talkies.

"The time is coming fast," said Mr. Weber, "when the only living thing around a motion picture house will be the person who sells you your ticket. Everything else will be mechanical. Canned drama, canned music, canned vaudeville. We think the public will tire of mechanical music and will want the real thing. We are not against scientific development of any kind, but it must not come at the expense of art. We are not opposing industrial progress. We are not even opposing mechanical music except where it is used as a profiteering instrument for artistic debasement."

Edward C. Rybicki, director of the New York City Free Employment Bureau, comes as closely in contact with unemployment as any other man in the country.

"Man has suddenly found himself swallowed up in a huge whirlpool of swift industrial and mechanical development," says Mr. Rybicki. "I would venture to say that four-fifths of the 500,000 men who are out of jobs in New York City find themselves in that plight because they have outlived their usefulness. Because new industries have sprung up with a new generation, leaving them to drift in decrepit and dying industries."

Dr. Lee de Forest, famous radio inventor, foresees an era of prosperity made possible by machines.

"Radio manufacturers," says Dr. de Forest, "are working on low power tubes and loud speakers for battery operation, which will give the unelectrified home reception comparable to that enjoyed by city dwellers. The use of such sets will create a market for 6,000,000 radios.

"Another forthcoming development in radio is the perfection of the pentode tube,

This maze of electrical equipment is used in making sound pictures which have put thousands of musicians out of work, replacing theater orchestras.

a British invention, to do away with the three tubes now used in audio-frequency circuits. American firms are now experimenting with that particular tube.

"Television will not be on the market this year and perhaps not for some time to come. Radio control of warships, airplanes, and tanks is also a long way in the future." But some day, it is safe to predict, television sets will become common—and when they do the manufacture of them will give work to thousands of men.

During 1930, which has gone down in the books of time as an Industrial Dark Age, a new business grew up and flourished almost overnight. This was the miniature golf course industry. It became a business in which more than $125,000,000 was invested, and it's still going strong. This stands as an example of the ability of a new invention to create new wealth.

Walter S. Gifford, president of the American Telephone and Telegraph Company, looks toward a future all the brighter because of machines and scientific develop-

Joseph N. Weber, president of the American Federation of Musicians, is leader of a magazine advertising campaign to educate the public to demand real orchestras in theatres, rather than "canned" music stigmatized by the Robot serenader.

Miniature golf stands as an example of how invention can create new jobs, new wealth. Over $125,000,000 was invested in these courses in less than a year. The above photo shows a typical layout.

ment. In passing, it may be remarked that Mr. Gifford's company is one of the largest employers of labor in the United States, and that this corporation is built up around a simple machine—the telephone.

"This depression will soon pass," Mr. Gifford has said, "and we are about to enter a period of prosperity the like of which no country has ever seen before. It is inevitable that business through science will work toward a social and industrial Utopia which will be gained by the perfection of the best and cheapest possible service consistent with financial safety."

Quite a different attitude is held by John Van Nostrand Dorr, famous engineer and former associate of Thomas A. Edison.

"We will eventually become lost in the multiplicity of things which sustain or amuse us unless we do more than invent things or processes," declares Mr. Dorr. "As a result, engineering might fulfill its proper purposes of meeting the simpler needs of men while, progressively, taking back from him the burden of labor, mechanics, physics, and chemistry should be made to serve art, music, philosophy, and literature by some such means."

Germany is coming into post-war prominence as a giant laboratory wherein the mechanical age finds its freest expression. She has produced the world's largest seaplanes, has led the world in constructing dirigible airships, and has produced inventions capable of altering the economic structure of vast industries. A case in point is the hydrogenation of oil by a German process, in which a gallon of crude oil is made to produce practically a gallon of gasoline, through the addition of hydrogen atoms, Usual methods now in use produce about half a gallon of gasoline from one gallon of oil. Here's an instance where factories may be built and men employed to carry out this new manufacturing process.

Over-production is, of course, the charge currently hurled against the Machine. That the world has at present a surplus stock of goods, from wheat to steel, is admitted. But the difficulty lies in the fact that the machine has given man leisure which he doesn't know how to dispose of. Not being able to employ his leisure to advantage, he goes on working at top speed, and his machines, which are after all under his control, are charged with over-production.

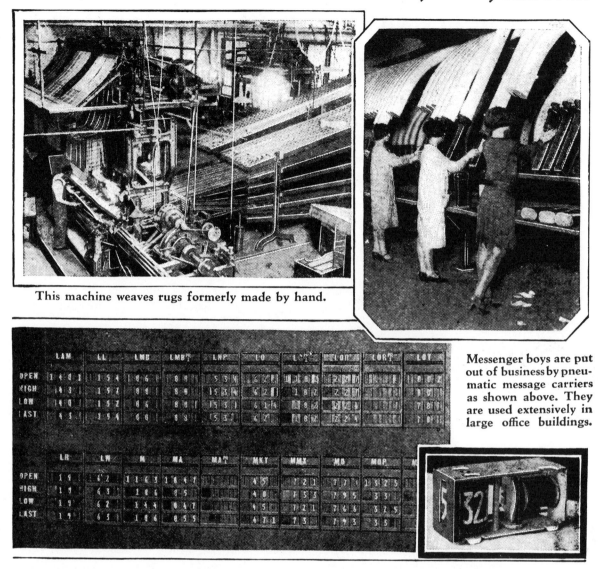

This machine weaves rugs formerly made by hand.

Messenger boys are put out of business by pneumatic message carriers as shown above. They are used extensively in large office buildings.

Stock market quotations are posted mechanically on the above board. The small photo at the right shows a unit of the machine. Men who formerly chalked up the figures lost their jobs, of course.

To remedy this, labor leaders have proposed a six-hour working day. In six hours the factory workman produces more goods, with the aid of his machine, than his fellow workman a hundred years ago could produce in a week.

The intricate construction of our modern industrial fabric can best be understood if one traces the uses to which a raw product is put, and observes the influence of machines in creating wealth from it. Machines, after all, have little to do with the overproduction of basic commodities such as wheat, which, although harvested largely by machines in this country, can trace its overproduction to countries such as Russia where the mechanical age has hardly begun.

Take cotton as an example. Formerly it was used almost exclusively as a fabric for clothing. Today more cotton is used in the manufacture of automobile tires than in the making of men's shirts. Can a grower of cotton, then, declaim against the machine age, which furnishes him with an outlet for his product which, if it did not exist, would force him to accept ruinous prices?

Civilization, unquestionably, has adjustments to make before it is entirely in tune with the age. But with inventive young Americans turning out new devices every day, creating new industries and outmoding old ones, it would seem safe to predict that both civilization and the machine will survive, and that it will be outdated conceptions of how industry should be run that will pass into the discard.

Wanted—Ten Billion-

by RAYMOND FRANCIS YATES

What are the inventions of tomorrow which will be worth billions of dollars to industry? Mr. Yates, member of the Institute of Radio Engineers and well-known writer on scientific subjects, here describes ten billion-dollar ideas. It will be interesting to make your own list and compare it with that of Mr. Yates.

THERE is at hand a new day of big rewards for inventors; rewards larger than dared to be dreamed of years ago. America is particularly anxious to stimulate its genius by the payment of huge sums of money to those who can solve the industrial problems that many of our large manufacturers are now facing. It has been said that competition is life of trade; it is more than that, it is the life of invention too. It has caused many of our great industries to establish their own laboratories in an attempt to better their products and widen their markets.

America needs more inventions today than it ever needed before and thousands of professional inventors have been hired to find these new things; these market builders. However, this, contrary to current opinion, does not mean that the independent inventor is no longer a factor or that his efforts are no longer needed. The

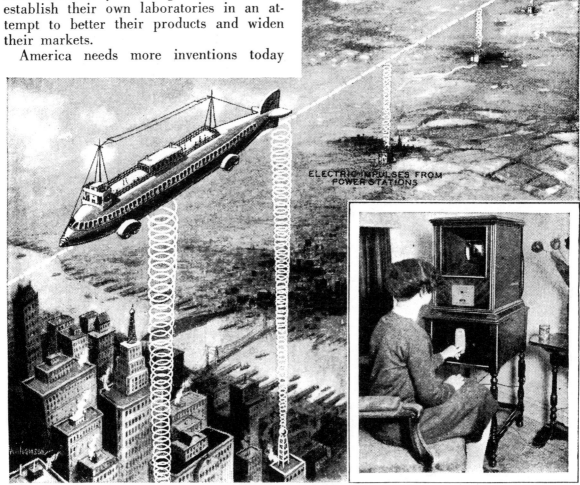

Electro-magnetic levitation, in which passenger cars are supported above the earth by electric impulses, is a billion-dollar transportation idea. Perfection of television likewise falls into the billion-dollar class.

Dollar INVENTIONS

At right above is Dr. Bruno Lange, German scientist who has succeeded in producing current from sunlight, in the manner diagrammed below.

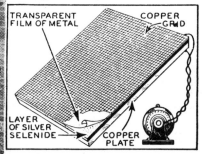

TRANSPARENT FILM OF METAL

COPPER GRID

LAYER OF SILVER SELENIDE

COPPER PLATE

Two metal plates, separated by a layer of silver selenide, produce an electric current when exposed to the heat of the sun.

The direct conversion of heat into electric energy will be worth a billion dollars to industry. With the perfection of this idea, it would be possible to turn the heat of the sun into electric current—a feat which is possible today, but not practical commercially.

records of the patent office prove quite the opposite. Manufacturers want ideas and they don't care where they come from. The fact that many of them have established their own laboratories just goes to show how tightly pressed they have been; how keenly they feel the onslaught of competition.

A short time ago the writer sat in the lounge room of a club. Two chemists, an electrical engineer, a mechanical engineer and a business man were present. The conversation drifted to invention and research and the business man finally asked those present to name what they thought were the outstanding problems of the day; to name what he was pleased to call "ten one-billion dollar ideas". At first there was some dissension but as the conversation wore on, agreement was at last reached and ten problems really in the billion-dollar class were laid down. It was not thought that inventors would receive this amount for their ideas. Rather, it was merely believed that the successful solution of the problems would be worth a billion dollars each to the industry to which they were related.

The first problem discussed had to do

A method of controlling rain scientifically would be worth countless billions to farmers, to property owners in the prevention of cloudbursts, and to railroad companies in the elimination of snowstorm tieups.

with a new source of power. Atomic energy was ruled out as being visionary and at present utterly beyond control, even if it could be produced. Also a substitute for gasoline was ruled out. Such substitutes are known but they have not as yet destroyed our gasoline markets nor do they jeopardize the millions that our gasoline manufacturers have invested in their refineries. It was decided, however, that electricity offers the most convenient, the most reliable and the most flexible means of power. What is needed is a cheap and effective means of storing large quantities of electricity in small light weight containers. Let us assume that a storage battery of new type is invented that will deliver a power of 25 horses for a period of 48 hours. What would this mean to transportation? What would this mean eventually to our gasoline market? In place of taking on ten gallons of gasoline at the gas station, we would simply take on a new container of electricity. During the night, when the service load on the public utility mains was relieved, current could be used to recharge such containers. Even such great water falls as Niagara might be "turned off" during the night and the power generated (some 7,000,000 horsepower) be used in this manner.

The electric automobile would be the ideal. Silent, fast and with a flexibility that can never be hoped to be reached in the gas car. Not only that, but it would be free of gas and it would require only an insignificant percentage of the lubrication needed for the gas machine. Surely that would be a billion dollar idea, and conservatively rated at that.

The discussion of this idea suggested the second billion dollar invention; the direct conversion of the heat from coal and other fuels into electric energy. At the present time, we burn coal, produce steam and permit the steam to expand in either a turbine or a steam engine. This is a very wasteful process and one that costs us many billions of dollars annually. It has been known for many years that when two dissimilar metals are brought together and heated at the points of their conjuncture, a small electric current is produced. On this principle a thermo-electric battery has been produced, but what we need is a thermo-electric generator of large size where the heat produced by the burning coal will be directly converted into electricity. By this process, at least fifty per cent more energy could be derived from the same amount of coal. And this aside from the advantage of junking almost half of the equipment now needed to produce power. To say that this is a billion-dollar idea is surely leaning toward conservatism.

A flying machine that will be able to operate vertically and horizontally is a much needed idea. True, we have the helicopter, but in its present form it by no means offers a solution to the problem. It is really a makeshift and but a passing fancy of designers. It can never endure. It is simply an airplane with two propellers.

When problems of invention and research are discussed, there always appears that old but none the less interesting sub-

A method of storing electrical energy is needed, so efficient that instead of gasoline motorists can use batteries.

A boon to the farmer would be a cheap nitrogen fixer for producing fertilizer from the air.

ject of light without heat. It was brought out for discussion on this particular occasion and it was decided to include it. Not only that but it was decided that we are getting dangerously close to its solution. The last year has seen the development of gas-filled lamps that offer a great deal of promise in supplying perfectly white light at very low cost. This new filamentless bulb has come as a result of researches into the conduction of electricity through gases. It is a billion-dollar idea but it has by no means been perfectly commercialized and it still awaits those final touches by some genius who is bound to receive a handsome reward for his efforts. Indeed, there is an odd race going on in this field of cold light research. Another

and highly revolutionary idea is that of painting the walls of a room with a luminous paint which is first "charged" with light and which continues to glow for hours after the charge has been received.

And then we might consider the elimination of static in radio as a problem of the first order. This is especially so since the advent of television, for it is obvious that static is going to interfere more with television than it has with voice radio. Imperfections are more discernible to the sight than to the hearing. It is no secret that a number of our very large electrical manufacturers are now ready and willing to pay one million dollars in cold cash to the man who can solve this ugly problem. Its solution will mean many billion of dollars to the radio industry in the years immediately ahead of it.

Harnessing the Power

Lowering one of the water pipes for the Claude power project in the sea off Matanzas, Cuba.

TEMPERATURE OF WATER AT SURFACE

80°

70°

60°

DEEP OCEAN WATER IS 30° COOLER THAN THAT AT SURFACE

50°

FLOATS

COLD WATER PIPE

When coal mines are exhausted, where is industry to obtain the power to keep its wheels turning? What sources of power are now lying dormant, waiting for some engineering genius to harness them? This important subject, of ever-present interest to scientist and layman, is fascinatingly discussed in this authoritative article.

DR. Georges Claude, brilliant French inventor, recently expended a million dollars and, after two unsuccessful attempts, succeeded in launching a mile long steel tube, some six feet in diameter, in the waters of the sea off Matanzas, Cuba. And most of the world is still wondering what he is trying to do.

The briefest answer is that Dr. Claude, who is best known in this country as the inventor of the neon lamp and sign, is attempting to harness the power of the sun.

Seems strange to go down under the sea to capture the power of the sun, but if he succeeds in doing on a large scale what he has already demonstrated in a small way

he may soon be generating enough power to run all Cuba, with a surplus to be exported by way of an undersea cable to Florida.

The sun heats the surface ocean water in the tropics to temperatures as high as 28 degrees, Centigrade, while 400 meters down the sea is as cold as 4 degrees, Centigrade. If the two bodies at different temperatures could be brought together water could be boiled, in a partial vacuum, producing power equivalent to a 300-foot waterfall.

In demonstrations before the Havana Academy of Science last year Dr. Claude showed that with the difference in temperature between ice at melting point and water

of the SUN

AIR PUMP UTILIZES VACUUM
FROM CONDENSER

WARM WATER BOILS
IN STEAM GENERATOR
IN PARTIAL VACUUM

DE-GASSING
TANK

DE-GASSING TANK
REMOVES GASES
DISSOLVED IN THE
SEA WATER

PUMP

WARM WATER
PIPE

COLD WATER CONDENSES
STEAM-LOWERING PRESSURE
IN STEAM GENERATOR

STEAM RUNS TURBINE AND
ELECTRIC GENERATOR

Prof. Claude, best known in America for his invention of the neon sign, is shown at left above demonstrating a model of his power apparatus.

at 68 degrees Fahrenheit—a difference of 36 degrees, sufficient vapor was released to run a small turbine at 5,000 r.p.m.

Following the launching of the tube Prof Claude announced that 4,000 cubic meters of deep sea water was being obtained each hour, at a temperature of 13 degrees Centigrade. The actual temperature at the lower end of the tube, 650 meters below the surface, was $10\frac{1}{2}$ degrees, so there was a tem-

The project of Prof. Georges Claude, French scientist, to obtain power from the warm waters of tropic seas, is one of the most ambitious yet advanced, and is scientifically sound. As shown above, warm surface water, at a temperature of 80 degrees, is pumped through a de-gassing tank into a steam generator in which a vacuum exists, causing the warm water to boil. Steam thus generated runs a turbine and electric generator, and passing on is condensed by cold water pumped from the sea bottom. In condensing, a partial vacuum is created which runs an air pump which lowers the pressure inside the steam generator. The process is thus self-sustaining.

perature rise of only one and a half degrees as the cold water was brought up through the warmer layers above.

In his power plant there is a huge tank filled with warm surface water. When the air in the tank is exhausted the water boils and provides the steam to operate the turbine driving the generator. The purpose of the cold water brought from the depths of the sea is simply to cool the exhaust steam at a rapid rate and so provide the vacuum to operate the air pump, which in turn exhausts the air from the warm water tank, and so converts the process into an endless chain.

The present plant, with a 50 kilowatt generator, is only an experimental affair, and, if successful, probably will be abandoned in favor of a much larger one located at some other spot in Cuba.

Sun motors, usually huge collections of mirrors set to capture the sun's rays over an area of many hundred square feet and focus them on a small spot, are not new. Such motors are working in California and in the

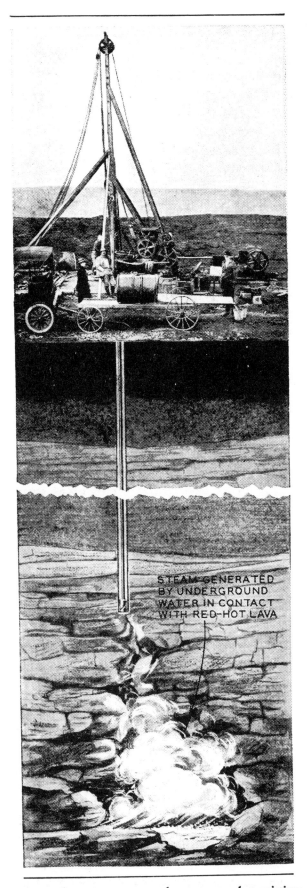

STEAM GENERATED
BY UNDERGROUND
WATER IN CONTACT
WITH RED-HOT LAVA

An early attempt to tap the steam pocket existing in the volcano Mauna Loa in Hawaii is depicted above. Inadequacy of drilling equipment caused the effort to be abandoned.

Sahara. But Dr. Claude's plan to trap the heat of the sun indirectly is the most ambitious sun power scheme ever conceived.

The sun motor can produce, in any of its present forms, only a fairly limited amount of power because the expanse of mirrors soon becomes too unwieldy to be moved and kept in focus, and the energy that may be trapped is limited to the amount of sun heat falling on a limited area during the hours of sunshine.

But with Dr. Claude's scheme power can be produced by night as well as by day, on cloudy days, and with no limitation on the total energy trapped. The surface water of the tropical sea does not cool enough on cloudy days or at night to make any great difference in the temperature spread between surface and the depths—even a drop of ten or fifteen degrees at the surface would still leave sufficient difference to work the thermal motor.

While a million, two hundred thousand dollars was spent on developing the plan and building the three tubes, the cost of a single tube is not particularly heavy. The one successfully launched cost $80,000 to build. If the plan works the cost of tubes would be much less than that of dams and penstocks for ordinary hydraulic power plants.

The search for new sources of power is one of the most absorbing of scientific hunts. The dream of releasing the latent energy in the atom—energy sufficient to make one drop of water drive a liner across the ocean—is still far in the distance, but there are other sources of power which are being tapped.

In California and Italy steam from volcanic vents, or fumeroles, is being used to run machinery. In Iceland the natives are piping the hot geyser springs to heat their homes. An adaption of the Claude plan might be used there to combine the heat of the geysers with the ice water from nearby glaciers and produce an abundance of cheap power.

The world's greatest reservoir of natural volcanic energy is owned by the United States, but probably never will be harnessed. For it is situated in the Valley of Ten Thousand Smokes, far out in the Aleutian islands, off Alaska, where literally thousands of fumeroles give off hot gases and boiling water the year around.

The earth offers an inexhaustible supply of power, if it can be tapped. A shaft a few

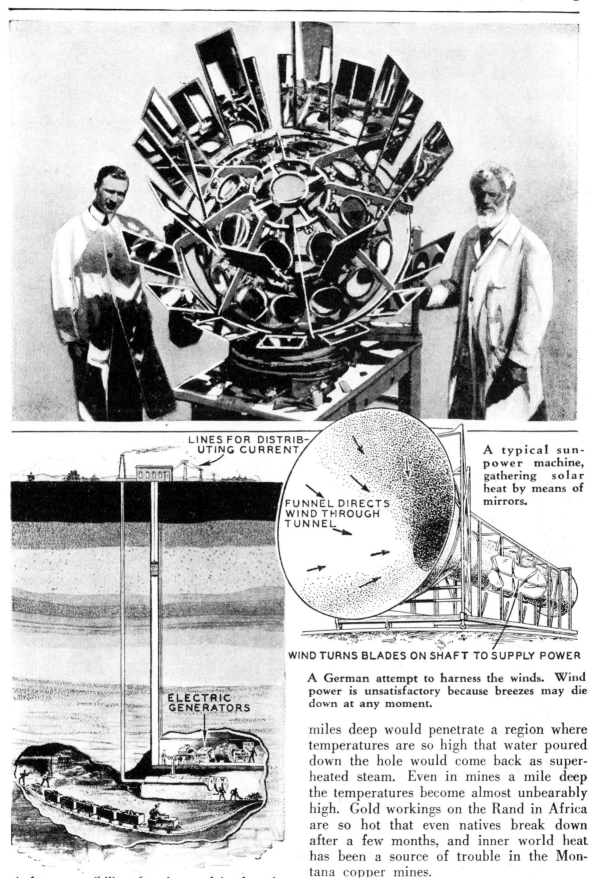

LINES FOR DISTRIB-
UTING CURRENT

A typical sun-
power machine,
gathering solar
heat by means of
mirrors.

FUNNEL DIRECTS
WIND THROUGH
TUNNEL

WIND TURNS BLADES ON SHAFT TO SUPPLY POWER

A German attempt to harness the winds. Wind power is unsatisfactory because breezes may die down at any moment.

ELECTRIC
GENERATORS

A future possibility—burning coal in the mines to generate current, thus saving transportation.

miles deep would penetrate a region where temperatures are so high that water poured down the hole would come back as superheated steam. Even in mines a mile deep the temperatures become almost unbearably high. Gold workings on the Rand in Africa are so hot that even natives break down after a few months, and inner world heat has been a source of trouble in the Montana copper mines.

COAL Costs Cut by Water-Pipe Shipment

Coal could be transported at 75 m.p.h. by grinding it to pea size, mixing with water, and pumping through pipe lines from the mine, in a scheme advanced by Reginald Bolton, New York engineer. A station similar to that shown above would separate the coal from the water at the receiving end. Coal could be piped from Scranton to New York in 2½ hours.

MOST of the selling price of a ton of coal represents the cost of transporting it —up out of the mine, across country to big cities, thence to small distribution centers, and finally to the consumer. But the day may soon come when coal will be *piped* from the mines to the city, at amazing savings in transportation costs.

If this idea sounds fantastic, consider the fact that most of the oil produced in this country is transported from well to refinery by pipe line. Coal, pulverized and mixed with water, can be moved through pipes just as efficiently as oil.

At the International Bituminous Coal conference recently held at Pittsburgh, Pa., Frederick Schulte suggested mixing powdered coal with air and pumping it through large pipes at a speed of 90 miles an hour. Laboratory experiments proved that speeds of 100 miles an hour could be attained by this method without difficulty.

Air as a carrying medium, however, is objectionable because of the possibility of explosion, so sponsors of this project are now experimenting with inert gas instead of air. Nitrogen, for instance, is plentiful and inexpensive, and would eliminate the danger of explosion.

Simpler yet, Reginald Bolton, a consulting engineer of New York, would grind the coal to pea-size and use water to pump it through pipe lines. At the receiving end, water would be drained from the coal as shown in the drawing above.

Machine Tells Your Brain Speed

IS YOUR brain and nervous system clicking at top speed? Here's a machine that will tell you in a hurry. On a revolving cylinder are 20 questions taken from standard intelligence tests. Each question has alternative answers, and during the moment the machine stops for each question you must answer by pulling a lever.

On a cylinder inside this machine questions with alternative answers are arranged, to be answered by pulling a lever.

Sun Furnace May Vaporize Diamonds

SUN 5300°C.

LENSES

REFLECTORS

MELTING POINTS OF METALS
TUNGSTEN - 3380°C.
PLATINUM - 1,755°C.
IRON - 1,535°C.
GOLD - 1,063°C.
NICKEL - 1,452°C.
TIN - 231°C.

4,500°C. EXPECTED TO BE DEVELOPED SUFFICIENT HEAT TO TURN A DIAMOND INTO VAPOR

COUNTERWEIGHT

Here's model of the experimental sun furnace.

A HEAT of 4500 degrees centigrade, intense enough to turn a diamond into vapor and to melt any known substance, is expected to be generated in an amazing new solar furnace which derives its heat directly from the sun. Eighty per cent of the sun's heat is expected to be captured by the furnace, which has been designed by scientists of the California Institute of Technology in Pasadena. It consists of a mounting similar to that of a telescope which always follows the sun, upon which are 19 lenses which focus the sun's rays on a central spot within the apparatus.

PULLING

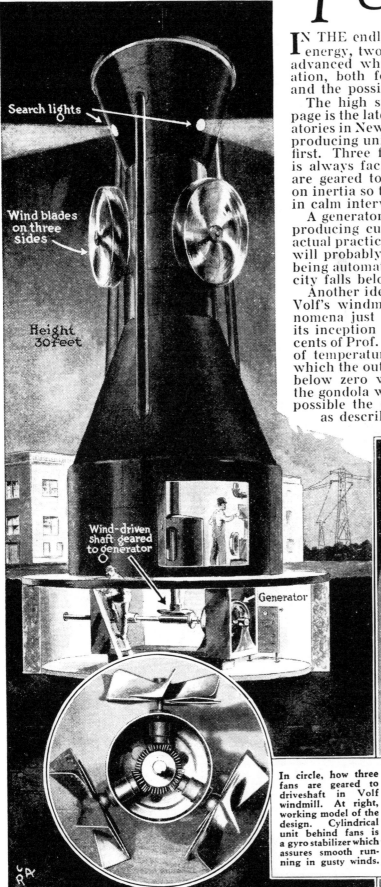

Search lights

Wind blades on three sides

Height 30 feet

Wind-driven shaft geared to generator

Generator

In circle, how three fans are geared to driveshaft in Volf windmill. At right, working model of the design. Cylindrical unit behind fans is a gyro stabilizer which assures smooth running in gusty winds.

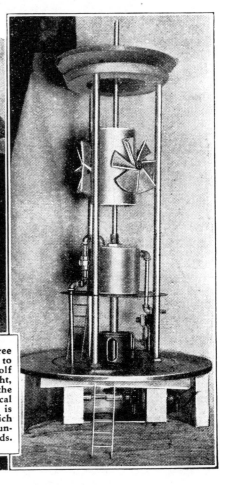

IN THE endless quest for cheap sources of energy, two proposals have recently been advanced which demand serious consideration, both for appeal to the imagination and the possibilities of practical operation.

The high speed windmill shown on this page is the latest development of Volf's laboratories in New York. The first of these power producing units will be in operation by May first. Three fans are provided so that one is always facing a wind current. The fans are geared to a gyro stabilizer which runs on inertia so that the fans will not run down in calm intervals between gusts of wind.

A generator is driven by the geared shaft, producing current for storage batteries. In actual practice three or four small generators will probably be used, one or more of them being automatically cut out when wind velocity falls below a certain point.

Another idea, less close to realization than Volf's windmill but involving natural phenomena just as dependable, partially owes its inception to the stratosphere balloon ascents of Prof. Auguste Piccard. The extremes of temperature encountered by Piccard, in which the outside air was around 75 degrees below zero while interior temperatures of the gondola were around 100 degrees, makes possible the operation of a thermal engine as described in detail on opposite page.

POWER *from the* SKIES

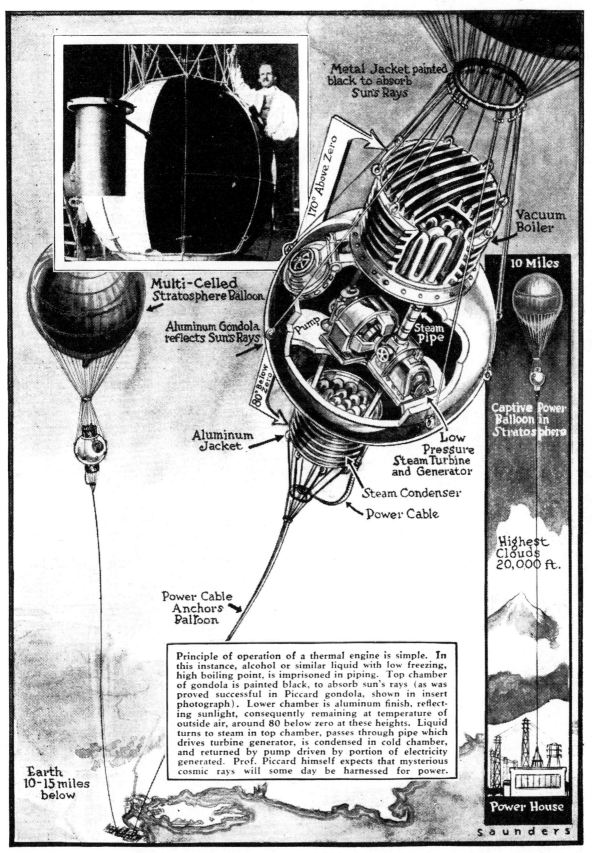

Metal Jacket painted black to absorb Sun's Rays

Vacuum Boiler

170° Above Zero

Multi-Celled Stratosphere Balloon

Aluminum Gondola reflects Sun's Rays

Pump

Steam pipe

80° Below Zero

Aluminum Jacket

Low Pressure Steam Turbine and Generator

Steam Condenser

Power Cable

Power Cable Anchors Balloon

10 Miles

Captive Power Balloon in Stratosphere

Highest Clouds 20,000 ft.

Earth 10-15 miles below

Power House

saunders

Principle of operation of a thermal engine is simple. In this instance, alcohol or similar liquid with low freezing, high boiling point, is imprisoned in piping. Top chamber of gondola is painted black, to absorb sun's rays (as was proved successful in Piccard gondola, shown in insert photograph). Lower chamber is aluminum finish, reflecting sunlight, consequently remaining at temperature of outside air, around 80 below zero at these heights. Liquid turns to steam in top chamber, passes through pipe which drives turbine generator, is condensed in cold chamber, and returned by pump driven by portion of electricity generated. Prof. Piccard himself expects that mysterious cosmic rays will some day be harnessed for power.

This thermal power plant, anchored by captive balloon high above the clouds to operate through heat of sun and cold of atmosphere, is an idea based on sound physical laws, demonstrated in Piccard balloon ascent a year ago.

More Leisure for Man in

Locating and extinguishing a fire automatically is the latest task performed by the electric eye, which searches the screen, as shown here, then operates relay to direct stream of chemicals from the extinguishers.

by L. Warrington Chubb
Director of Research, Westinghouse Electric & Manufacturing Co.
As told to J. EARLE MILLER

Mr. Chubb describes in this remarkable article a number of the amazing inventions recently developed which promise to free man from toil at machines, to better health, and to add greatly to the comforts of home life.

L. Warrington Chubb.

IN A ROOM down the hall an electric eye is busy at a task that human eyes and hands have always performed. Nearby an electric organ fills the building with the deep, soft notes of a cathedral instrument. Across the way a facsimile machine receives and dispatches exact copies of written or printed pages, a cathode tube flickers with the moving picture of electricity in transit, and a beam of polarized light passing through a piece of celluloid is telling its master that railroad rails are being made with too much steel near their base and not enough just beneath the flange on which the car wheels glide.

Those widely different activities, together with a host of others like them, are the first light beams marking the dawn of the automatic age, when electrons will be harnessed to perform many of the tiresome, laborious tasks that human brawn has been mobilized to do in the past.

The past fifty years or so have been known as the machine age, but now comes the automatic era to emancipate man from the machine. The old bugaboo, that labor will starve unless it can work at back-breaking tasks, immediately arises. But the history of machine development has shown that when science frees one man from wearisome labor it creates new fields to utilize his released talents. And without modern machinery men would still be working 12 and 14 hours a day for a mere pittance, earning scarcely enough to clothe and feed a family, and having only bare necessities of life.

The field of probabilities in the new era opened by the harnessing of the electron are as vast as electricity itself. One of the chief problems we are considering at the Westing-

the AUTOMATIC AGE

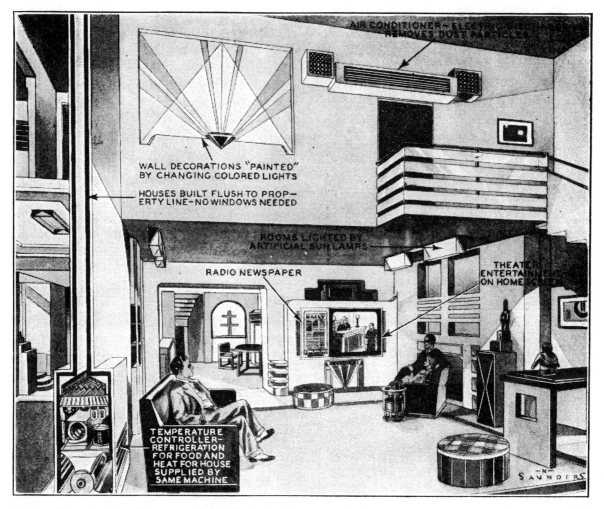

WALL DECORATIONS "PAINTED" BY CHANGING COLORED LIGHTS

HOUSES BUILT FLUSH TO PROPERTY LINE—NO WINDOWS NEEDED

AIR CONDITIONER—ELECTRIC DISCHARGE REMOVES DUST PARTICLES

ROOMS LIGHTED BY ARTIFICIAL SUN LAMPS

RADIO NEWSPAPER

THEATER ENTERTAINMENT ON HOME SCREEN

TEMPERATURE CONTROLLER—REFRIGERATION FOR FOOD AND HEAT FOR HOUSE SUPPLIED BY SAME MACHINE

This artist's drawing illustrates the logical development of the typical home of the future. Health-giving artificial sun lamps will eliminate windows, while an electric machine will warm rooms with heat extracted from air, and also purify the atmosphere and furnish proper humidity in the same process.

house research laboratories is the home of the future. It isn't enough that the electrical industry should provide a welded steel framework and fill it with light and with labor saving appliances. The scientifically created home of the future should be heated in winter and cooled in summer by electricity; it should have washed air of the proper degree of humidity; it should be lighted with the proper mixture of health giving ultraviolet rays.

Such a home can be built to the property line, eliminating both windows and light and air shafts, and its inside rooms, lighted by artificial sun lamps, will be more healthful than the outside rooms of the present. Some day we may combine the heating plant and the refrigerator, and the operation of mak-

ing ice will heat the house. Heat can be extracted from air by compressing it, and the dust removed by an electrical discharge. This discharge will also give washed air without the disadvantages of applying water, as it will be extracting the moisture to obtain the proper humidity. The heat extracted from the air can be applied to a water heating apparatus, or even stored for future use.

Our facsimile transmitter opens a new field for the home of the future, which not only can have radio entertainment and television, but also a radio newspaper. Such a receiver is quite simple. literally a development of the old-fashioned electric pencil, or stylus, writing on a sheet of paper dipped in iron oxide—a device which many young experimenters in years past have built.

ENDLESS Belt SUBWAY

This cross section drawing of model shows spiral driving gears and two-way line of subway seats.

Amazing non-stop belt system would permit passengers to get on and off and take 70,000 past a given point every hour at moderate cost and, wonder of wonders, all travelers would be seated in future.

WITH giant skyscrapers being built in almost every large city of the nation and still larger and taller and greater ones projected for the future the traffic problem is growing daily more acute. Merchants and customers are wondering how they can get together without spending the major portion of their time in travel.

Out of this endless maze there has come the plans and the practical suggestions of Herman E. Taylor, supervisor of traffic for the Detroit Department of Street Railways, and because it seems practical and adaptable to all large cities it is being given serious study by city authorities, technical engineers and University authorities who have recently interested themselves in the national situation.

Mr. Taylor's method calls for a system of rapid transit, either subway or elevated, capable of carrying 70,000 persons past a given point every hour, every passenger seated and the system making no stops, but passengers permitted to board or alight at any point along the system with absolute safety!

Sounds fantastic, does it not? Especially when its sponsors insist that it will do twice as much as any two-track subway system,

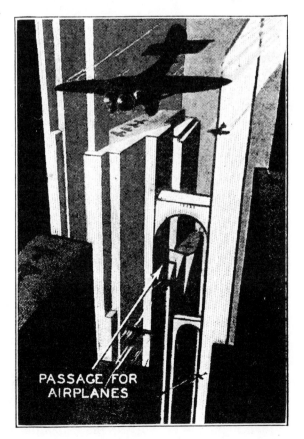

Futuristic conception of city skyscrapers to facilitate the use of airplanes in traveling.

to EXPEDITE TRAFFIC

CHAIRS MOVING ON ENDLESS BELT

ENTRANCE

The girl above has stepped onto a slow moving outer "belt" which will speed up to same pace of belt carrying seats and permit her to sit down.

and at one-half to three-fourths the cost.

A model of the proposed system has been completed and grinding out miles without a breakdown for many weeks.

The system is in the form of two endless belts, one immediately inside the other and each 5 feet wide, built in 12-foot sections. The inner belt, separated from the outer belt by an endless succession of automatically controlled gates, would move continuously at 20 to 25 miles an hour. Its outer edge would carry the seats, all facing in the forward direction, this belt known as the "constant speed platform."

Traveling on wheels and tracks, the 12-foot sections are built as solidly as the modern type street car floor and articulated at either end to fit the next section.

The outer "belt", or variable speed platform, is set off from the subwalk—in case the system is constructed underground—by another set of automatic gates. This platform would move at frequent intermissions at three-quarters of a mile an hour, at which times the gates would open to permit passengers to board from the subwalk. In nine seconds the variable speed platform would be accelerated to the same speed as the constant speed platform, permitting passengers to move through the inner gates, automati-

Herman E. Taylor, designer of "belt" subway.

cally opening for the purpose, and to take seats on the constant speed platform.

The entire system could be built only to move in one direction under the sidewalk on one side of the street and in the other direction under the sidewalk on the opposite side, Mr. Taylor says, a width of only 86 feet being necessary for turnings.

The system would be driven by electric motors, eight being required each side in each mile. Eight hundred horse-power per mile would start the lines, and 400 horse-power per mile would drive the system, Mr. Taylor says, as compared with four 50-horsepower motors now required as power for each two-car surface train.

Airport in the Heart of a City Provided by Logical Design

NEON WARNING LIGHTS
GUARD WALL
FLOOD LIGHTS
RAMP ELEVATOR
STORAGE FLOOR
CROSS-SECTION OF LANDING RAMP

CONTROL STATION

PLANES CIRCLING AWAITING SIGNAL TO LAND

FLOOD LIGHTS

GUARD WALL

NEWARK MUNIC'. AIRP

ELEVATOR

WIND DIRECTION POINTER

NEON TYPE FIELD LIMIT LIGHTS

AIRPORT BUILDING

ELEVATOR WELL

STORAGE AND SERVICE FLOOR

WARNING LIGHTS

AIR-CAR EXIT

DOUGLAS ROLFE

ALLEY
ELEVATOR
CONTROL STATION
AVENUE
AIRPORT BUILDING
STREET
STREET
OVERHANGING APRON
AVENUE

Visualized by Douglas Rolfe as the type of city airport which must inevitably come, this drawing foretells the trend of development in a graphic manner. A concrete runway, built atop neighboring skyscrapers, has arresting devices which bring the landing plane to a quick stop. An elevator lowers the entire plane to the service floor beneath the runway, where passengers alight and go about their business in the heart of the city. No time lost on long taxi rides from the present type of outlying airport.

Here's cross-sectional view showing layout of city airport.

WILL THE CITY OF THE FUTURE LOOK LIKE THIS?

ELEVATED express highways passing through special "motorway" buildings are a feature of a plan proposed by engineers of the Automobile Club of Southern California for handling traffic problems in metropolitan areas. In the photograph above, showing a scale model of "Every City" designed to illustrate the plan, such a highway is seen entering a miniature building near the center of the model.

Marvelous Movie Miniatures

Nine lanes of traffic, all moving on belts, are shown on the ground level.

THE scenarist's dream of New York City in 1980 has been done in miniature at Hollywood for "Just Imagine," a motion picture fantasy. This model took five months to complete and cost approximately $200,-000. It was built in an old blimp hangar once used by the U. S. Army balloon corps and covers a ground area 75x225 feet, representing the most extravagant effort yet conceived by the American cinema industry.

Lofty office buildings 250 stories high, canals carried overhead on suspension cables, airplanes that land on a few square feet of flat space on the side of tall structures, streets with nine lanes and nine levels of traffic, are among the interesting features. Although the model city is futuristic, its construction violates no engineering practices. It is really engineering skill carried a bit farther than today.

A crew of 200 technical experts and artisans moulded and built the miniature, which is raised on a plat-

The city of the future should be a pedestrian's paradise with foot bridges crossing the traffic at each corner.

Portray CITIES of the FUTURE

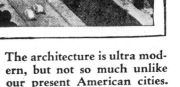

The architecture is ultra modern, but not so much unlike our present American cities. Note subway at lower left.

form above the ground. More than five tons of plaster, to say nothing of hundreds of pounds of lumber, glass and other materials, were employed in this "giant" miniature, the tallest tower of which is 40 feet high — which would be close to 2000 feet in actuality. The model is built to a scale of one-fourth inch to one foot.

The utmost fidelity to truth was observed in making this set. No details of exterior construction were left undone. Even real glass was used for windows, and the plaster was colored just the same as in real structures.

STREET TRAFFIC ON MOVING BELTS

Night in the miniature city. Note helicopter aprons on the tower.

Six-Story Speed Highways of Tomorrow

Here is an artist's conception of the amazing multiple highway plan of Dr. John A. Harriss, former health commissioner of New York City. The plan calls for six traffic levels. Each level is for designated traffic. There is an express traffic level, two one-way levels for bus traffic and other plans to expedite traffic. This proposal of Dr. Harriss is gaining in favor as one of the most feasible of many schemes advanced to adequately handle the constantly increasing motor and pedestrian traffic.

Cross U. S. In 48 Hours On Proposed Road

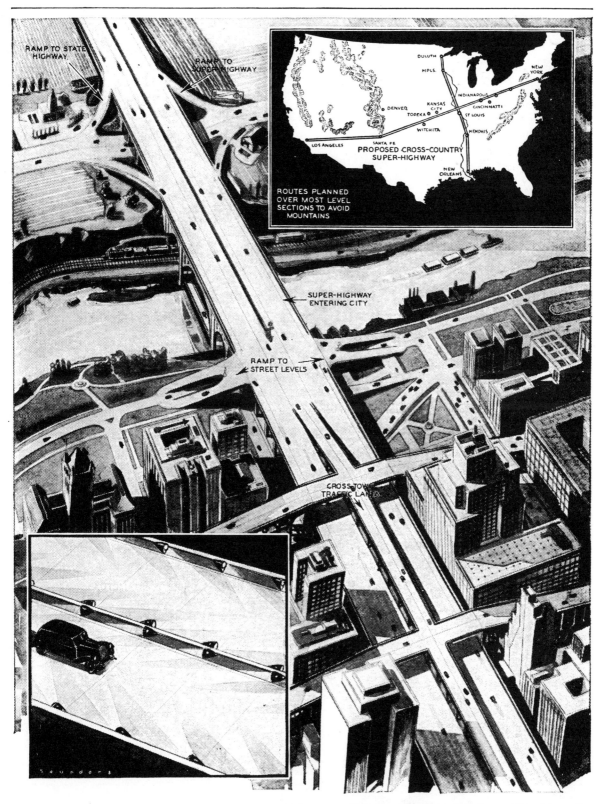

RAMP TO STATE HIGHWAY

RAMP TO SUPER-HIGHWAY

PROPOSED CROSS-COUNTRY SUPER-HIGHWAY

ROUTES PLANNED OVER MOST LEVEL SECTIONS TO AVOID MOUNTAINS

DULUTH

MPLS.

NEW YORK

INDIANAPOLIS

DENVER

KANSAS CITY

CINCINNATI

TOPEKA

ST LOUIS

WITCHITA

MEMPHIS

SANTA FE

LOS ANGELES

NEW ORLEANS

SUPER-HIGHWAY ENTERING CITY

RAMP TO STREET LEVELS

CROSS-TOWN TRAFFIC LANES

An artist's drawing of the proposed coast-to-coast super highway on which automobiles may travel at speeds of 100 miles an hour, making the trip between New York and California in forty-eight hours. Road builders are now working on plans for a four-lane highway with all grade crossings eliminated. The super roadway will be elevated through towns with ramps furnishing access to the main road through a central lane. Night travel is expected to be fully as safe at high speeds as day touring. Parapet walls two feet in height and made of opal glass bricks are intended to flank the black-surfaced roadway. Imbedded in the walls and spaced about twenty feet apart, as shown in insert, the engineers intend to put lights whose hoods will direct the light on the pavement below the eye level of the automobile driver.

Big Cities to Have COOLED Sidewalks

COOLING big cities by means of underground air ducts has long been the dream of inventors and sweltering citizens alike. A plan is now being seriously considered by a Chicago scientist, Dr. Gustav Eglov, of the American Chemical Society.

Dr. Eglov believes that huge refrigeration plants built at intervals of a mile and a half along city streets would rid the canyons between sky scrapers of humid hot air. Giant blowers in the plants would force the cooled air into the streets through ducts, as illustrated in the accompanying drawing. The cold air would hug the streets and walks, displacing the warm air, which would be forced upward. The plan could also call for piping into skyscrapers so as to provide office buildings with air conditioning. A practical street cooling system would be welcomed by store owners in crowded districts, it is believed. The increased patronage would be expected to more than pay for operation of the plants.

COOLED AIR OUTLET

WARM AIR INTAKE

COOLING OFFICES BY REMOTE CONTROL

DUCTS TO OFFICE BUILDINGS

AIR CONDITIONING PLANT

OUTLETS AT HALF-BLOCK INTERVALS

STREET COOLED AIR OUTLET

BLOWER

UNDERGROUND COLD AIR DUCT

COOLED AIR SPREADS OVER STREET DISPLACING HOT AIR

Artist's drawing shows how central air conditioning plants will service streets and offices with cooled air to keep city's inhabitants comfortably cool even in hottest weather. Shops on such streets expect increased patronage to pay costs.

French Engineer Plans Huge Floating Mid-Ocean City

The above drawing shows the model, built by a French engineer, of the proposed $2,000,000 mid-ocean city to be established midway between Bordeaux, France, and St. Johns, Newfoundland. The outer steel network will act as a breakwater, and the harbor inside will serve as a trans-Atlantic hydroplane station.

WHEN the continents of the world have become overcrowded and trans-oceanic airplane travel is as common as travel by steamers at present, we may see the establishment of huge mid-ocean cities such as is shown in the above drawing, which illustrates the plans recently made by Leon Feoquinos, a French engineer of Marseilles.

The foundation is to be a network of steel sections, held together with cables, to act as a gigantic breakwater against the heavy seas. In the center there will be a large enclosed harbor that will serve as a landing place for hydroplanes and a port for ocean liners. Later other features will be added, such as a spacious hotel, gaming casino, and four huge towers.

Liner Staircases Imperil Lives

THE wide staircases and spacious halls and passages of a great ocean liner may add to the attractiveness of the ship for passengers so long as nothing happens, but they may become veritable death traps if the vessel gets into trouble at sea and takes a strong list to one side or the other.

As the staircases are virtually unclimbable when tilted, members of the crew must carry passengers up from the lower decks, and in case of a rush to the boats many passengers, being unable to negotiate the stairway, may be left helpless to drown. Mr. E. F. Spanner, British merchant marine architect, has urged that several narrow stairways be provided.

Modern SCIENCE Predicts

Egyptians 5,000 years ago may have attempted to control weather by building the great pyramids. The Pyramids of Gizeh may have brought rain to the desert.

MAN'S greatest problem is the weather. It destroys crops; it kills thousands of persons annually; it causes disastrous floods, tornadoes and cloudbursts; in the form of a drought it brings starvation, disease and suffering.

In three weeks of August, 1896, a "heat wave" caused 2,036 deaths from sunstroke in the United States alone. Two years earlier a hot spell destroyed $50,000,000 worth of crops in the single state of Iowa.

Hot weather, too, has been known to increase crime. Records of the New York City police department show that cases of assault and battery increase well over 70 per cent when the mercury hovered in the nineties.

No wonder then that man, probably since the dawn of civilization, has attempted to change weather to suit his needs. Recent theories bring out the possibility that the Pyramids of Egypt, built 5,000 years ago, may have been one of the earliest great efforts to control climate.

Rockets shot through clouds have shattered storms in Germany. The rocket allows the wind to break up clouds.

These massive structures, towering 500 feet in height on the borders of the desert, have always been mysteries to scientists. They are known to be the tombs of Pharaohs, but this question always arises: "Were they built for burial places only?"

To erect a Pyramid today would involve an expense of $156,000,000 and it would take 22,000 men about seven years to build it. It seems probable, then, that the Pyramids had another purpose—to bring rain and to break the force of hot winds laden with sand.

This warm, moist air, sweeping up from Central Africa or down from the Mediterranean, struck the sloping sides of the Pyramid. As it swept upward, the wind revolved about the triangular shaped structure. This spinning column of warm air continued to rise, it is believed, until it came in contact with cold air. Here condensation took place, clouds formed, and rain eventually fell.

It is said that this phenomenon still can be noted in Egypt. There is little doubt that the Pyramids break the force of sandstorms. The Sphinx, standing beside the

Dry ice scrattered over clouds will cause condensation and start rain. The experiment was successful in Holland.

Made-to-Order WEATHER

The canyons of modern cities formed by tall skyscrapers are great ventilating shafts that have reduced deaths from heat waves. The drawings below illustrate wind action.

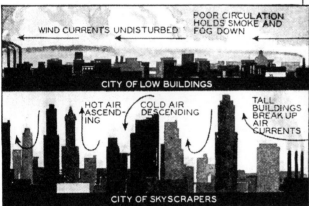

Great Pyramids of Gizeh, has almost been buried in sand deposited by winds.

For the same reason the modern city with its skyscrapers provides better air and temperature than a crowded city of low flat buildings. Weather bureau records show that heat prostrations in cities have been reduced considerably during the last generation. Warm air striking a skyscraper is forced to circulate upward around the building, forcing cold air down and reducing temperature in the streets.

This 70 story building in Radio City, New York, without the conscious effort of the designers is improving weather conditions in the world's largest city through air control.

Make Street Intersections PAY a PROFIT

RECORDS show that busy street intersections are the favorite spots in which traffic accidents occur. To eliminate these danger spots, J. G. Van Zandt, an engineer of Pittsburgh, Penn., has patented the idea of a safety-tower which practically eliminates the possibility of crossing collisions and at the same time returns a profit to the community.

Space above and below street level at intersections belongs to the city. Mr. Van Zandt's towers would be constructed at the intersection, as shown in the drawing below, and would contain stores, offices, and parking facilities which would return a handsome revenue to the builders.

The safety feature is provided for by the two-level roadway. North-south traffic travels on one level, with east-west traffic passing above it, doing away with the need for stop and go signs, since traffic is continuous. Crossings for pedestrians are provided at street level; autos travel below and above the street, but not on its surface at the intersection.

Motorists making right turns pass underneath the pedestrian bridges. Left turns are not permitted. Parking facilities are provided for beneath the street level.

Revenue produced would depend largely on conditions at individual intersections. In many cases, Mr. Van Zandt believes, small cities can well afford to construct a safety-tower as a civic center building, satisfying local needs for city hall, banquet halls, public rest rooms, etc.

It is a simple matter to locate an air beacon on the top of the tower.

FIXED BEACON POINTS TO LOCAL AIRPORT

REVOLVING AIRCRAFT BEACON LIGHT

BALLROOM

OFFICES, RESTAURANTS, CONCESSIONS, AND BUS DEPOTS IN BUILDING

PASSENGER ELEVATORS IN PIERS

ONE STREET GOES UNDER, THE OTHER OVER, THE SIDEWALK LEVEL

COLD-WAVE REFRIGERATORS

GARAGES AND PARKING UNDER RAMPS

ALL RIGHT TURNS MADE UNDER PEDESTRIAN BRIDGES. NO LEFT TURNS

This safety-tower, to be constructed at street intersections, reserves street level for pedestrians and permits cross traffic to flow continuously, without regulation of stop and go signs. Rental of parking space, offices, and stores would return sufficient revenue to pay a profit on the tower's construction. This unique idea has been patented by J. G. Van Zandt.

Fighting skyscraper fires is already a serious problem in the larger cities. Fires in these tall buildings must be fought entirely from the inside if the blaze is above the fifteenth story. This would present a serious problem if the fire and the smoke should prevent firemen from getting close to the blaze. Chief Kenlon, of the New York City Fire Department, expects to see the day when fires in these lofty skyscrapers will be fought from special types of airplanes. Here is an artist's conception of how this will be done. Helicopters will be used so that the firemen may hover over the spot, directing streams of chemicals from high pressure tanks carried on these "fire planes." Stranger things have happened.

Hurricane House

WEATHER-VANE DWELLING DESIGNED FOR

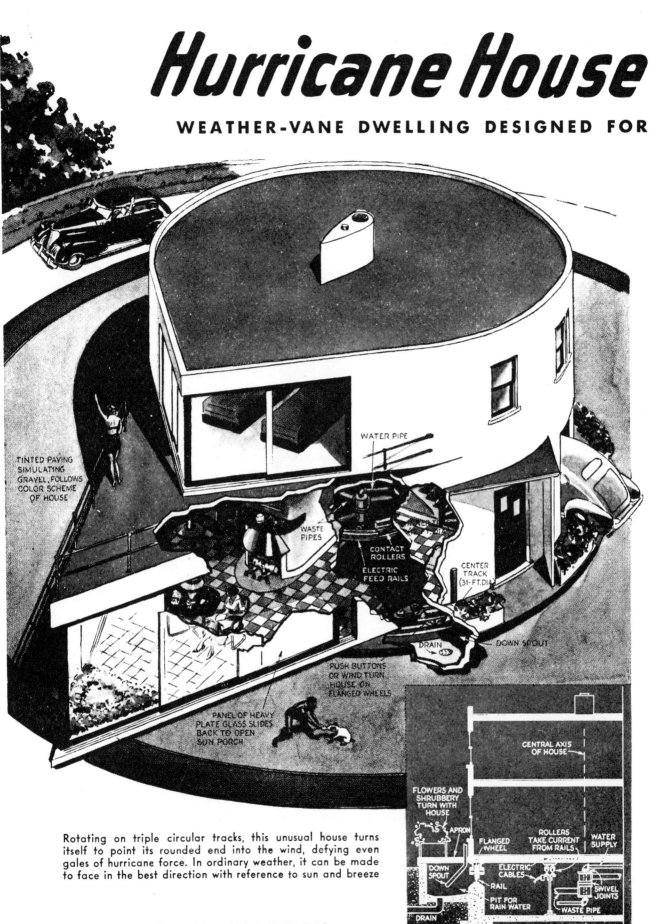

TINTED PAVING SIMULATING GRAVEL, FOLLOWS COLOR SCHEME OF HOUSE

WATER PIPE

WASTE PIPES

CONTACT ROLLERS

ELECTRIC FEED RAILS

CENTER TRACK (31-FT. DIA.)

DRAIN

DOWN SPOUT

PUSH BUTTONS OR WIND TURN HOUSE ON FLANGED WHEELS

PANEL OF HEAVY PLATE GLASS SLIDES BACK TO OPEN SUN PORCH

CENTRAL AXIS OF HOUSE

FLOWERS AND SHRUBBERY TURN WITH HOUSE

APRON

FLANGED WHEEL

ROLLERS TAKE CURRENT FROM RAILS

WATER SUPPLY

DOWN SPOUT

ELECTRIC CABLES

RAIL

PIT FOR RAIN WATER

SWIVEL JOINTS

WASTE PIPE

DRAIN

Rotating on triple circular tracks, this unusual house turns itself to point its rounded end into the wind, defying even gales of hurricane force. In ordinary weather, it can be made to face in the best direction with reference to sun and breeze

By CARL WARDEN

Turns with Wind

BOTH SAFETY AND COMFORT

WHEN raging storms whip across the land, accompanied by violent gales that uproot trees, tear the roofs from houses, and turn a trim countryside into a scene of desolation, there could probably be no safer refuge than the interior of a novel hurricane house designed by Edwin A. Koch, New York City architect. Streamline in the form of a mammoth teardrop, this amazing dwelling would revolve automatically to face into the oncoming storm, meeting it like the wing of an airplane and passing it smoothly around its curving sides toward its pointed tip.

Although planned for areas subject to periodic winds of gale force, the unique home has other unusual features that adapt it to luxurious living in any climate. Constructed of light steel channels and I-beam sections bolted together, the house has insulated walls faced on the exterior with semiflexible waterproof plywood. The entire structure rests on flanged wheels similar in construction to those found on a highway or railroad drawbridge. These run on three separate circular tracks: an inner track twelve feet in diameter, a second, placed just below the exterior walls, measuring thirty-one feet in diameter, and an outside, sixty-eight foot track for a wheel located at the pointed tip of the dwelling and cleverly concealed by an indoor living-room flower-bed.

A cantilevered floor covered with boiler plate extends beyond the outside walls for a distance of four feet to prevent driving rains from beating into the pit below the house, and to form an apron for the garage, a platform for the entrance doorways, and a ledge for flower boxes. Electricity enters the building through the inner track, while the water-supply and sewage pipes come in underground at the axis on which the house turns, swivel joints being provided to connect the stationary exterior pipes with those which are attached to the dwelling.

Inside the house, the first floor provides an entrance hall, a triangular living room with a built-in dining section on one side and a built-in library nook on the other, a kitchen, laundry, heater room, and a garage having space for a workbench and a trapdoor that provides access to the piping, wiring, and track mechanisms in the foundation pit below. Upstairs there are three large bedrooms, two baths, and a spacious open sun deck. Garage doors, and most of the broad expanse of glass windows, slide into the walls.

Merely by selecting the desired push button on a central control board, the entire house may be rotated to face rooms toward or away from the sun or to point bedroom windows toward a cooling breeze.

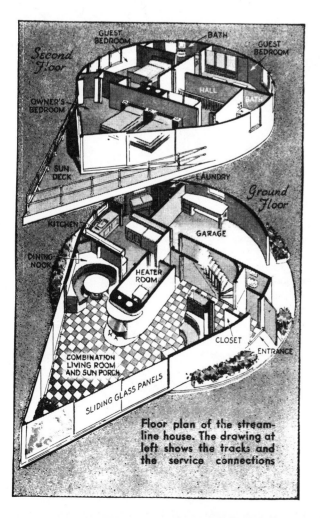

Floor plan of the streamline house. The drawing at left shows the tracks and the service connections

London to Build Mid-City Air Port

YORK ROAD

WIND VANES

R.R. STATION

FLOODLIGHTS

ENTRANCE TO HANGARS

ELEVATOR TO BUS STATION

BUS TERMINAL

ELEVATOR TO STREET

RAMP TO STREET

SAUNDERS

Here is an artist's conception of completed London aerodrome, built over roofs of buildings in heart of city, making landing field easily accessible to air passengers.

Mr. Clever with his model of air port to be built over buildings.

WITH the rapid growth of airplane transportation, the air port of the future may be moved up into the center of the city where it will be easily accessible. A bold step in this direction has been taken by Charles Clever, a London architect, who has constructed a model for a proposed airport to be located in the heart of London. The landing field consists of four runways arranged in the form of a giant wheel, the entire structure being supported by the buildings over which it is erected, as illustrated.

Giant Air TOWER to GUARD PARIS

TO GET defense aircraft into action more quickly, architects of Paris have worked out plans for a huge aerodrome tower, more than a mile in height, which will literally hurl planes into the air at the 5000-ft. level, ready for combat.

High-speed elevators would bring planes from the roof-top-level landing field up to each of the three aerodrome platforms. Swooping downward after leaving the inclined take-off platform, planes would reach flying speed with little loss of altitude.

Towering into skies for more than a mile, proposed Paris aerodrome tower would have three decks, with roof-top landing field built around base. Artist's sketch shows how structure, if built on river Seine, would dwarf Eiffel tower.

Cutaway sketch below shows how Paris defense planes stored in lower aerodrome of tower are taxied down sloping platform, gaining momentum for dive into space from outlet ports. Left: cross-section of upper third of tower shows elevator leading to top aerodrome.

HEIGHT 6550 FEET

ARMORED BOMB PROOF ROOF OVER PLATFORM

AIRPLANE OUTLET PORTS

PLAN OF ELEVATOR AT TOP AERODROME

STORAGE PLATFORM

TAKE-OFF PLATFORM

SLIDING ELEVATOR DOORS

ARMORED BOMB PROOF ROOF

VIEW SHOWING INTERIOR OF AERODROME

AIRPLANE OUTLET PORTS

RADIO TOWERS

EIFFEL TOWER 984 FT HIGH

PLAN OF ELEVATOR ARRANGEMENT AT PLATFORMS UP TO SECOND AERODROME IN TOWER

DOOR POCKETS

ELEVATORS

Electric Home Laundry Scientifically Planned Like Factory

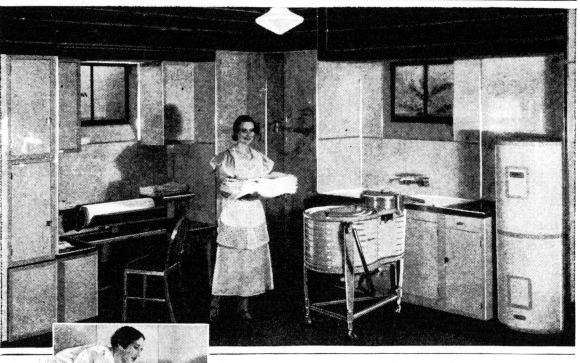

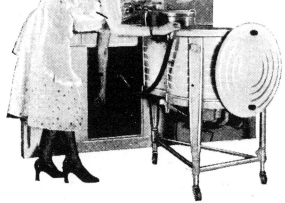

Clothes come from the bin at the foot of the washer and therefore require minimum foot work in moving. Every little detail like this has been carefully thought out by Westinghouse engineers.

Scientifically planned by industrial engineers, this Westinghouse model laundry will delight the heart of any woman. Mangle is located so plenty of light falls on the ironing.

ENGINEERS have stepped out of the factory and have invaded home planning fields with singular success. The results of the engineering method of thought when "factoryizing" the home are little short of remarkable.

Today, thanks to the efforts of engineers of the Westinghouse Electric and Manufacturing Company, every function of the serious business of making a home and keeping it has been reduced to its simplest elements and then mechanized, so that getting a meal, sweeping a floor, or doing a washing is "pie."

Look at the laundry pictured here! Yes, it's in the basement, but you'd never know it. The walls are of Micarta, and the whole room can be cleaned to nickel plate spotlessness with a moist rag. Oils, stains, soap suds, splashes and other gummy concomitants of the laundry are cleaned off this

remarkable wall surfacing with a swipe of a rag, so impervious and hard and glistening is the surface of Micarta.

And the arrangement of the machines! And the number of them! Let's look—The washing machine is right at the bottom of the clothes chute, which is of metal, washable and hence vermin proof. The laundry tub looks like a De Mille version of a Roman bath tub, but it is very inexpensive, is trimmed with non-rusting monel metal, and is placed conveniently near the washer.

A mangle in its own nook, with a comfortable chair and plenty of light, together with a water softener and heater bolstered up with numerous closets, all of metal.

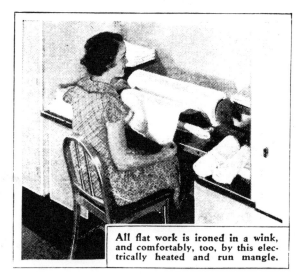

All flat work is ironed in a wink, and comfortably, too, by this electrically heated and run mangle.

Pleasure-Tower Half Mile High

HOW CARS ASCEND TOWER ON RAMPS

Spiral ramps by which the cars climb the tower will be supplemented by a series of elevators within the structure.

BEACON 2,300 FEET HIGH

RESTAURANT FOR 2,000 GUESTS

GARAGE TO HOUSE 500 CARS

SPIRAL RAMPS FOR ASCENDING TOWER BY AUTOMOBILE

CONCRETE WALLS

EMPIRE STATE BUILDING 1,100 FT.

EIFFEL TOWER 984 FT.

BAY OF BISCAY

LONDON

SPAIN

ENGLISH CHANNEL

HAVRE

BELGIUM

FRANCE

PARIS

Towering almost half a mile above the ground, dwarfing such gigantic structures as the Empire State Building and the Eiffel tower, a huge concrete tower 2300 feet high, surmounted with a beacon and built with a spiral ramp for autos to climb up its sides, stuns the imagination with its vastness. It is the design of the French engineer, M. Freyssinet, intended for the 1937 Paris Exhibition. He estimates the cost at less than half the Eiffel Tower, or in the neighborhood of $2,500,000. It will be called the "Phare du Monde," or Lighthouse of the World. The project appears far removed from the visionary and a new all-time "high" in buildings seems in a fair way to being achieved.

UP or DOWN by BELT

AUTOMATIC RELEASING GEAR

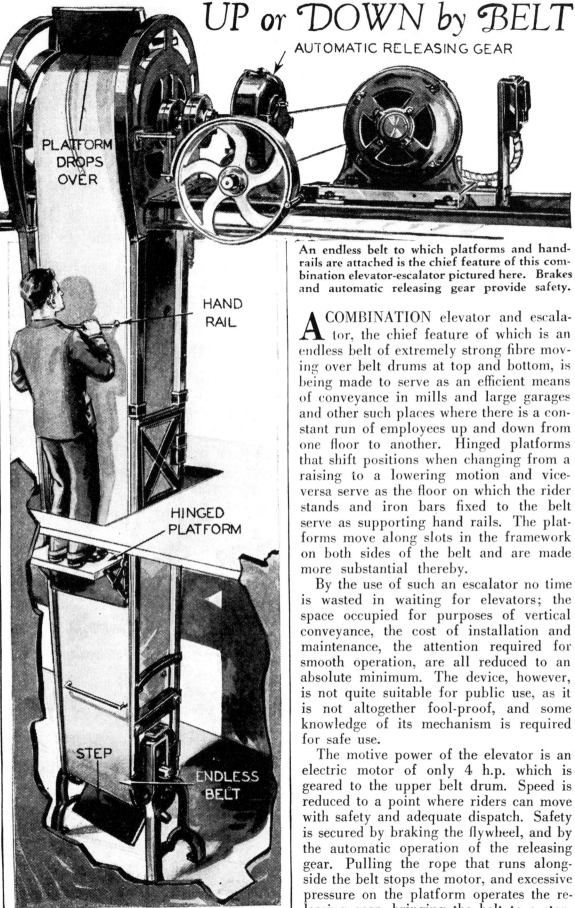

PLATFORM DROPS OVER

HAND RAIL

HINGED PLATFORM

STEP

ENDLESS BELT

An endless belt to which platforms and handrails are attached is the chief feature of this combination elevator-escalator pictured here. Brakes and automatic releasing gear provide safety.

A COMBINATION elevator and escalator, the chief feature of which is an endless belt of extremely strong fibre moving over belt drums at top and bottom, is being made to serve as an efficient means of conveyance in mills and large garages and other such places where there is a constant run of employees up and down from one floor to another. Hinged platforms that shift positions when changing from a raising to a lowering motion and vice-versa serve as the floor on which the rider stands and iron bars fixed to the belt serve as supporting hand rails. The platforms move along slots in the framework on both sides of the belt and are made more substantial thereby.

By the use of such an escalator no time is wasted in waiting for elevators; the space occupied for purposes of vertical conveyance, the cost of installation and maintenance, the attention required for smooth operation, are all reduced to an absolute minimum. The device, however, is not quite suitable for public use, as it is not altogether fool-proof, and some knowledge of its mechanism is required for safe use.

The motive power of the elevator is an electric motor of only 4 h.p. which is geared to the upper belt drum. Speed is reduced to a point where riders can move with safety and adequate dispatch. Safety is secured by braking the flywheel, and by the automatic operation of the releasing gear. Pulling the rope that runs alongside the belt stops the motor, and excessive pressure on the platform operates the releasing gear, bringing the belt to a stop.

Glass Banks Will Foil Hold-Ups

BANK hold-ups may soon become things of the past if the common-sense but revolutionary ideas of Francis Keally, New York architect, are put into effect. He suggests that banks be constructed with glass walls and that office partitions within the building likewise be transparent, so that a clear view of everything that is happening inside the bank will be afforded from all angles at all times.

The glass wall would be double, with an air space between which would be maintained at even temperature to keep the surface clean of frost and steam. Tellers would not be caged behind barred wickets or bullet-proof windows, but would transact business over an ordinary counter, keeping a minimum amount of currency at hand. Cash reserves of the bank would be kept in a huge basement vault, connected by a pneumatic tube system for carrying money to and from the tellers. The money vaults would be windowless and admittance would be barred by massive doors, but workers would be provided fresh air by means of modern ventilating systems.

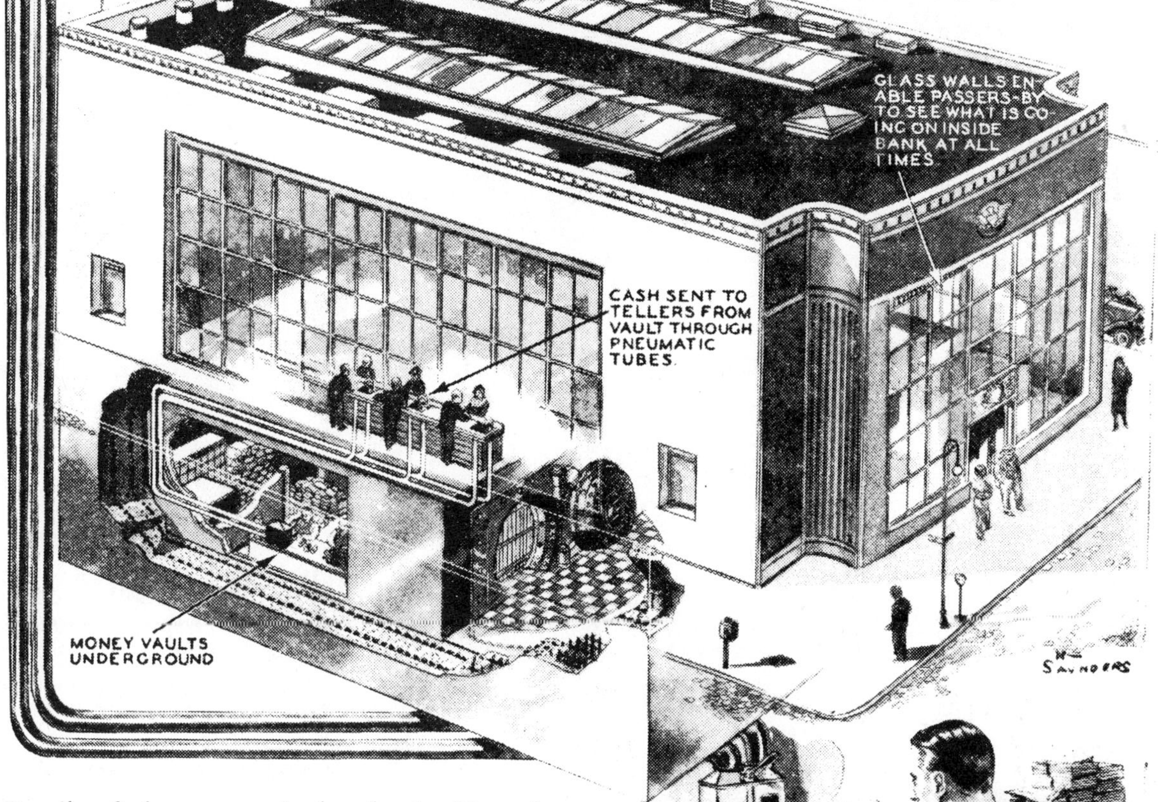

GLASS WALLS ENABLE PASSERS-BY TO SEE WHAT IS GOING ON INSIDE BANK AT ALL TIMES.

CASH SENT TO TELLERS FROM VAULT THROUGH PNEUMATIC TUBES.

MONEY VAULTS UNDERGROUND

Details of the suggested glass bank. Note that passers-by on the street have a full view of what is going on inside the building, and can thus give warning if a hold-up is in process. However, even if bandits attempted a hold-up, their loot would be small, inasmuch as tellers in the glass bank would keep only a small amount of cash at hand. Money vaults would be hidden underground, and communication would be effected through a pneumatic tube system as illustrated in drawing above.

SKYSCRAPERS DOOMED

The doom of Manhattan's towering skyline, above, may be sounded by the centrifuge, left, below. Construction models placed in this machine are whirled about until centrifugal force equals the pressure to which the full-size buildings are subjected by earth in actual sub-surface conditions.

by WILLIAM JENNINGS

SAFE from bomb attacks—free from disease and changing temperatures—living in cities a mile beneath the surface of the earth—such is the dream of science for the man of the future, a not impractical dream which may doom the towers of Manhattan and every other large city to destruction.

Despite its towering skyline, the trend of building construction in New York City has been ever downward. Today the island of Manhattan and its surroundings are honeycombed with a vast network of underground facilities. There are more than 130 tunnels and underground areas in the metropolitan district; more than 2800 miles in the subterranean sewage system, and about 600 miles of subway trackage carrying 5,000,000 passengers every day.

With habitable space growing more scarce every year in the crowded centers, architects and scientists freely predict that vertical cities, built from the earth's sur-

face downward, may eventually supplant the skyscrapers of today.

The reasons for their belief in the practicability of such a plan lies in the recent successful tests of a machine known as the "centrifuge" invented by Professor Philip B. Bucky, of Columbia university.

Explained in its most simple terms, Professor Bucky's machine is a device into which accurate scale models of underground structures may be placed and whirled about in such a way that the centrifugal force equals the actual earth stress to which full sized construction would be subjected.

Built of the same materials as the structure to be tested, the model is placed on the centrifuge and whirled at speeds up to 4000 revolutions a minute until the centrifugal force tends to pull the model apart.

A movie camera simultaneously records each revolution of the machine. When the film is run off on the screen it shows up the stress and strain under varying degrees of force up to the collapse of the model.

Heralds New Building Era

From these technical tests a new science of foundation engineering is expected to develop. Lack of a yardstick with which to measure the stresses of the earth has hitherto kept architects from planning extensive underground projects.

Testing depths up to 6000 feet, the centrifuge opens up an amazing vista of life in the future. It will be possible to have business blocks under airports with the

by UNDERGROUND CITIES?

surface left clear for planes. Vast subterranean caverns could be constructed, capable of sheltering entire populations against enemy bomb attacks. Office buildings, factories, homes and theaters—all could be sunk into bedrock.

Life underground would be different only in the respect that conditions, under scientific control, would be more sanitary and healthful. Conditioned air would prevail and the sun's absence compensated for by the use of ultra-violet lamps. The temperature would be constant at about 62 degrees. Coal bills would no longer worry the householder and bacteria would be killed.

Professor Bucky does not venture to make extravagant predictions. His centrifuge does not construct; it merely tests. The advantage of the machine lies in the fact that the safety of underground buildings may be absolutely proven by testing miniature models.

Photo at right shows one of the three-tube subway tunnels, part of the vast network underlying New York City. This picture is a possible forerunner of the future underground city shown below. Note elevator shafts which will carry city cave dwellers from one level to another, the giant air conditioning tubes and the enclosed roadway, leading from left to right, for through traffic. Lower part of drawing shows an underground apartment fronting on a street lined with stores and shops furnishing all necessities.

TUBES FOR THROUGH TRAINS

WARM AIR AND VENTILATING PIPES TO INCREASE TEMPERATURE 65° TO 73°

ELEVATOR TO UNDERGROUND CITY

ENCLOSED WALKS

RAPID TRANSIT SUBWAY TRAINS

SUBWAY STORES

UNDERGROUND APARTMENTS

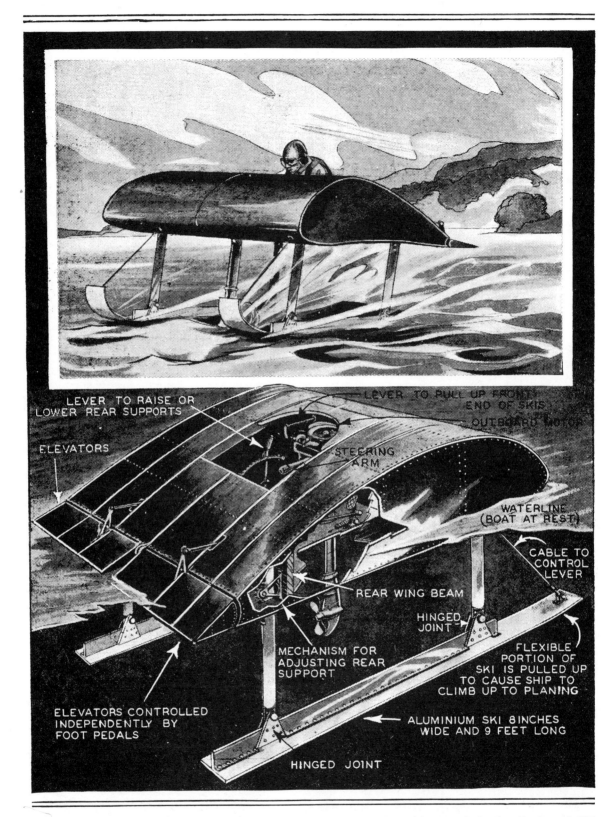

The oddest contraption which has been brought to our attention this month is the Outboard Ski-Plane now being constructed by C. T. Elle, of Chicago. The idea is that when the boat gets up speed the front of the skis will be raised, causing the boat to come to the surface. When wind gets under the wing it is supposed to furnish enough lift to permit the boat to skip over the waves.

Garage Without WALLS for Car Parking

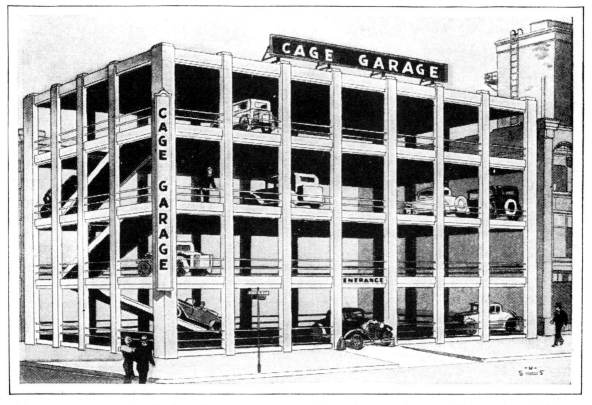

This new garage can be built at low cost on vacant lots, solving parking problems in crowded areas.

A TYPE of garage built on entirely new lines has been designed and patented by Samuel Eliot, a real estate operator and building manager of Boston, Mass. Known as a "cage garage," it is an open-air parking space stepped up three or four stories, with no side-walls or windows, no heat, no elevators or electric lighting. It has a low stud of eight feet, staggered floors and a twenty per cent pitch double ramp that takes up the space of only two cars. The construction is of reinforced concrete, and the inventor says that such buildings can be constructed at the low cost of ten cents a cubic foot, and can accommodate as many as 800 cars easily.

It is estimated that such garages will be able to earn five times the amount earned by the more expensive types of public garages. The cars are run up the ramps under their own power and parked as on an ordinary open lot, with room to run them out when wanted. The buildings are strictly fireproof and are easier of access to fire apparatus than the expensive enclosed public garages.

A company is being formed to build these garages throughout the country. The plan is to lease ground space near the business districts of large cities.

New Toothbrush Has Rubber Disks

SANITARY rubber disks are now used in a new toothbrush which is very easy to keep clean. The disks are thin enough to enter easily between the teeth.

Rubber disks of brush fit easily between the teeth.

Canvas House Costing But $1000 to Be Home of Future

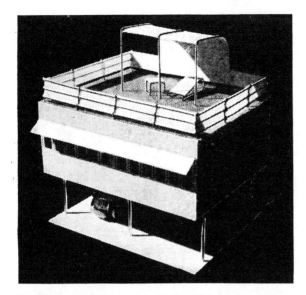

Model of new cotton summer house which can be constructed anywhere in country for less than $1000. Open lower floor serves as garage. Top floor is used for sun-baths.

"Ergometer" Checks Pensioners

DISPUTES between pensioners and government officials at Hamburg, Germany, as to their working capacities are now being settled by the "ergometer," a machine which registers electrically the capabilities of different people for all sorts of work.

The queer machine is first adjusted to the height of the person.

A mask is adjusted over the face to meter the amount of air breathed in and out. The patient then cranks a device which records electrically the amount of work being done. From this reading a fair pension allotment can be found for any person. The machine will expose persons who claim disability when they are too lazy to work.

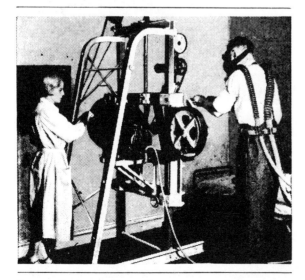

German "ergometer" machine measures energy used up by patient while doing measured amount of work. Pensions can now be allotted according to working capacity.

CANVAS is now being considered by architects as an attractive and economical building material for the small homes of the future. Canvas can now be treated with preservative paints to make it waterproof and fireproof.

A summer home which can be built anywhere for less than $1000 uses canvas almost exclusively as a surfacing material. The open lower deck, raised one foot off the ground to avoid dampness, is used for garage, storage, and shower bath. The main floor 8 feet above is reached by a folding stairway, as is the sun-deck above.

Largest Golf Club Weighs 100 Lbs.

Three persons perched atop a stepladder are needed to swing this giant golf club. Head is 36 inches long; club weighs 100 lbs. Ball set on giant tee is 13 inches in diameter.

THE world's largest golf club, with a head 36 inches long, and other dimensions in proportion, is being used at opening ceremonies for various golf tournaments in California.

Three players perched on a step ladder are needed to drive off the 13 inch diameter golf ball atop its gigantic tee.

Cheese Now Ripened in Tin Cans

CHEDDAR cheese, heretofore sold only in slices, can now be merchandised in sealed tin cans of convenient size. The green cheese is packed in cans and sealed. A new safety valve permits gases formed during the ripening process to escape.

Mechanical Grocery Store Walks Around the Customer

MOVING TRAYS CONTAINING GROCERIES

STATIONARY BINS

Endless belt carries groceries to customer.

INSTEAD of tiring herself out walking around the store and selecting what she wants from the shelves, the housewife who patronizes the newest type of grocery sits down comfortably while the store "walks around" her. Literally, of course, it doesn't quite do that, but the entire stock of the store passes before her on an endless belt and she merely picks out what she wants, placing the items in a bin beneath a stationary counter, as shown in the illustration at right. When she has completed her purchases, she presses a button. The bin goes to a wrapping room.

Machine Reads Books Aloud

INVENTED by Dr. George Schutkowsky, an engineer of Berlin, Germany, the extraordinary machine shown below is designed to convert printed matter into vocal sounds, thus making ordinary books and newspapers "readable" by the blind. No details of the operating principles of the device are available.

This mechanism is claimed to convert type into sound.

Making Auto Doors Open Easier

TO SUPPLY auto door latches with a constant source of lubrication, preventing their sticking and becoming hard to handle, a new little device has been put on the market which slips under the plate which forms the door latch. Only two screws need be

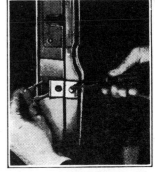

loosened to install the lubricator. Two prongs fit under the plate out of sight and only the lubricant end protrudes, where the door catch comes in contact with it.

One in Four Dies of Heart Disease

CALCULATIONS of a large life insurance company indicate that one in every four adults over the age of 50 will die of heart disease, now the commonest single cause of death in the United States. For white boy babies at birth, one out of every five will eventually be carried off by the ailment. Women are more susceptible.

Stove Top Oven Among New

"What won't they think of next?" the surprised householder asks as a compressed air toothbrush is added to the month's discoveries.

AIR BRUSH FOR TEETH

CAKE TIN OVEN

An air gun which sprays the teeth with compressed air and carbon dioxide has been introduced in England at South Kensington, where dentists of the right little, tight little isle recently convened. Pressure and chemical action do the work. The action is said to be non-painful and harmless to the teeth.

A brand new idea in ovens is one which fits the individual cake tin and can be used on top of the stove instead of in the regular big oven which takes a lot of gas to run. It has a funnel shaped opening in the base of the bake pot which gives even distribution of heat. Being sealed it preserves the moisture of the object which is baking and therefore does a better bake job.

WAFFLED STEAKS

ROTARY ICE CHOPPER

For cooling bottled beverages a convenient unit is now available which stores the beer in a hexagonal tub over which is a rotary ice chopper which shaves ice cubes into chopped ice. The steak waffler shown at the right will make the toughest flank steak taste like tenderloin. The rotary knives break the fibers up into units that cook easily.

HOUSEKEEPING *Ideas*

Waffled steaks, oxygen beauty baths and serve-all scissors are among the latest gadgets introduced to the home.

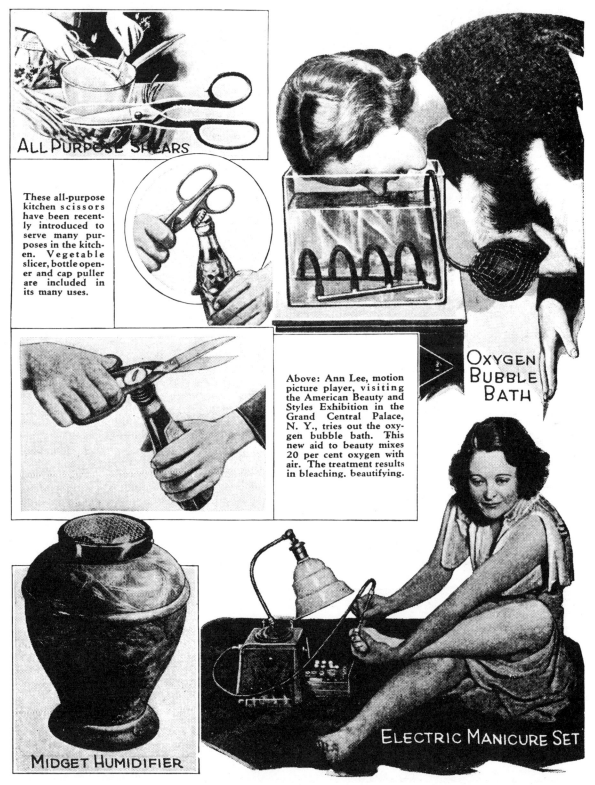

ALL PURPOSE SHEARS

These all-purpose kitchen scissors have been recently introduced to serve many purposes in the kitchen. Vegetable slicer, bottle opener and cap puller are included in its many uses.

OXYGEN BUBBLE BATH

Above: Ann Lee, motion picture player, visiting the American Beauty and Styles Exhibition in the Grand Central Palace, N. Y., tries out the oxygen bubble bath. This new aid to beauty mixes 20 per cent oxygen with air. The treatment results in bleaching. beautifying.

MIDGET HUMIDIFIER

ELECTRIC MANICURE SET

Above is shown a silent portable humidifier for use in rooms difficult to keep comfortable. Right, above, shows new portable home manicure set which much is claimed for, including its ability to do the difficult task of polishing toenails.

"I Can Whip Any
by
JACK

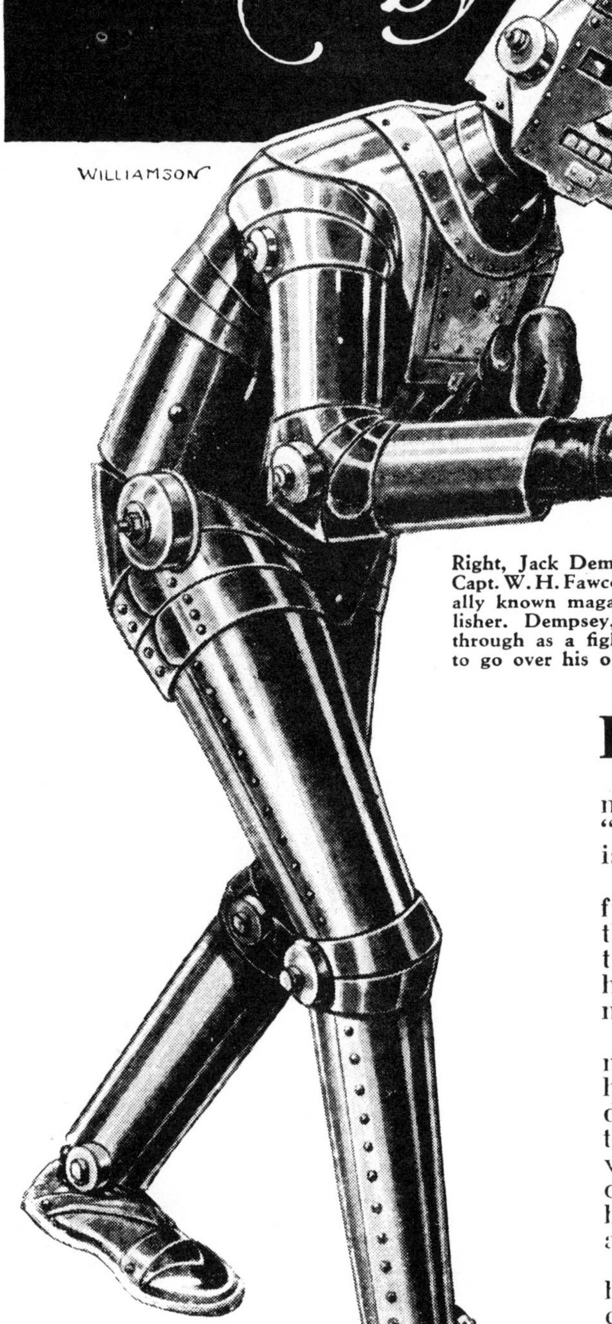

WILLIAMSON

Right, Jack Dempsey, and Capt. W. H. Fawcett, nationally known magazine publisher. Dempsey, although through as a fighter, likes to go over his old battles.

Jack Dempsey wouldn't be afraid of this mechanical man. He tells why in this article.

I CAN whip any mechanical robot that ever has or ever will be made.

Maybe that sounds a bit egotistical, maybe you will say it's just the voice of a "has-been," but I assure you that neither is true.

I was talking over old times with my friend Captain W. H. Fawcett and during the course of conversation he remarked that undoubtedly mechanical ingenuity has done much to improve the work of many boxers.

"That's true," I answered, "but nothing mechanical will ever be able to whip an honest to goodness boxer. Even right now, despite the fact that I am definitely through with the ring as a fighter, I wouldn't be afraid of any robot or mechanical man. I could tear it to pieces, bolt by bolt and scatter its brain wheels and cogs all over the canvas."

The reason is simple: Engineers can build a robot that will possess everything except brains. And without brains no man can ever attain championship class in the boxing game. It is true enough that we have had some rare intellectual specimens in the higher frames of boxing glory, but I can truthfully say that no

Mechanical Robot "DEMPSEY

Picturesque former champion of world tells mechanical side of boxing. Challenges any robot.

man ever attained genuine boxing recognition without real headwork. The best punch in the world is not worth a whoop if the boxer doesn't know what to do with it.

The most damaging of all blows is the short, straight-arm punch to the solar plexus—the punch which came into being when Fitzsimmons took the championship from Jim Corbett in one of the boxing game's greatest surprise victories.

In hitting to the solar plexus, that spot just below the meeting point of the ribs, the blow travels only about six or eight inches and the result is comparable only to the terrific effect of being struck by a piston which moves forward as its arm slides out. There never has been and never will be a boxer who could remain on his feet after being struck by a mechanically perfect solar plexus punch.

Another blow, almost equally devastating, is the left hook to the "button." This likewise travels only about six inches, but the impulse for this blow comes from the body as it moves forward, pivoting slightly at the hips. When, with the piston's hard-driving precision, the fist and elbow turn instantly to travel over that six-inch span to the point of contact, the fighter's previous forward motion gives him the greatest power it is possible for a human to achieve in the ring.

And here is Jack Dempsey, the Manassa Mauler. Jack lets you in on a few of his secrets in this article.

The Great Wall of China

An artist's conceptior of how the great wall of China will appear when converted into an elevated boulevard extending fifteen hundred miles westward from the city of Peking.

The plans of the Nationalist Government of the Republic of China for converting the great wall into a major motor highway are revealed to the world for the first time in this exclusive story.

Vehicles like this will be scarce along the Great Wall Highway. It would take this cart about 50 days of continuous travel to cover its full length.

THE Great Wall of China, long considered one of the most remarkable engineering feats in the world, may soon become one of the greatest and most unusual motor highways on earth if the plans of the Nationalist government are carried through.

The great wall was built about 220 B. C. by the first emperor of the Tsin Dynasty as a protection against the roving bands of Tartars, which were then in the habit of descending from the Mongolian plains and making sporadic raids upon the Chinese cities to the south. After 2150 years the wall is still in a remarkable state of preservation considering that only twice, in the fifteenth and again in the sixteenth century, were any extensive repairs made upon the structure.

The height of the wall ranges from twenty to forty feet, while at intervals of about two hundred yards are towers about 25 feet higher than the wall. The northern parapet of the entire fortification is loop-holed to protect the defenders from the missiles of the enemy, while the towers are surmounted by such a parapet around all four sides. Many of the towers are roofed over, and were no doubt used as barracks by the Chinese soldiers, while sentries were posted at the other towers.

to be Motor Highway

The wall is from fifteen to thirty feet wide at the base, and tapers inward to an average width of about twelve feet on top. Two solid masonry parallel walls from eighteen inches to four feet in thickness were first built, and the space between was then filled with loose stone and earth. Owing to lack of care, these outside walls have crumbled in places, but not to such an extent that their repair would be exorbitant.

Imagine, if you can, such a wall stretched across the United States. Starting at Washington, D. C., it would extend north to Cincinnati, then south around Cairo, Ill.; north again to Marshall, Missouri, south of Wichita, Kansas, and west to about fifty miles from Denver, Colorado—a serpentine path more than 1,500 miles in length.

With a smooth motor road laid on top of the wall its value to China would be enormous; for besides its unquestioned military value, enabling the government to stamp out the incessant banditry in the interior provinces, it would do much toward helping the rehabilitation of those who are isolated in this mysterious interior country, and who sometimes starve to death because food, plentiful on the coast, cannot be transported inland in time.

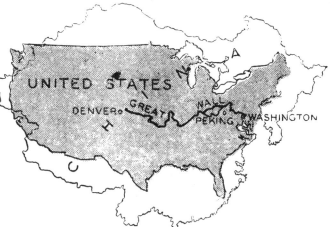

A typical section of the Great Wall showing how its winding course follows the high ground. Above is a map of the United States superimposed upon that of China to show the relative size of the wall.

CARS IN MOTION SWING OUTWARD GIVING BIRD'S EYE VIEW OF PYRAMID.

Mammoth flying swings erected atop the pyramids, when Egyptian government's consent is obtained, is amazing project planned by engineers to give tourists a thrilling bird's eye view of the huge desert structures.

CARS AT REST

ELECTRIC MOTOR

GANGPLANK

Mammoth Flying Swing to Give Bird's Eye Pyramid View

BOOK READS ITSELF ALOUD!

After 500 years, books are given voice by a clever Detroit inventor.

The Duston book, or record, is dependent upon photo electricity for its active principle. Put on this machine, voice is reeled off.

Merle Duston, of Detroit, with the fifteen-cent tape which records an hour's talk or music.

Contrasted with the strip of paper which not only records the words of a book, but which actually talks them from the surface of the paper through marvelous photo electric machinery, the original Gutenberg press, shown above, is the 500-year-old ancestor of Duston's Talking Book.

In 1455 Gutenberg used this crude method of melting metal and casting his own type which he used in the press above. It would take a year by this method to cast the type needed in recording the thought contained in Duston's fifteen-cent reel of chemically treated paper tape.

THE talking book is here at last!

Merle Duston, young Detroit inventor, has succeeded in recording spoken thought in a new way, infinitely cheaper than the present printed method, and on a medium by which machinery does the reading of the thought!

Ordinary paper, treated chemically, is run through a simple machine in which the modulations of a voice are recorded by photo-electric tubes by a reflected light process.

Entirely new is this method of recording, and new also is the fact that there is no further treatment required to develop the sound track.

Electric impulses bring forth the sound track lines, but just how the black lines emerge on the impregnated paper Mr. Duston is frank to say he does not know. Electrodes connected to the output terminals of an amplifier rest on the paper and darken portions of it. An ordinary pickup is used to play back, and the same machine may be used for recording and reproducing.

Radio Power will Revolutionize

Nikola Tesla, electrical wizard, foresees the day when airplanes will be operated by radio-transmitted power supplied by ground stations, as shown in the drawing above.

THE world will soon enjoy the benefits of electricity transmitted by radio. Huge and expensive transmission lines will be unnecessary. Bulky and unsightly distribution systems will be done away with. A little receiving device in your home will give you all the power you can use—and for only a fraction of present-day costs.

We will soon be communicating with other planets, where it is entirely possible that there is civilization far ahead of ours.

Tomorrow we will see rocket planes flying through stratosphere at a speed of a mile a second or 3600 miles an hour.

Fanciful dreams? No! Just conclusions based upon knowledge of what has been done, what is being done and what can be done in the future. I speak along practical lines and with a practical knowledge of what I am talking about.

Power transmission by radio is going to change our present civilization materially. The transmission of energy to another planet is now only a matter of engineering. I have solved the problem so well I no longer regard it as doubtful. I am also certain there are creatures on other planets whose ways are like ours. The new era will see amazing developments in interplanetary relations.

Every other planet has to pass through the same phase of existence this earth did, and life is started on them during that favorable phase by the rays of some sun. It develops in the presence of moisture, heat and light in much the same manner as life does here. We know that light propagates in straight lines, and consequently our perceptions of the forms through the images projected on the retina must be true.

Therefore, it should not be hard to establish intelligent exchange of ideas between two

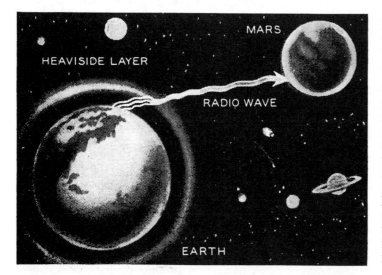

By using ultra-short waves, science expects to penetrate the heaviside layer, or gaseous medium surrounding the earth, and establish radio communication with Mars and other distant planets, as shown in drawing above.

the WORLD

by NIKOLA TESLA
As told to
ALFRED ALBELLI

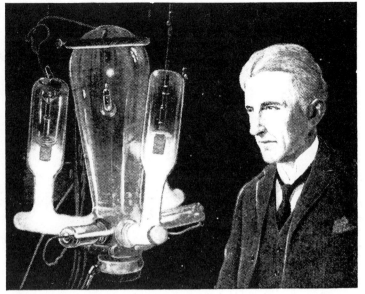

Nikola Tesla is shown in his laboratory with late type mercury arc rectifier tubes. When operating, these tubes give off a violet glow.

Who Is Tesla?

Radio Pioneer Nikola Tesla was born in Hungary, came to the United States in 1884 and has since developed more than 100 devices and improvements in electrical technology.

Once associated with the late Thomas A. Edison, Tesla sent a radio impulse around the world almost 40 years ago. He discovered the rotating field principle in alternating currents and is considered one of the greatest living electrical scientists and radio authorities.

planets. The earth we inhabit might be the beneficiary. It is conceivable that there is civilization on other planets far ahead of ours. If communication could be established by the earth the benefits to human beings would be incalculable.

As far back as June, 1900, in discussing my experiments at the beginning of the century, I said that my measurements and calculations showed that it was perfectly practicable to produce on our globe an electrical movement of such magnitude that, without the slightest doubt, its effect would be perceptible on some of our nearer planets, as Venus and Mars.

Interplanetary Communication Probable

Thus, from mere possibility, interplanetary communication has entered the stage of probability. In fact, that we can produce a distinct effect on one of these planets in this novel manner, namely, by disturbing the electrical condition of the earth, is beyond any doubt.

In order to make myself clearer I shall delve still further into the preliminary discoveries made in what I call my pioneering days, which was long before any other scientist had made any progress in this field. I have always chosen to remain in the background.

Some years ago I urged the experts engaged in the commercial application of the wireless art to employ very short waves, but for a long time my suggestions were not heeded. Eventually, though, this was done, and gradually the wave lengths were reduced to but a few meters. Invariably it was found that these waves, just as those in the air, follow the curvature of the earth and bend around obstacles, a peculiarity exhibited to a much lesser degree by transverse vibrations in a solid.

Recently, however, ultra-short waves have been experimented with and the fact that they also have that same property was hailed as a great discovery, offering the stupendous promise of making wireless transmission infinitely simpler and cheaper.

It is of interest to know what wireless

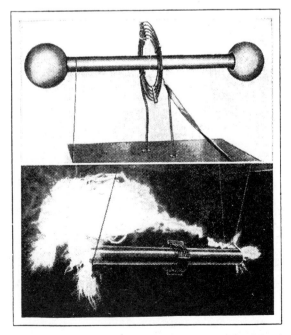

Top photo shows the famous Tesla coil, used to transmit early radio signals. Below, the coil in actual operation.

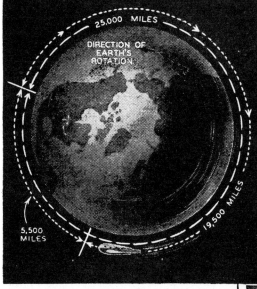

Future rocket planes may circle the globe in 5½ hours. At 3600 m.p.h., the plane travels about 19,500 miles. Earth's rotation adds 5500 miles to total. Right, lights directed against giant reflectors may furnish constant daylight in future, if radio-power projects prove successful.

experts have expected, knowing that waves a few meters long are transmitted clear to the antipodes. Is there any reason that they should behave radically different when their length is reduced to about half of one meter?

As the knowledge of this subject seems very limited, I may state that even waves only one or two millimeters long, which I produced thirty-four years ago, provided that they carry sufficient energy, can be transmitted around the globe. This is not so much due to refraction and reflection as to the properties of a gaseous medium and certain peculiar action.

Short Waves Provide Increased Channels

The chief object of employing very short waves is to provide an increased number of channels required to satisfy the ever-growing demand for radio appliances. But this is only because the transmitting and receiving apparatus, as generally employed, is ill-conceived and not well adapted for selection.

Because of this and other shortcomings, I do not attach much importance to the employment of waves which are now being experimented with. Besides, I am contemplating the use of another principle which I have discovered and which is almost unlimited in the number of channels and in the energy three-electrode tubes.

This invention has been credited to others, but as a matter of fact it was brought out by me in 1892, the principle being transmitted.

It should enable us to obtain many im-

portant results heretofore considered impossible. With the knowledge of the facts before me, I do not think it hazardous to predict that we will be enabled to illuminate the whole sky at night and that eventually we will flash power in virtually unlimited amounts to planets.

I would not be surprised at all if an experiment to transmit thousands of horsepower to the moon by this new method were made in a few years from now. We must establish transmission of power in all its innumerable applications. This has been my life work, and although I am now close to 78, I unhesitatingly say that I hope to see its fruition.

I have been fortunate in the evolution of new ideas, and the thought that a number of them will be remembered by posterity makes me happy indeed. I am confident

What About Today's Scientists?

"The scientists from Franklin to Morse were clear thinkers and did not produce erroneous theories. The scientists of today think deeply instead of clearly. One must be sane to think clearly, but one can think deeply and be quite insane.

"Today's scientists have substituted mathematics for experiments and they wander off through equation after equation and eventually build a structure which has no relation to reality."

—Nikola Tesla.

Radio Power to Revolutionize World

that my rotating field and induction motor and the wireless system I have given to the world will live long after I have gone.

You ask me about atomic energy? I experimented with the atom, and achieved similar ends, long before the wave of ballyhoo swept over the country in recent years. The idea of atomic energy is illusionary but it has taken a powerful hold on the mind and there are still some who believe it be be realizable.

Tesla's Vacuum Tube

I have disintegrated atoms in my experiments with a high potential vacuum tube I brought out in 1896 which I consider one of my best inventions. I have operated it with pressures ranging from 4,000,000 to 18,000,000 volts. More recently I have designed an apparatus for 50,000,000 volts which should produce many results of great scientific importance.

But as to atomic energy, my experimental observations have shown that the process of disintegration is not accompanied by a liberation of such energy as might be expected from the present theories.

And as for the cosmic ray: I called attention to this radiation while investigating Roentgen rays and radioactivity. In 1899 I erected a broadcasting plant at Colorado Springs, the first and only wireless plant in existence at that time, and there confirmed my theory by actual observation. My findings are in disagreement with the theories more recently advanced.

I have satisfied myself that the rays are not generated by the formation of new matter in space, a process which would be like water running up hill. According to my observations, they come from all the suns of the universe and in such abundance that the part contributed by our own sun is very insignificant by percentage. Some of these rays are of such terrific power that they can traverse through thousands of miles of solid matter.

Properties of Solar Rays

They have, furthermore, other extraordinary properties. This ray, which I call the primary solar ray, gives rise to a secondary radiation by impact against the air and the cosmic dust scattered through space. It is now commonly called the cosmic ray, and comes, of course, equally from all directions in space. If radium could be screened effectively against this ray it would cease to be radioactive.

The scientists from Franklin to Morse were clear thinkers and did not produce erroneous theories. The scientists of today think deeply instead of clearly. One must be sane to think clearly, but one can think deeply and be quite insane.

Today's scientists have substituted mathematics for experiments, and they wander off through equation after equation, and

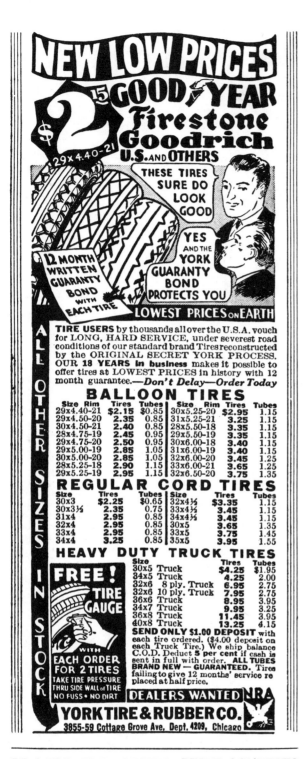

Radio Power to Revolutionize World

eventually build a structure which has no relation to reality.

I work every hour that I am awake but not with a feverish tempo. Although I live in the midst of the hustle and bustle of New York, I do not time my scientific experiments to the hectic, jazz rhythm of the hysterical metropolis. I work for the future—build for the future. Just as today I see the realization of experiments carried on fifty years ago, I am now working with a view toward still greater achievements which will come to pass a half century hence.

That is my method. After experiencing a desire to invent a certain thing, I go on for days, months, even years with the idea in the back of my head. Whenever I feel like it, I play around with the problem without giving it any deliberate consideration. This is the incubation period.

How Tesla Works

Next comes the stage of direct effort. At this point the solution is somewhere in my subconscious mind, although it may take some time before it reaches the level of consciousness.

As my conceived device begins to take form, I make mental changes in the construction, improvements are figured out, and I even operate it. All of this is preliminary work—all in my mind. When the machine itself is finished, I slip my imaginary job over it and find they coincide to the minutest detail.

A great development can be expected in rocket propelled machines for purposes of peace and war. With such machines it will be practicable to attain speeds of nearly a mile a second (3600 miles per hour), through the rarefied medium above the stratosphere.

I anticipate that such machines will be of tremendous importance in international conflicts of the future. I foresee that in times not too distant, wars between various countries will be carried on without a single combatant passing over the border.

Infernal Gas Machines

At this very time it is possible to construct infernal machines which will carry any desired quantity of poison gases and explosives, launch them against a target thousands of miles away and destroy a whole city or community.

If wars are not done away with, we are bound to come eventually to this kind of warfare, because it is the most economical means of inflicting injury and striking terror in the hearts of the enemy that has ever been imagined.

My paramount desire today, which guides me in everything I do, is an ambition to harness the forces of nature for the service of mankind. As I see it, we are on the threshold of a gigantic revolution based on the commercialization of the wireless trans-

Radio Power to Revolutionize World

mission of power. The principles for this have been discovered by me.

As this wireless energy is converted into a commodity for the use of the masses, transport and transmission will be subjected to tremendous changes. Motion pictures will be flashed across limitless spaces by my system. The same energy will drive airplanes and dirigibles from one central base.

In this new era man will be able to travel safely, and at great speed, to any part of the world—the jungle—the arctic—the desert—mountain tops—over oceans. The instruments by which these wonders will be achieved will be amazingly simple.

These things will come to pass. Some of them are already within the realm of realization. But like those wonders which I predicted and helped perfect nearly fifty years ago—in the early 80's—power transmission is just around the corner. It's coming.

Today I repeat again what I said to contemporary scientists of those earlier pioneering days:

The scientific man does not aim at an immediate result. He does not expect that his advanced ideas will be readily taken up. His work is like that of the planter—for the future. His duty is to lay the foundation for those who are to come, and point the way. He lives and labors and hopes.

TELEVISION Now Gives

These engineers are testing television's practicality. At the rear is the television projector which picks up the image of the speaker's face.

The television apparatus is concealed in the front of the booth, as shown above. The speaker's face is scanned with the disc above and the received image is reproduced on a screen with the disc beneath.

TWO way television, whereby two persons at opposite ends of a radio circuit may see images of each other as they talk. has finally become a practical working reality.

Before a group of skeptical witnesses the practical application of television was recently demonstrated by engineers of the American Telegraph and Telephone Company at their laboratories in New York City.

Although television is as yet outside the limits of commercial exploitation and cannot be used in homes as are broadcast receivers, the engineers are confident that this new radio development will be as popular within the next three years as is broadcast music now.

Back in April, 1929, the possibilities of television were first realized when President Hoover's face was "televised" from Washington to New York City. Then the next year Dr. Herbert Ives, head of the Bell Telephone Research Laboratories, reproduced via television, an outdoor tennis game. In 1929 television made another stride forward when colors were sent over the wire. A watermelon and a red rose were reproduced at a distant station with a perfect

Radio EYES and EARS

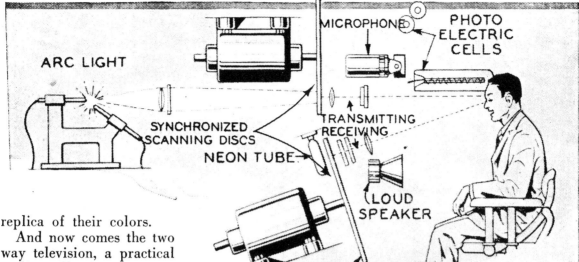

replica of their colors.

And now comes the two way television, a practical reality, allowing two people to look each other in the eyes as they talk.

At the recent test the demonstrator entered the three-sided television booth and seated himself in a swivel chair, facing a glass screen about a foot square, and marked with the words "Ikonophone—watch this space for television image." Above was a small aperture through which the scanning beam played on the speaker. Behind the booth, though all invisible to the speaker, was concealed the intricate transmitting and receiving apparatus, only the frame and the aperture being visible.

When the current to the apparatus was turned on and transmission about to begin, the face of the demonstrator became illuminated by a faint glow of blue light which was given off by the photo electric cells stationed at various points around the booth. These photo electric cells, known as "radio eyes," are the means whereby the image of the speaker is picked up and transmitted to the distant receiving station where the other speaker is seated.

Even though the speakers were situated three miles apart, it would not have made a particle of difference, the engineers stated, if they had been located an entire continent apart.

When transmission begins the words on the glass frame facing the speaker vanish as if by some magic trick, and there appears the animated image of the speaker at the other end of the circuit. The features are sharp and distinct, and are shown forth in black and white on a pinkish background.

While the demonstrator was watching the

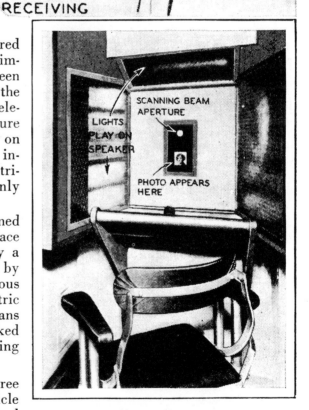

Above: A diagrammatic sketch of the combined radio and television apparatus. The voices and images of the speakers are being transmitted simultaneously. Below: Booth with the photo-electric cell lights which pick up the man's image, and the reproducing screen.

figure of the other person, his face was in turn being scanned for transmission— that is, his features were being swept 18 times a second by a scanning beam and

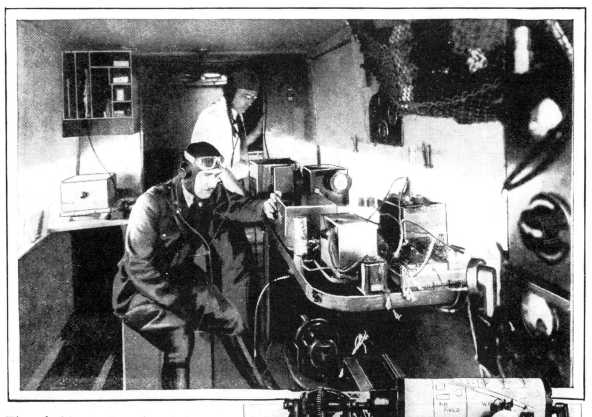

The television station aboard the army airplane from which maps of enemy territory and movements were sent during air maneuvers. At right is the receiving cylinder reproducing the map.

transmitted by the impulses set up in the light sensitive photo-electric cells above his head. The flickering blue light created by the cells is in reality very bright, and would be hard on the eyesight, were the rays not run through a blue glass, creating a light to which the human eye is insensitive.

When the demonstrator speaks his voice is picked up by a microphone concealed overhead and the other speaker's voice is in turn reproduced by a loud speaker, also concealed within the booth.

Television has also proved its serviceability for war time use in the recent air maneuvers held at Mather field. Here the entire activities of the planes were directed by radio, and maps of supposed enemy territory were charted out by a plane flying over the area and transmitted by television to the headquarters.

The chart was placed on a television cyl-

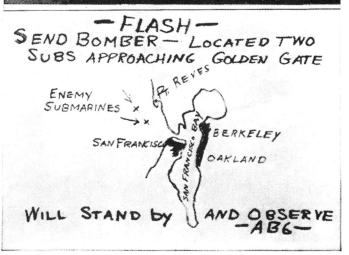

The above map, sent by television from an airplane gives some idea of the value of television in wartime.

inder in the plane and the details of the map were picked up by a photo electric cell and transmitted to "GHQ", where another synchronized disc reproduced the chart, thus informing the commanding officers directly as to the nature and position of enemy forces.

Television Movies Brings Distant Program to Theater

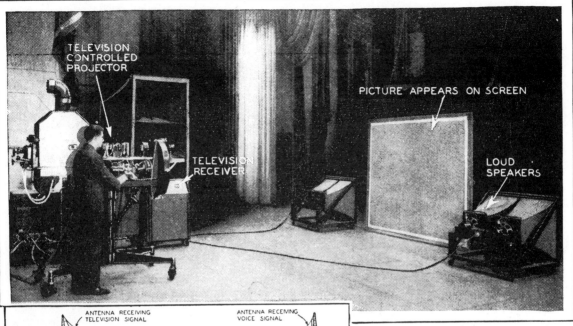

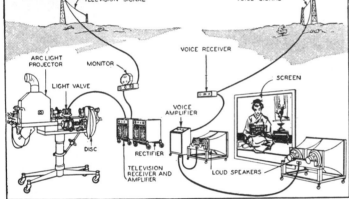

This diagrammatic sketch shows the television and radio-phone receivers which bring in both signals simultaneously, thus giving synchronization to the voice and the image.

A photo of the television equipment, showing receivers, projector, screen, and loud speakers, set up in the Schnectady theater for the first television movie show in history.

THE latest and most spectacular advance of television equipment took place recently at a vaudeville theatre in Schenectady, which the General Electric leased for a demonstration of television movies. This performance was the result of years of experimentation on the part of Dr. E. F. W. Alexanderson and his colleagues.

When the curtain parted, revealing a six-foot screen, Dr. Alexanderson stepped forward and modestly announced that the audience was about to hear and witness on the screen television images and voices of vaudeville actors performing at his laboratory about a mile away.

Immediately a pair of black faced comedians appeared on the screen cracking jokes and doing a song and dance. Then the leader of the orchestra appeared on the screen, baton in hand, and directed his orchestra which was located in the pit.

At Dr. Alexanderson's studio, images of the performers were being picked up by photo electric cells, and the television signals created by the light impulses broadcast along with the voices of the entertainers. At the theater where Dr. Alexanderson was acting as operator of the television movie projector, the voice and image signals were received simultaneously, the voice signals issuing from the loud speakers, while the television signals were transformed into light impulses, which controlled the projector beam.

A small device called a monitor telopticon transformed the radio waves into the electrical impulses which operate the sensitive light valve in the projector. This valve, a recent invention which makes television movies possible, controls the light from the arc, which is projected through the valve and the rotating disc. This disc breaks up the light in synchronism with the scanning disc at the transmitting station.

The entire television and voice receiving apparatus was located behind the screen.

Home Movies From Phonograph Records

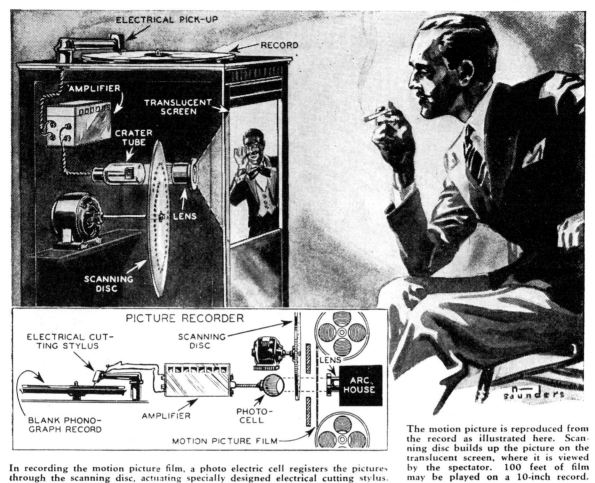

In recording the motion picture film, a photo electric cell registers the pictures through the scanning disc, actuating specially designed electrical cutting stylus.

The motion picture is reproduced from the record as illustrated here. Scanning disc builds up the picture on the translucent screen, where it is viewed by the spectator. 100 feet of film may be played on a 10-inch record.

PLAY a moving picture from a phonograph record!

When Baird, the English television experimenter, suggested this system several years ago, he did not realize how soon it would be before his prophecy would come true.

Those who have listened to television programs know that the signals become audible in the form of a shrill whistle in the loudspeaker. This whistle carries the picture elements in the form of modulated sound.

If we pass this sound through suitable apparatus it becomes capable of reproducing a picture. It is obvious, then, that we could record this sound on a phonograph record and "can" a picture just as we now "can" sound in the form of music.

The sound, in the form of electric current, is taken from the phonograph record by means of a specially designed electrical pick-up. From this point it is carried to an amplifier and thence to a television crater tube. At this point the image is thrown on the screen.

While much remains to be done to develop this apparatus, we may look forward to the day when our moving pictures will come in this new and convenient form.

Auto Chair for Crippled Vets

AS a means for making life more comfortable for crippled war veterans, a German mechanic has designed an "auto chair" which conveys the ex-fighters from place to place with utmost convenience. The motorized chair, shown below, is driven by a motor of low horsepower, and is easily maneuverable in the closest places. Bicycle-size tires add comfort.

Crippled German war veterans are enabled to transport themselves in this special "auto chair," powered by motor.

Television Shown in Theaters

TELEVISION in theaters, already a success in England, may soon entertain American audiences. Just opened in a New York office building, a demonstration "theater" exhibits the Baird system used abroad, which throws brilliant images as large as fifteen by twenty feet upon the screen. Installed in a number of British theaters, it offers televised news scenes to supplement regular movie shows, and all-television programs of major sporting events.

Occupying the center of the theater, the projection booth contains all the essential apparatus and controls, except for a special receiving aerial on the roof and high-tension power supply from a 50,000-volt rectifier. One of its two duplicate receiver-projectors serves as a stand-by, in case of tube failure, while the other is in operation. Each set employs twenty-seven tubes, including a cathode-ray tube of new design, whose intensely bright four-by-five-inch image is magnified by the projection lens. From the same booth, the operator controls the accompanying sound and all stage lights.

ALUMINUM SCREEN
(9' BY 12')

LOUD-SPEAKER

TWIN CATHODE-RAY-TUBE PROJECTORS
—ONE SERVES AS SPARE

CATHODE-RAY TUBE

PROJECTION BOOTH—OPERATORS CONTROL IMAGE WITH DIALS ON PANEL— EACH PROJECTOR HAS OWN RECEIVER AND AMPLIFIER

CABLES LEAD TO ANTENNAS ON ROOF

50,000-VOLT RECTIFIER SUPPLIES CURRENT FOR PROJECTORS

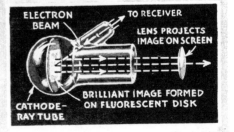

ELECTRON BEAM

TO RECEIVER

LENS PROJECTS IMAGE ON SCREEN

CATHODE-RAY TUBE

BRILLIANT IMAGE FORMED ON FLUORESCENT DISK

THEATER AUDIENCES WATCH EVENTS AS THEY HAPPEN

How television programs are presented in a theater under the Baird system commonly employed in England. Drawing above shows the manner in which the bright image in the cathode-ray tube is projected onto the screen

Giant Receiver *gives*

R. A. Fox, manager of Lorain, Ohio, wired entertainment system, working in his studio

By Robert E. Martin

Programs, Retransmitted over Telephone Lines, Go to Loudspeakers in Many Hundreds of Residences

Out of this 22-inch cone speaker, with volume control, comes the relayed radio programs

MUSIC that had filled the studio stopped as R. A. Fox, the man who entertains Lorain, Ohio, for eighteen and one-half hours a day, turned a switch. Fox snapped another switch, and began talking into a microphone standing on the desk in front of him:

"Ladies and gentlemen, we're going to bring you the Cleveland-Chicago baseball game as received through station WGN at Chicago. Because of noise and interference, we are going to re-broadcast the program instead of providing a direct hook-up."

He then started a crowd-noise record to provide a suitable background, and proceeded to describe the game as it was played. While Fox was telling about the game, baseball fans in several hundred Lorain homes were grouped around cone-type loudspeakers that stand on three legs. Wires run from these speakers to wall terminals, thence parallel to regular telephone wires to the nearest exchange building. On the back of each speaker is a switch and volume-control knob.

The baseball news that issues from such speakers is but one item on a program that runs from 6:30 in the morning until 1:00 o'clock the next morning. During all of this eighteen-and-one-half-hour period, the listener simply turns the speaker on or off as he pleases. For $2.50 the wired-entertainment subscriber gets, each month, over twenty-three solid days of music, news, word pictures of local and national events, and occasional novelty programs.

The heart of the Lorain system is a room at the central telephone office. A panel-type amplifier not unlike that to be seen in any radio broadcasting station or talking-picture house, occupies one corner of the room. It takes audio-frequency cur-

rents that come to it from any of several sources, steps them up, and then feeds them out through a maze of wires to subscribers or to other amplifying panels at the three branch stations. These branches, one at Amherst, seven miles away, and the other two in East and South Lorain, relay programs to individual subscribers.

The amplified sound, at audio frequency, goes out to homes and business places on separate lines. That is, while the regular telephone facilities such as conduits are used, separate cables are laid for entertainment purposes. Of these, nearly three-fourths are underground, so that static and other disturbances usually associated with radio reception, are almost entirely eliminated.

The capacity of the amplifier at the main station is 300 speakers. The East Lorain station serves 200 more, and the

South Lorain and Amherst exchanges, 100 each. A maximum of four speakers can be operated by each line that goes out from the amplifier. Whenever such a line becomes grounded, a buzzer sounds and a light glows on the switchboard, so that the trouble can be remedied at once.

Although the entertainment generally is selected by operators of the system, a subscriber can have a favorite radio program "put on the wire" by calling the studio at the telephone office at least a half-hour beforehand. Such requests are

Dark-colored wires in this maze are ones that carry music and news to hundreds of subscribers

RADIO *to Whole City* ·

SOUND PARTS OF MOTION PICTURES OF PARTICULAR INTEREST ARE USED OCCASIONALLY →

LOCAL EVENTS REPORTED WITH AID OF PORTABLE REMOTE CONTROL EQUIPMENT

RADIO RECEIVING STATIONS PLACED IN STRATEGIC POSITIONS IN OUTLYING DISTRICTS PICK UP CHAIN BROADCAST PROGRAMS AND RELAY THEM BY SPECIAL WIRES TO "CENTRAL"

DISTRIBUTING RACK TO SUBSCRIBERS' SPEAKERS

LOCAL HOTEL BALLROOM DANCE ORCHESTRA FURNISHES MUSIC BY REMOTE PICK-UP

SUBSCRIBERS IN NEAR-BY TOWNS RECEIVE PROGRAMS THROUGH LOCAL SUB-STATIONS BY SPECIAL WIRE

"CENTRAL" STATION IN LORAIN RECEIVES, AMPLIFIES, AND DISTRIBUTES PROGRAMS BY SPECIAL LINES TO SUB-STATIONS AND NEAR-BY SUBSCRIBERS

LARGE CONE SPEAKER FURNISHED BY PHONE COMPANY IS THE ONLY APPARATUS NECESSARY IN THE HOME TO RECEIVE PROGRAMS

SUB-STATIONS IN NEAR-BY COMMUNITIES RECEIVE PROGRAMS THROUGH SPECIAL TRUNK LINES, AMPLIFY SIGNALS, AND SEND THEM TO LOCAL SUBSCRIBERS BY SPECIAL WIRES

Drawing shows clearly the various steps in the operation of the community radio system

not frequent, Fox says, because programs always are made up of features that are known to be popular.

Often Fox is asked why regular telephone wires are not used for carrying programs into homes. This was tried, but found unsatisfactory. Carrier current was super-imposed on the telephone lines at such frequencies that it did not interfere with ordinary conversation. However, the carbon-grain microphone that forms the sound-converting part of each telephone transmitter persisted in acting as a detector, rectifying radio-frequency currents and making programs audible through the telephone receiver. Of course, this played havoc with regular service. An investigation revealed that the trouble could be overcome by installing choke coils in each telephone box, and making other changes; but the cost would have been prohibitive.

The system now in use, which consists essentially of a giant radio receiving set with hundreds of loudspeakers scattered over several square miles of territory, has been found satisfactory. The all-day-long entertainment for the price of a telephone has proved popular with those who do not want to be bothered with a complete radio receiver, or dislike paying for one.

Television in Three Dimensions

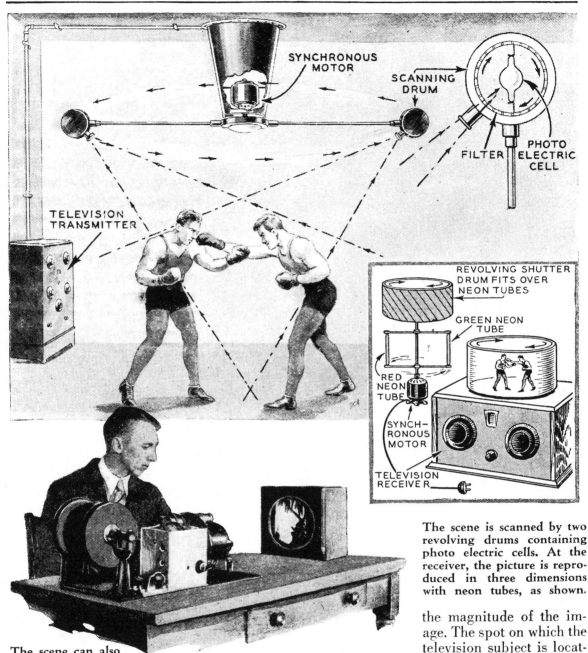

The scene can also be reproduced on a screen by means of a television controlled projector.

The scene is scanned by two revolving drums containing photo electric cells. At the receiver, the picture is reproduced in three dimensions with neon tubes, as shown.

A DEVICE which can produce a 360 degree picture by television through a stereoscope scanner has been invented by Leslie Gould, a radio engineer of Bridgeport, Connecticut. With Mr. Gould's television system it is possible to televise a boxing match, a play, an orchestra, or any other spectacle whose scene of action can be compressed into a reasonable space.

The new invention makes use of neon tubes of various sizes and colors, depending upon the magnitude of the image. The spot on which the television subject is located is scanned by beams from two rotating arms, as shown in the drawing above. At the extremity of each arm is a scanning drum containing a photo electric cell, which picks up the images to be televised.

The scene which is going to be televised must be flooded with a great quantity of strong light. Each electric eye catches the light reflected through the apertures in the revolving drums from the light portions of the body, and flashes to the transmitter the electric impulses set up by the variations in light.

BUILD YOURSELF A
Wrist-Watch Radio

TUNING CONTROL.

6A8 TUBE

TUNING CONDENSER (C-4)

R-5

C-2

C-5

C-1

L-1

R-4

L-2

8-PRONG WAFER SOCKET

ANTENNA.

MIDGET TUNING COIL

Detail view of the receiver with the flanged cover removed to show compact arrangement of parts. Below, wiring diagram of circuit

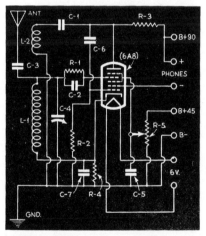

The midget receiver being used as a wrist radio. Flexible wires, anchored at the armpit, lead to the battery power supply on the belt

TINY enough to be worn on your wrist, carried in your pocket, or fastened to your belt, this homemade "two-tube" broadcast receiver sets a new record in compactness. By careful planning, its seventeen standard parts have been crammed into a midget cabinet measuring two and a half inches square and less than one and three quarters inches deep.

Built around a single dual-purpose metal tube (type 6A8), the circuit consists of a screen-grid detector resistance coupled to a triode audio stage. Being in reality two tubes in one, the 6A8 provides all of the necessary elements in a single casing. As shown in the diagram, one six-volt filament or heater serves the combination tube, saving additional space.

For simplicity, the sheet-aluminum cabinet is made in two parts; a simple U-shaped piece serving as the chassis, and a similar U-shaped unit provided with flanges serving as the cover. To keep the cabinet as small as possible, a square hole should be cut in its upper end to take the projecting head of the 6A8 tube.

Although standard parts are used throughout, a few minor changes must be made in the interest of compactness. For instance, the standard A.C.-D.C. antenna coil used can be shortened considerably by cutting off the excess cardboard tubing that projects from each end of the coil. Similarly, the wafer-type tube socket can be cut down all around with a pair of sharp scissors. One other minor alteration consists of providing the air-padding condenser (C_4) with a suitable control knob.

In wiring the circuit, follow the placement of the parts shown. First wire the potentiometer, fixed condensers, and resistors, and do not mount the tuning coil, tuning condenser, and tube socket permanently until all the connections have been made. To save space, the coupling condenser (C_6) is mounted inside the hollow core of the tuning coil.

When connected to a ten or fifteen-foot antenna, the set should give good earphone volume. Should the circuit fail to

oscillate, switch the connections to the tickler coil (L_2). Some experimenting may be necessary to obtain the right polarity for the winding.—ARTHUR C. MILLER.

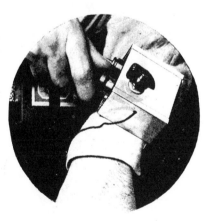

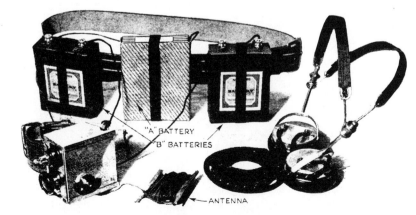

"A" BATTERY

"B" BATTERIES

ANTENNA

An idea of the size of the set can be gained by comparing it with the portable "B" batteries

PARTS NEEDED

C_1.—Mica condenser, midget, .0005 mfd.
C_2.—Mica condenser, midget, .0001 mfd.
C_3.—Mica condenser, midget, .00025 mfd.
C_4.—Air-padding condenser, variable, 100 mmf.
C_5 and C_7.—By-pass condensers, .05 mfd.
C_6.—By-pass condenser, .01 mfd.
L_1 and L_2.—Midget A.C.-D.C. antenna coil, broadcast.
R_1.—Resistance, 3 meg., ½ watt.
R_2.—Resistance, 300,000 ohm, ½ watt.
R_3.—Resistance, 250,000 ohm, ½ watt.
R_4.—Resistance, 350 ohm, ½ watt.
R_5.—Potentiometer, 50,000 ohm.
Miscellaneous.—Eight-prong socket, 6A8 tube, two knobs, aluminum case, batteries, wire, earphones, solder, bolts, nuts, etc.

A Fan Motor Television

by L. B. ROBBINS

Here is a simple and easily-built type of television receiver with which you can pick up the television images now being transmitted over the air from a number of stations.

When tuning in television images on the receiver, the room should be darkened for best results.

THE time is now ripe for radio fans who build their own sets to construct a television receiver. Several broadcasting stations are on the air transmitting on both long and short waves, and have so perfected their apparatus that a simple receiver like that illustrated in the accompanying drawings will bring out the pictures with a fair degree of clarity and brilliancy.

The construction of a television receiver is actually not so complicated as the construction of a broadcast receiver, and the expense is probably less. The one herein described utilizes the simplest of parts, and constructional details are simplified as much as possible. Many dimensions are not given because the builder may wish to use certain parts which he has on hand, that are well suited for the purpose.

First, build a cabinet of ½-inch soft wood about the dimensions shown in Fig. 1. The

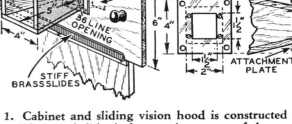

Fig. 1. Cabinet and sliding vision hood is constructed as shown. The panel slides in brass strips to any of the openings. Position of the neon tube is adjusted from the side.

top is shown in three sections, the ends of which cut with a miter box to make a good joint. These joints are glued and nailed to cleats underneath. Such a top adds much to the appearance of the cabinet, but may be discarded if simplicity is desired, and a flat top substituted instead. The back can be

Receiver for Experimenters

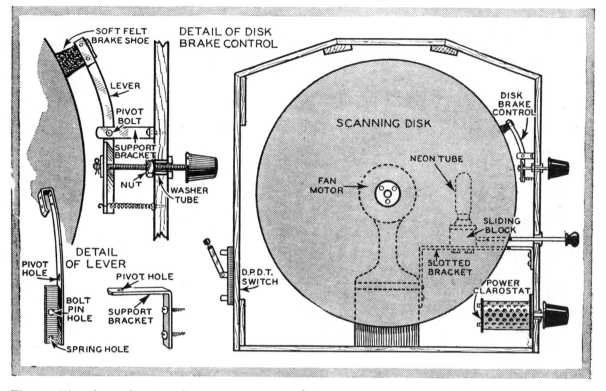

Fig. 2. The above drawing shows arrangement of the parts in the cabinet, and details of the brake which regulates disk speed. The motor table is built so that the motor shaft lines up exactly opposite the center mark on the cabinet front. The D.P.D.T. switch throws receiver from speaker to neon tube.

made from a sheet of stiff wallboard or from boards. You can finish the cabinet in any manner you desire.

The front door should consist of one single piece of plywood 30 in. square if possible, reinforced along the back edges with thin battens.

Hinge it to the right hand edge of cabinet and supply a pair of hooks for closing it. Two cleats nailed to the inside of left hand edge of the cabinet keep the front flush with the edge.

The viewing apparatus is then attached to the face of this hinged front as shown in Fig. 1. First strike a point on the hinged front of the cabinet representing the exact center. From that point draw a horizontal line across the front to the right hand edge. This is the center line for three holes, which are 1½ in. square and 1½ in. apart as shown, cut in the front. The left hand hole should be 4¼ inches from the center spot on the front of the cabinet.

Now over and below these holes attach two stiff brass slides, as shown, into which can easily slide the movable observation panel. This panel is 12 in. long, 6 in. wide and ½ in. thick. In the exact center of this panel is cut a 1½-inch square hole. Over this hole is mounted the vision hood, which is made of thin wood of the dimensions specified in Fig. 1. An attachment plate serves to hold the hood to the panel as shown. Now, scribe a short vertical line under the exact center of each hole in the hinged front and the single hole on the panel. Then when the mark under the panel hole coincides with that under one of the front holes, the hood opening and the hole in the front are properly aligned for viewing. Number the hinged front mark nearest the center with a 24, the next, 36, and the right hand hole, 48. These designate the portions of the scanning disk to be viewed over those numbers. Finally, finish the inside of the hinged front, the back of the movable panel and the inside of the hood in dull black and paint the outside to match or to contrast nicely with the rest of the cabinet.

MAY, 1938
VOL. XX - NO. 1
W. H. FAWCETT
PUBLISHER

MODERN MECHANIX

A PRIVATE newspaper with any spot in your home as the press room, the world's best editors and reporters on your staff, and the radio as your copy boy—this is not the dream of Jules Verne—but an actual accomplishment, available today to anyone in the United States owning an ordinary radio receiver.

No thundering press will deafen you when your paper is printed, but instead, equipment contained in a small, attractive box, will silently print your "latest edition" while you sleep, completing it in time for reading at breakfast.

Facsimile transmitters and printers have been announced by two manufacturers, Finch Telecommunications Laboratories, Inc., of New York City, and RCA Victor, of Camden, N. J.

Predicted to be in wide-spread use within the year, many large broadcast stations have started tests with the system, and actual broadcasts on a definite schedule will be an accomplished fact as

soon as these tests are completed. Of great significance is the fact. that the Federal Communications Commission has granted the broadcasters permission to operate the facsimile equipment on the regular broadcast frequencies. Translated into actual use, this means that when the householder is through listening to his favorite station, he merely turns a switch which will, at the correct time, again turn on the radio for reception of the same station, but this time instead of sounds emitting from the loudspeaker, an up-to-the-minute newspaper will unfold.

At present one of the largest eastern broadcast stations, WOR, is supplying this type of transmission, though not yet on a regular schedule. It is being done both on the regular broadcast channels as well as on the ultra-short waves. Plans are under way for regular service of facsimile transmissions early this spring.

Among other stations that have received F.C.C. permission to make facsimile broadcasts are WGN,

YOUR NEWSPAPER BY RADIO!

Chicago; KSD, St. Louis; WHO, Des Moines; WGH, Norfolk, Va.; WHK, Cleveland; KSTP, St. Paul; KMJ, Fresno, and KFPK, Sacramento.

The facsimile recorder will be sold at a price no higher than the average good broadcast receiver. When production is increased the price is expected to be reduced to that of the average medium priced midget receiver. With the exception of the recorder, no special equipment is required except the broadcast receiver itself.

This new medium of entertainment and education is not to be confused with television, differing most widely from it in that its operation produces a tangible newspaper on which appears the printed word, photographs, drawings, sketches and even adver-

tisements. As the newspaper is produced, it can be removed from the machine and preserved if desired, differing from the conventional type only in size.

Briefly, the operation of the transmitter and recorder is as follows: The copy to be transmitted—whether it is pictures, news flashes, line drawings or comic strips—involves no special printing or preparation because the material itself can be inserted directly into the transmitter. An electric bulb, throwing a spot of light, moves back and forth across the copy to be transmitted. This action is similar to that of the human eye as it sweeps from left to right across a line of type. In its movement across the copy, the spot of light is reflected back into a light-sensitive photo-electric cell. When the scanning light strikes the white portions of the copy, it returns a full reflection to the light-sensitive cell. When it strikes a black area, no light is reflected, while for the shaded areas, a corresponding reflection is obtained.

Because of the action of intermittent light at the cell, these reflections are changed into electrical energy or impulses. At the receiver or recorder, these impulses operate a stylus sweeping in synchronism with the scanning light at the transmitter.

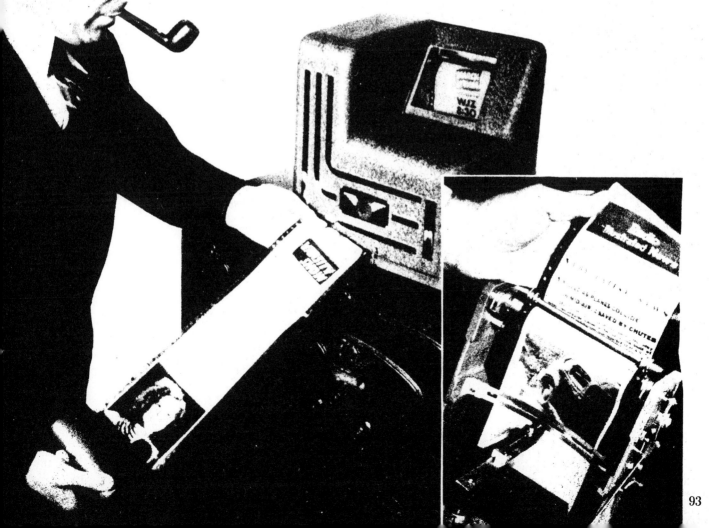

Inventor William G. H. Finch holding a newspaper printed by the recorder he developed. Below, right is shown the printing section of the Finch recorder. The arm swings back and forth across the paper in synchronism with the beam of light scanning the copy at the transmitter. While television remains hiding around the mythical "corner," facsimile brings news, photographs, sketches, and drawings into the home today.

"Vibrometer" Makes Radio Music Visible

Music and voice from radio is produced in sound patterns on the screen of the "vibrometer," as shown in drawing above.

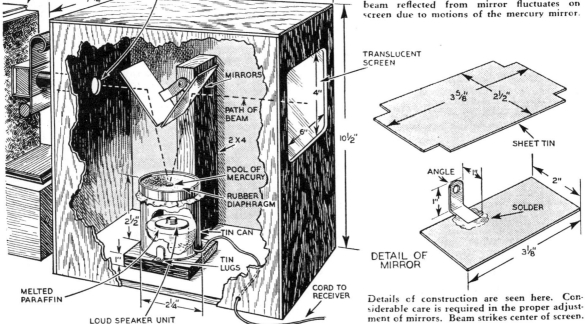

Interior view of the "vibrometer" shows how mirrors are mounted on the 2x4. Beneath is seen the can over which is stretched the rubber holding the pool of mercury. Light beam reflected from mirror fluctuates on screen due to motions of the mercury mirror.

Details of construction are seen here. Considerable care is required in the proper adjustment of mirrors. Beam strikes center of screen.

WITH the simple little instrument here described, a whole new world of radio experimentation is opened to the amateur. On a screen you are enabled actually to see the strange effects of sound waves and the endless variety of patterns, many of them curiously beautiful, that are produced by the incoming music and voice in a radio receiver.

The pattern producing instrument is made by placing a small radio loudspeaker unit, preferably of the Baldwin type, in a tin can in the manner illustrated in the drawings above. A half pint lacquer or paint can is just the right size to accommodate the average small unit.

Two tin lugs are soldered to the can to hold it down to the baseboard. Inasmuch as a dead sound chamber must be produced between the loudspeaker unit and the rubber diaphragm, it will be necessary to pour melted paraffine in the space that exists between the loud speaker unit and the tin can.

The rubber diaphragm must be very thin for best results. The writer used a rubber balloon and strong rubber bands to bind it over the top of the can. The degree of tautness of the rubber diaphragm will depend somewhat upon the power the loudspeaker and the current fed into it. It's mainly a "cut and try" job.

Television Programs Sent on Light Beams

TELEVISION SIGNALS TRANSMITTED OVER BEAMS FROM TOWER LIGHT

PHOTO-ELECTRIC CELLS, FOCUSED ON STATION LIGHT, PICK UP BEAM

TELEVISION STUDIO

LEAD TO HOME TELEVISION RECEIVER

MICROPHONE

PHOTO-CELLS RECEIVE VOICE ON LIGHT BEAM

FOG-PENETRATING LIGHT

Airport supervisor directs plane landing over voice-modulated beam of light. Photo-cells on plane pick up beam, which is transformed back into voice speaking directions.

Artist's drawing above illustrates system whereby television programs in future may be broadcast from a powerful arc light mounted atop a tower high above the city. These modulated light waves will be picked up in the homes by individual photo electric cells, or "electric eyes," instead of the present type of wire antenna.

TELEVISION transmitted on a light beam, opening the way to a new era in the art of broadcasting, has been successfully demonstrated at Schenectady, N. Y. by Dr. E. F. W. Alexanderson, noted radio engineer.

In the laboratory tests, instead of the electric impulses being fed into the radio transmitter as heretofore, they were modulated into high frequencies on a light beam from a high-intensity arc. This beam was projected the length of the laboratory into a photo-electric tube, which transformed the light waves back into electric impulses. These latter impulses reproduced the original image by means of an ordinary television receiver.

Light-transmitted television points the way to the development of a new method of communicating with planes whereby a fog penetrating light, modulated into voice waves, is projected to photo-electric cells on the wings of a plane, so that landing directions may be transmitted through fog for prevention of smash-ups.

Robot With Mechanical Brain Thinks Up Story Plots

FORMERLY robots were merely mechanical devices that could perform a variety of stunts under the guidance of a human being, but now a robot has made its appearance that thinks, has a soul of a kind, creative imagination, and other qualities necessary for writing a modern stereotyped short story. This robot, the invention of Wycliffe Hill, a Los Angeles scenario writer, is declared to be able to build up millions of plots, no two alike, for magazine stories or movie plays.

Mr. Hill has equipped his robot with an index chart, divided into eight sections, one devoted to each of the eight elements of a story—background, character, obstacle, problem, predicament, complication, crisis and climax—and with an assortment of variations. The robot selects the material as required from this inexhaustible source and builds plots that could never be imagined by the author

Mr. Wycliffe Hill demonstrating his new story writing robot, which can think up any kind of plot with its mechanical brains.

without the aid of the mechanical brain. Now if you want to become a successful author simply obtain a robot and put it to work.

London Bobbies Broadcast Crime News With Five-Pound Portable Radio

The portable radio carried by London bobbies.

RADIO is fast becoming one of the most dangerous foes of the modern criminal. Often before he has fairly finished committing his crime, the news has gone out to all the police, broadcast over a powerful central radio station and picked up by squad cars cruising the streets.

In London, the police officials have carried the development a step further and equipped each individual Bobby with a sending and receiving set by means of which he is enabled to phone headquarters at any minute.

The new equipment, devised by H. W. Adey, a London radio expert, is no larger than a lantern and weighs between four and five pounds. The box, which is provided with hooks so that it can be carried on the belt, contains a two-tube transmitting and receiving set having a radius of ten to twenty miles. A wire a hundred feet long wrapped around a specially devised helmet worn by the Bobby serves as the antenna.

When equipped with one of these combination transmitter-receivers, the Bobby is enabled to flash the news of a crime immediately to the central station, which in turn broadcasts it to the police all over the city.

Radio Controlled Robots Stage a Realistic Boxing Match

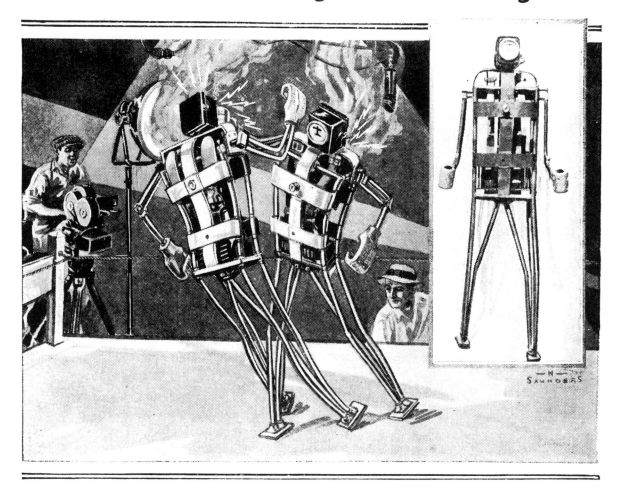

TWO pugilistic robots, built by the Ver-onda brothers, of California, recently staged a furious six round boxing match in which they slugged each other's metal bodies with all the realism of a human fight. The actions of the mechanical fighters were controlled by short wave radio. At the height of the fray, however, the wires got crossed somewhere. With smoke rising from their innards the fighters lost their heads and began lashing out wildly, dealing terrific clouts with both fists. Finally one robot went down and the other collapsed on top of him.

Giant Whale Makes 3000-Mile Trip Across the Country on a Trailer

PEOPLE living inland, who have never seen the ocean, to say nothing of a whale, will have the opportunity to satisfy their curiosity when this gigantic 32-foot whale, shown in the photo at the right, passes through their town on its 3000-mile overland journey from Los Angeles to New York. The great fish will be carried on a trailer, so that the curious can get a good view of its peculiarities. The whale's flesh will be treated with chemicals that will preserve it against decay.

Trailer will convey this whale across country for exhibition.

Golf is Now Played Like Roulette

A SCRAMBLING of the ancient Scotch game of golf and the somewhat less Scotch game of roulette has resulted in the creation which beats all for novelty—golf played on a roulette wheel. In the center of a circular pit a gaming wheel, marked like the table variety, spins merrily, while the golfer attempts to knock a golf ball into the winning compartments.

Introduced recently in Los Angeles, the new game is winning increasing favor among West Coast golf fans seeking the thrills of both roulette and golf. The putting tee is located in a recess in the side of the pit, and the ball, shot from there, flutters around the wheel and finally settles into some compartment. Located out of doors to give full health benefits, the wheel is cleverly decorated with flashing lights and illuminated numbers for night playing.

The latest in mergers—a combination of golf and roulette. The player knocks golf ball into compartments of gaming wheel.

Straw Hat Autos for Hot Climes

For protection against torrid rays of sun, motorists of Madeira Islands have encased autos in woven straw as shown in the photo above.

IN THE torrid Madeira Islands, automobiles have donned straw hats to provide the last word in comfort for motorists. Experimenters there have found that woven straw is much less heat absorbing than the customary metal cover, and so have equipped their cars with an overall sheathing of this airy material. Hood, body, running boards, mud guards, and even wheels are encased with woven straw and motorists report that they no longer suffer from the terrific heat when their cars are exposed to sun rays. An auto which has gone straw hat is shown in the photo above.

Gov't Builds Hoosegow on Wheels

DID you ever hear of a hoosegow on wheels? Well, the government has recently rigged one up for the transportation of prisoners to the state penitentiaries. From the outside it looks no different from a regular passenger coach, but you may be assured that the bars on the windows are quite adequate to frustrate the most violent attempts at jail break. The interior is so arranged that a formidable army of guards is no longer necessary, four instead of the usual twenty being sufficient to prevent escapes.

Separate compartments provide accommodations for both male and female prisoners, totalling more than a hundred.

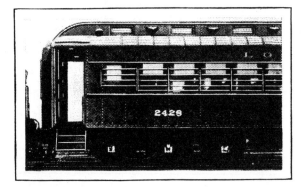

The new government hoosegow on wheels, built for transportation of convicts. Steel compartments and bars over window make escape impossible.

New Automatic Device Answers Phone, Records Message

PAUL H. ROWE, a Los Angeles sound engineer, has perfected a nearly human robot that answers his telephone perfectly when he is out.

The ringing of the telephone bell starts this ingenious machine operating, and whatever the caller says is received by a microphone and recorded. When Rowe returns, he is able to listen to whatever messages have come in.

Expert Tastes Soap for a Living

TESTING soap by taste is one of the chief duties of Joseph Strobl, chief soap maker for a Los Angeles company. He samples the cooking product much like an expert chef. Chemical tests take too long at critical stages and are said to be less accurate than Strobl's tongue.

Photo shows expert testing soap by tasting sample from caldron.

Paul H. Rowe demonstrating his ingenious telephone robot which takes and records messages phoned in his absence. He predicts these machines will soon be in wide use.

Auto-ship Runs on Land or Water

A PRACTICAL amphibian run-about has been designed and built from odds and ends by a California man, who has made several successful trial runs with it on highways and waterways near Sacramento.

In the water it is driven by a motorboat propeller, and on emerging the power is transferred to the rear wheels. Power is supplied by a two-cylinder, eleven horse power motorcycle engine, equipped with a fan for cooling at the high r.p.m. attained when the propeller is used. The vehicle is steered like a common automobile.

This unique amphibian, made by William Faulkner of Sacramento, Cal., from odds and ends of automobile and motorcycle parts, can travel twelve miles an hour on water, and reaches a speed of about fifty miles an hour on land.

Shooting the Rapids—Thrill

All the thrills of a breath-taking roller coaster are combined in this new mammoth amusement park ride. Glass-topped boats shoot the rapids and go over the falls. The invention would bring to any city a realistic section of the Grand Canyon with its pueblo villages, rock formations and trails.

This boat is shooting the rapids of the Grand Canyon ride and is about to dive over the falls. Drawing shows wheels and guide rails which eliminate all possibility of the boat upsetting in the canyon walls.

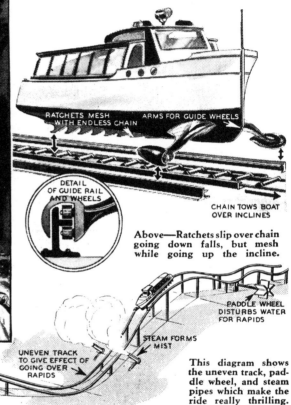

Above—Ratchets slip over chain going down falls, but mesh while going up the incline.

This diagram shows the uneven track, paddle wheel, and steam pipes which make the ride really thrilling.

THE Grand Canyon of Colorado gave two inventors the idea for a new, unusual and thrilling amusement park ride.

The inventors, F. H. Michaelson and Ray Durie of Portland, Ore., would bring to any world's fair or amusement park a true reproduction of a section of the Grand Canyon. Within its walls they would build a ride that would have all thrills of a roller coaster and speed boat ride combined.

Glass topped boats to protect passengers from spray are to be fitted with guide wheels. These wheels will run along undulating tracks under the water channel in the canyon reproduction.

Paddle wheels under the water will churn up the stream to give the effect of rapids. Riding over the uneven track through the rough water the boat would shoot the rapids very realistically.

During the ride the boat would take a breath-taking dive over falls. Steam pipes ejecting mist will add to the effect, but the dive would be quite safe as special guide wheels will hold the boat to the rails during the entire trip.

When the boat reached the bottom of the dive, ratchets along its keel would mesh with an endless chain. This would pull the boat up the incline. The boat will be provided with a motor to drive it at varying rates of speed through the scenic ride.

The inventors plan to reproduce the walls of the Grand Canyon to a height of 100 feet. The entire reproduction will be surrounded by a wall at the top of which will be a scenic walk. From this walk spectators can see the boats riding through the channel, shooting the rapids and going over the falls.

A suspension bridge will lead to the Pueblo Village that will closely resemble those found in the southwest. The rocks of the canyon will be built of composition material and painted to match the varied colors of the real Grand Canyon.

# of Grand Canyon Scenic Ride

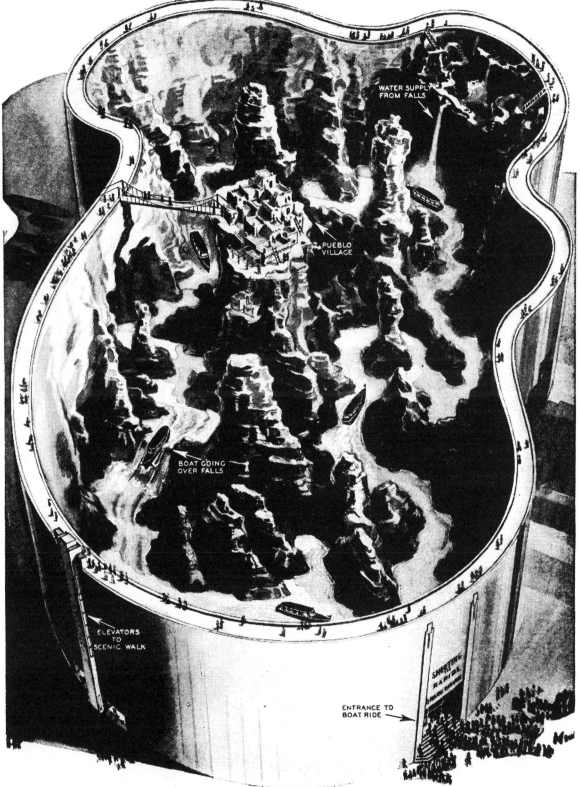

The Grand Canyon amusement park ride will be a great undertaking, as shown clearly in the above drawing. The walls would be about one hundred feet high. Within would be a realistic reproduction of the Grand Canyon of Colorado.

At one point the scenic walk will lead to a trail going down to the headwaters of a waterfall that is the source of supply for water in the channel. Two entrances are provided for: one to the boat ride and the other to the scenic walk.

Japan's GASOLINE Gun Whirls Death

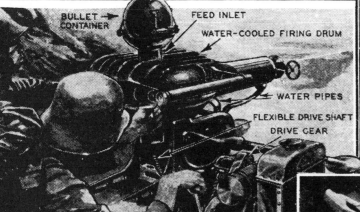

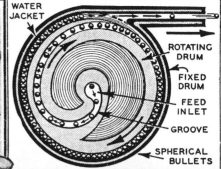

Japanese gun, driven by gasoline motor, is capable of expelling 9,075 bullets a minute, making it one of the most effective war weapons developed to date. At upper right is diagram showing how it works. Bullets are fed into groove through hopper.

A POWDER-LESS gun capable of firing 9,075 bullets per minute, almost one half ton of steel per minute, has been perfected by a Japanese inventor after years of secret experimentation. The new weapon is scarcely heavier than a machine gun.

Steel bullets resembling ball bearings are whirled outward at tremendous velocities just as fast as they are fed into the hopper. A small gasoline engine spins a steel disc at an estimated speed of 60,000 r.p.m. Bullets fed into the center of the disc are hurled outward and through the muzzle by the terrific centrifugal force.

A gun of similar design perfected just after the war in 1918 by L. W. Lombard and Earle Ovington was turned down by the United States government and later bought by Great Britain.

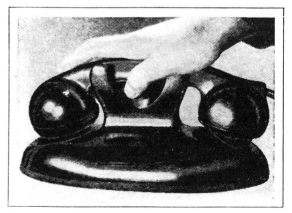

This gun, practically the same as that now used in Japan, was developed in 1918 by Levi W. Lombard and Earle Ovington, shown in photo. Turned down by the United States, it was sold to the British for a large sum of money.

Streamlined Phone Is Attractive

SMALL, efficient and attractive because of its unique design, this latest telephone is proving very popular in offices and homes. The handset and base are each moulded in one piece. Tone quality is very good. Streamlined after the fashion of new model automobiles and trains, it is welcomed on any busy man's desk because it takes up so little room.

Now You Can Watch Air Program

This light, attached to your radio, flashes on, off with volume of voice coming through set.

A MYSTERIOUS phosphorescent light attached to any radio enables listeners to "see" their programs. The light, which can be had in white, blue, or red depending upon the type of crystal used, varies in strength with the current passing through the loudspeaker.

The light will show three flashes if some radio actor says "Come here, John."

Here's the streamlined phone. Put your hand on your desk set and compare with photo to get an idea of size.

Modern "Super-Artists" Make Nightmares in Metal

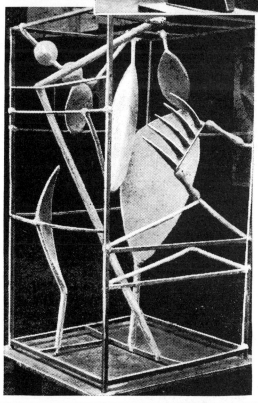

You'd never guess it, but the masterpiece at the upper right is "The Kiss." Paris super-independent artists work in metal, using welding machines and shears for brushes.

IRON and steel are replacing the canvases of a group of super-independent artists in Paris, who weld together iron castings, forged steel shapes, and pieces of tin to form grotesque figures looking more like nightmares than works of art.

Needless to say, the works of these modern artists are infinitely symbolic, aiming to reflect moods rather than pictures of the subject or action chosen.

Film Winds, Unwinds on Same Reel

A NEW projection camera for short movies, using only one film-holding reel, runs a roll of film over and over again. The film is spliced into an endless loop, and wound in such a way that as it unwinds from the outside of the roll it winds up on

In this automatic movie projector the film unwinds from the outside of reel and at the same time winds on inside.

"Back to the Land" is the title of this art masterpiece, one of the most unusual displayed at the recent super-independent artists' exhibit in Paris. Or is it just a nightmare?

the inside. The camera is automatic in operation, and can be used for continuous movies in store windows.

A roller resting on the moving band of film is connected to an electric switch, so that power is cut off when the film breaks.

Salesmen can use the new projector for showing short films to their clients.

Mechanical Contraptions

by JAY EARLE MILLER

When the season opens for amusement parks this spring, you'll find a number of new mechanical fun-makers ready for your entertainment. Mr. Miller attended an exposition of carnival men recently, and he tells here of the ingenious contraptions which were on display there.

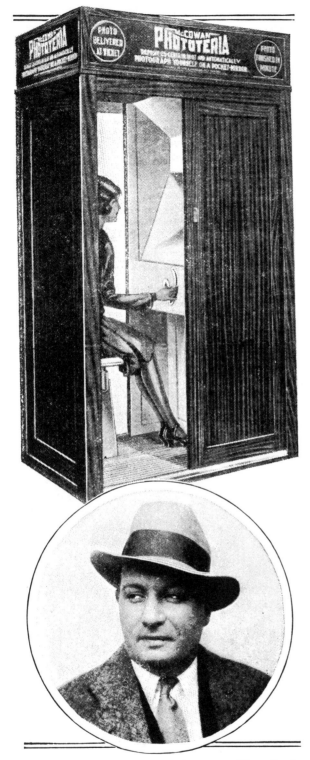

Newest of the automatic photo machines is the Phototeria, shown above. Drop a quarter in the slot, and three minutes later your photo is delivered to you encased in a neat round frame. Mr. Miller took his own picture, reproduced above in actual size. Four photos a minute is the capacity of the machine which is entirely automatic.

HOW are you going to spend your money when you go to the amusement park next summer? What will they offer to entice your nickels, dimes and quarters?

If you want the answer drop in with me at the winter exposition when the outdoor showmen of America—circus men, carnival men, and state and county fair executives—meet to transact business. Here are all the new things thought up to give you a thrill or a laugh.

Over here there's a hiss of compressed air escaping, and a blase showman from a small town carnival park, with a diamond stickpin in his tie, is getting the surprise of his life —and showing it too—fighting the buckin'est imitation airplane ever conceived. A knot of fellow carnival men stands around convulsed with laughter, but at the same time sizing up the thrills that trick flight training machine will give the general public.

Down the aisle there's a "ping" and a white hole appears in the side of one of five small deer on an illuminated target on the wall. The demonstrator shoots each deer square in the heart with his "radio gun" as he calls it. Actually the machine is a picture projector, throwing the target picture on the wall, and each time he pulls the trigger a needle punches a hole in the film, and so registers the exact location of your aim. Five shots, five cents, pull a lever and the machine cuts off your piece of film and delivers it, with the holes punched to prove your marksmanship.

Around the corner a barker is getting ready to chop off a smiling lady's head with a very realistic reproduction of a French guillotine. The big steel blade falls, apparently just behind the ears, the supposedly severed head,

to keep you ENTERTAINED

This "radio gun" uses movie film for targets. The film is projected on the wall and when the rifle is fired a needle punctures the film at the exact spot at which you aimed. The film is delivered to you as a record of your marksmanship. Several examples are shown in the lower right corner of photo.

apparently wrapped in a red cloth, is transferred to a sword apparently lying across the arms of a chair, is turned, with appropriate patter, into a cabbage, then back to a head, and finally vanishes. Then, in more serious vein, the barker talks "turkey," to the assembled showmen, for this is a business show at which next year's attractions are bought and sold. The "nut," he explains, meaning the operating cost, is so much a week, and then he goes on to estimate the possible profits.

Next door an automatic machine, which works something on the principle of the production line in an automobile factory, is turning out an endless stream of a frozen delicacy faster than an attendant can scoop it into ice cream cones and pass them around. Going to a showman's show is fun, because everything is free. Attendants stand around

with hands full of slugs, or real pennies, nickels and dimes, ready to drop them into any machine. If you pause in front of the penny arcade exhibits, artist's models or Nights in Paris are flickering before your eyes as fast as a salesman can feed the pennies into the slot.

Stop and look at the baseball machine, which is the newest successor to the old "hit the nigger's head" game, and a handful of balls are thrust on you. The baseball machine looks like an ordinary batter's cage, with a painted batter and catcher, life size, at the end. You throw the ball to hit the bat, and if you hit it hard enough it swings all the way around and rings a bell.

Air Bomb Releases Sky Advertisement

BURSTING high overhead with a loud explosion to attract attention, a novel aerial bomb for advertising purposes has just been introduced. At the first glance, spectators see only a huge cloud of smoke as the bomb bursts. In a moment, the smoke clears and a giant object—an oversize copy of the bottle, food package, automobile tire, or other product being advertised—is revealed floating in space. Made of lightweight, silky paper, the advertisement weighs only about nine ounces, though it may have a surface area of sixty-five square feet and be as much as fifteen feet in length. It requires from two to ten minutes to float back to earth, being borne up by rising air currents entering a hole at the bottom. Weights at the bottom hold the parachutelike advertisement upright. Developed for use wherever large crowds gather outdoors, the compact bomb is shot from its mortar at a safe distance. It rises 360 feet before a time fuse explodes it, and the giant "flying signboard" is released. At a seaside resort, the practice is to shoot the bomb aloft from a boat cruising a short distance off the bathing beach.

How the aerial advertising bomb is fired. On bursting, it releases a balloonlike copy of product advertised

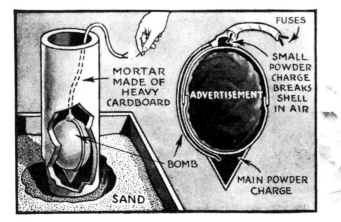

MORTAR MADE OF HEAVY CARDBOARD

FUSES

SMALL POWDER CHARGE BREAKS SHELL IN AIR

ADVERTISEMENT

BOMB

MAIN POWDER CHARGE

SAND

Projector Makes Living Movies

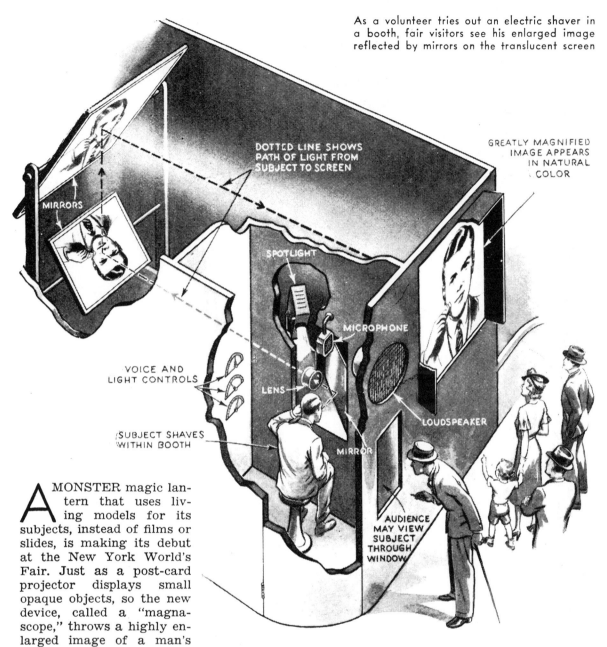

As a volunteer tries out an electric shaver in a booth, fair visitors see his enlarged image reflected by mirrors on the translucent screen

MIRRORS

DOTTED LINE SHOWS PATH OF LIGHT FROM SUBJECT TO SCREEN

GREATLY MAGNIFIED IMAGE APPEARS IN NATURAL COLOR

SPOTLIGHT

MICROPHONE

VOICE AND LIGHT CONTROLS

LENS

SUBJECT SHAVES WITHIN BOOTH

MIRROR

LOUDSPEAKER

AUDIENCE MAY VIEW SUBJECT THROUGH WINDOW

A MONSTER magic lantern that uses living models for its subjects, instead of films or slides, is making its debut at the New York World's Fair. Just as a post-card projector displays small opaque objects, so the new device, called a "magnascope," throws a highly enlarged image of a man's face upon a translucent screen. Meanwhile, a microphone picks up the voices of the subject and operator, and the audience hears them through a loudspeaker, so that the effect is that of a talking motion picture projected as fast as it is produced.

In its first application, the magnascope gives spectators a close-up view of what happens when a man shaves with an electric razor. Unshaven chins look like forests of tree stumps upon the screen, and the bristles fall like cordwood as the razor sweeps across them.

Chosen at random from crowds of visitors to the exhibit building, a subject sits within a booth where powerful spotlights illuminate his face. His reflection from a slanting mirror is picked up in turn by a series of condensing and magnifying lenses, and two larger mirrors. The last mirror reflects the image to the screen, where the audience sees it. By adjusting the positions of the mirrors, the operator regulates the degree of magnification, which the inventor, William Herrschaft, declares may be stepped up to as many as thirty diameters without distortion. Spectators may peer also through a window of the projection booth and see the subject.

Movie Trains Big-Game Anglers

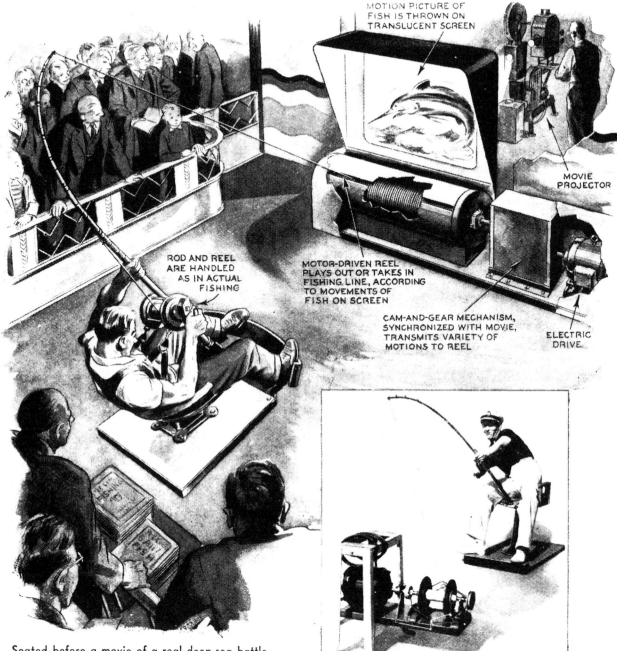

MOTION PICTURE OF FISH IS THROWN ON TRANSLUCENT SCREEN

MOVIE PROJECTOR

ROD AND REEL ARE HANDLED AS IN ACTUAL FISHING

MOTOR-DRIVEN REEL PLAYS OUT OR TAKES IN FISHING LINE, ACCORDING TO MOVEMENTS OF FISH ON SCREEN

CAM-AND-GEAR MECHANISM, SYNCHRONIZED WITH MOVIE, TRANSMITS VARIETY OF MOTIONS TO REEL

ELECTRIC DRIVE

Seated before a movie of a real deep-sea battle, the angler has all the thrills of landing a fish

This simplified and smaller version of the device employs the motor-controlled drum, but no movie

ALL the thrills of deep-sea fishing, from hooking a giant swordfish to fighting it in toward a boat, are provided for the entertainment of sportsmen on land by an ingenious amusement device. Seated before a translucent motion-picture screen, the angler grasps an actual big-game fishing rod and reel fitted with a line that runs to a revolving drum placed just below the screen. A movie of an actual deep-sea fishing battle flashes on the screen, and the fight is on. As the giant fish darts, leaps, and thrashes about on the screen, a cam-and-gear mechanism operates the motor-driven drum to reproduce the exact tugs that the angler would feel on his line if the film fish were real. Matching his wits against the mechanical fish, the angler strives to play the fighting giant toward his "boat," as though landing a real deep-sea fighter on the open water.

Movie Slot Machine Shows Pictures of Latest News Events

MOTION-PICTURE newsreels are on view for a nickel in a modern version of the old penny-arcade, animated-picture machine recently displayed at a Chicago, Ill., convention of manufacturers. As shown at the right, the device has a motion-picture projector installed in the base of its cabinet. Film images are thrown on a small mirror that reflects them up to a ground-glass screen near the top of the cabinet, where they are viewed through an eyepiece by a customer. Designed for hotel lobbies, railroad stations, taverns, and other public places, the movie machine is entirely automatic, running through four separate scenes when a nickel is dropped into the slot, and rewinding for the next customer when the film ends.

Inserting a nickel starts the newsreel movie which is viewed through an eyepiece. How the mechanism is arranged is shown in picture above

This watch fits the curve of any part of the wrist

New Watch Can Be Worn on Any Side of Wrist

A WRIST watch just put on the market can be worn anywhere on the wrist—top, bottom, or side—according to the owner's taste. Flexible bars at the ends of the watch automatically adjust themselves to the contour of the wrist, making it possible to move the timepiece to any position. Gold-plated, the watch has raised gold numerals that are stamped by means of a special process on the face of the dial.

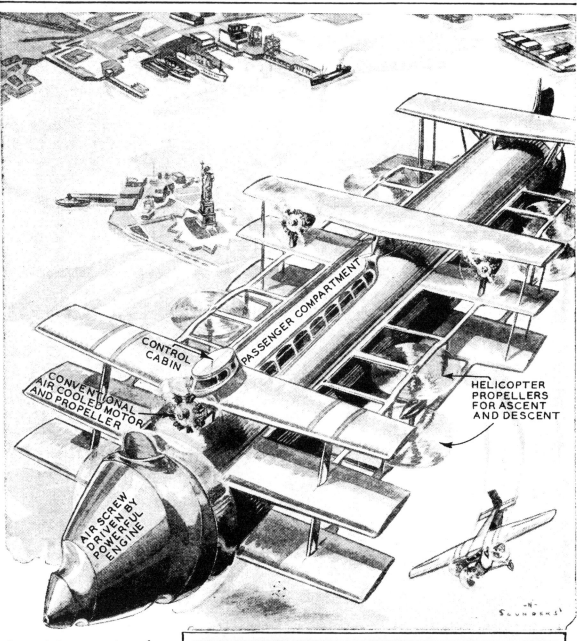

An artist's conception of Mr. Knott's air liner.

THE most unusual design brought to our attention this month is the air liner invented by Mr. R. Knott of Lewisham, England, who hopes to cross the Atlantic with a ship of this type carrying 600 passengers in from 12 to 15 hours.

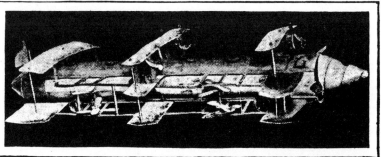

Here is a photograph of the model of this unusual ship which the inventor calls a heliplane. With eight horizontal propellers, the plane is supposed to be able to rise straight off the ground without any preliminary run and to land safely in almost its own length.

Science Shows NOISE Causes Indigestion

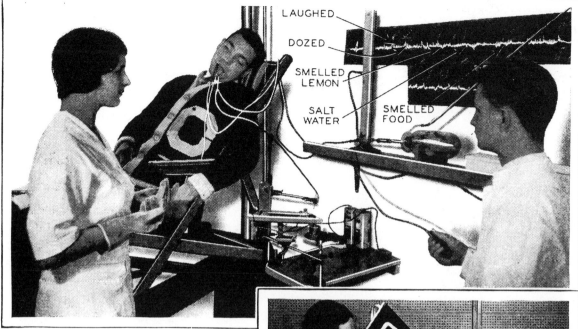

LAUGHED
DOZED
SMELLED LEMON
SALT WATER
SMELLED FOOD

In conducting the experiment to ascertain the effects of noises on the digestive secretions, the subjects submitted to having a tube placed in their stomachs so that the flow of gastric juice could be checked when noises, ranging from whispers to the din heard in the noisiest section of New York City, were applied. It was found that the flow of the juice was impeded directly as to the amount of the noise. The glass apparatus, shown on the wall in the above photo, was used to make the measurements of the frequency and strength of the stomach contractions. Right—the test revealed that smell alone will stimulate or impede the muscular activity of the various digestive organs, a personal resistance.

In this test as noise from the loud speaker was increased, it was found that the secretion of saliva was decreased. Under influence of excessive noise the flow was stopped almost entirely. Action became normal when noise ceased.

WORKING with various intricate devices that record the effects of sound waves on the digestive processes, scientists have found that a lot of digestive troubles are directly attributable to noises. Dr. Donald A. Laird, of Colgate University, has discovered the effects of various noises on the digestive juices.

Using two different methods on a chosen group of healthy men, the experimenter measured the effect of discordant sounds upon the flow of saliva. It was immediately evident that many sounds had a distinct effect. For example, when the sounds increased in volume comparable to the noises in a quick lunch restaurant, the secretion of saliva decreased to almost half of the normal quantity.

When the noise increased still more and became as loud as din heard at Fifth Avenue and Forty-Second Street, in New York City, the flow of saliva almost stopped.

Gastric Juice Flow Affected by Noises

The scientist and his associates went a step further in their measurements. Using tubes that reached down to the stomach, they had the subjects take a meal test and then watched the flow of gastric juice. Practically without exception, din, uproar and racket had a marked ill effect. As the noise increased, the gastric juice flowed less freely, preventing proper digestive action. The subjects showed all the effects of suffering from lowered stomach secretion when eating was accompanied by excessive noises.

In both instances, when the noise ceased the digestive juices began to flow normally.

World's Greatest Underground Fortifications Guard France

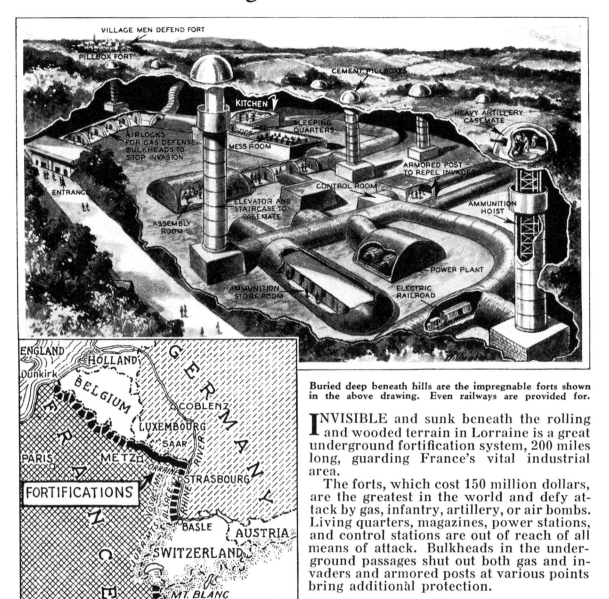

Buried deep beneath hills are the impregnable forts shown in the above drawing. Even railways are provided for.

Solid black line shows location of 200 mile system of French underground forts, opposite disputed Saar basin.

INVISIBLE and sunk beneath the rolling and wooded terrain in Lorraine is a great underground fortification system, 200 miles long, guarding France's vital industrial area.

The forts, which cost 150 million dollars, are the greatest in the world and defy attack by gas, infantry, artillery, or air bombs. Living quarters, magazines, power stations, and control stations are out of reach of all means of attack. Bulkheads in the underground passages shut out both gas and invaders and armored posts at various points bring additional protection.

German Rises Six Miles in Rocket

IN HISTORY'S first successful rocket flight, Otto Fischer, brother of the inventor of the rocket plane, was shot 32,000 feet into the air in a shining 24-foot steel projectile.

With a blinding flash the rocket ship shot out of its steel framework and disappeared into the sky. It reappeared a few minutes later, dangling from a parachute, its pilot maneuvering to land on the little island of Rugen in the Baltic Sea, where the flight started.

The pilot was quoted as saying, "I left the ground in a deafening roar and lost consciousness for a moment. When I came to my senses the altimeter was flickering at 32,000 feet. It began to drop rapidly. I pulled the parachute release ring."

Moisture Fan Bests Tropic Heat

NEW air conditioning fans, tiny but wonderfully efficient, are being installed in every French government office in the tropics.

A drum filled with ice water or other liquid revolves inside the unit, throwing liquid out through short capillary tubes into blades of two fans turning at 4000 r.p.m. Large halls can be cooled and humidified in 10 min.

In this French air conditioning unit, the fan blades, driven at a speed of 4000 r.p.m., cool rooms with washed air.

Rotary Golf Game Affords Winter Practice

INVETERATE golfers who insist upon keeping their swings grooved the year 'round will welcome a new device which combines practice and pleasure in a novel manner.

The apparatus consists of 10 tubular metal coils, 15 feet in diameter. These surmount a 20 foot funnel-shaped approach, set at an angle of 25 degrees to the driving tee.

The distance traveled by the ball through the metal tubes indicates the length of the drive. At intervals of 15 yards a red neon light, attached to a sensitive mercury switch, shows the player what yardage he has attained.

Only hard, perfectly hit drives register in the 300 figures. Hooks and slices penalize the golfer as in actual play. The ricocheting action of an off-line ball naturally slows the forward motion and cuts down the theoretical yardage. Netting protects players and spectators from wild shots.

In addition to registering yardage by neon lights, device drops golf balls through funnels to score various holes. A return pipe brings the balls back to the driving tee.

Artist Makes Pasteboard Masks

A NEW sculptor's medium has been devised by Stanislaw Raczinsky, Polish artist, who utilizes colored pasteboard, skillfully cut and clipped together, to make striking, modernistic masks.

Shown above are two of the masks skillfully fashioned from colored pasteboard by the Polish artist, Raczinsky.

"Cabin" Life Preserver Tested

SHIPWRECK at sea may be robbed of some of its terrors with the introduction of a new de luxe life preserver resembling a small-sized navigation buoy. The "cabin," or upper part of the device, is equipped with a combination door and window which may be closed against the threat of heavy waves.

Made of inflated rubber, the device is composed of two sections, as a safety measure. Thus, if one section becomes deflated, the other still serves as a spare. Atop the preserver is a small flag to attract the attention of any possible rescue craft.

Closeup of cabin life preserver, showing observation window.

Pulsating Wing to Drive Prop-less Plane

LACKING both propeller and tail assembly and driven only by a 10 H.P. motor, an Austrian plane is expected to take the air this summer. The motor drives a compressed air pump which expands and evacuates a large series of pneumatic air cells in the wings. It is planned that pulsations of these cells will furnish lift and driving power for the ship. By altering the stroke in the rear wing cells, which act as a propeller, the plane is expected to climb, bank, dive, hover and go forward or backward. The forward wing is used primarily for the higher speeds. The framework of the ship is constructed of welded steel tubing.

Workmen are shown building the many-celled wings which are expected to furnish the power for the strange craft.

New Motor Clamps to Boat's Side

A NEW swivel motor which clamps to the side of the boat solves the transportation problem for hunters and fishermen whose skiffs are decked over and cannot be fitted with an outboard motor in the stern.

Easily mounted, the one cylinder, 2 h.p. motor consumes about a quart of gasoline per hour and drives the boat at 7 to 11 miles per hour. Water for cooling is taken up by a folding inlet pipe and is discharged through the hollow propeller shaft. Propeller blades are protected by a shear-pin.

The engine is started by a cord and controlled by a single throttle lever. The magneto supplies the ignition and sufficient current for lights.

Model Violin Is Perfect

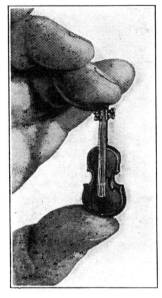

This miniature violin is a perfect scale model of full-size instruments. Size, 1¾ inches.

BUILT by a noted violin maker of Pasadena, Calif., this unusually tiny instrument is perfect in every detail. The miniature violin is made of seasoned wood throughout and is fashioned with the same fidelity as in full-size instruments. It has a carved back and front, ebony keyboard and tiny strings. The model weighs slightly less than 1/32 of an ounce. Months of labor were necessary to complete it.

This new sideboard motor can be attached to any boat, collapsible or otherwise. Weighing only twenty-four pounds, it develops a speed of from 7 to 11 miles per hour.

UNDER-SEA *Tractor*-SPHERE ROAMS OCEAN FLOOR

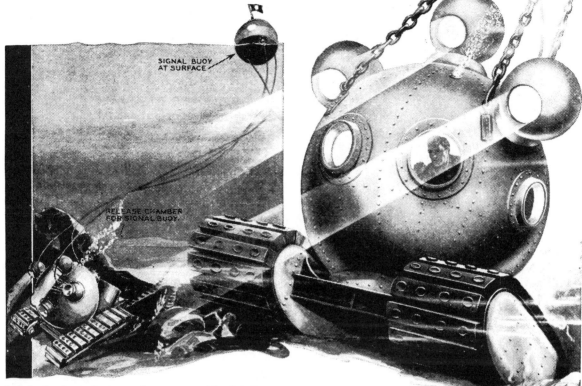

Artist's drawings of tractor-sphere proposed by Otis Barton, designer of Beebe bathysphere. At left emergency buoy has been released, carrying air lines and guide cables to surface. At right chains have been lowered for hoisting sphere.

NEWEST of mechanical monsters intended for under-sea exploration is the tractor-sphere being designed by Otis Barton, builder of the bathysphere used by Dr. William Beebe in setting a new world's diving record of 3028 feet.

The new invention, intended to be driven into the sea from the beach level under its own power, might be classed as a bathysphere mounted on caterpillar treads. Powerful electric motors operating from sealed-in storage batteries would move this undersea tractor over the rocky slopes and pinnacles of the ocean floor.

Under ordinary conditions there would be no contact with vessels at the surface as the tractor-sphere roamed about the ocean bottom. In case of emergencies such as engine failure a large buoy would be released, carrying airlines to the surface. Hoisting cables could then be slipped down the guide cables to the automatic chain-coupling devices on the sphere itself. Sphere, tractor, and all would then be hauled on board the ship for repairs.

Where oceanic explorations are to be made some distance from shore, ships

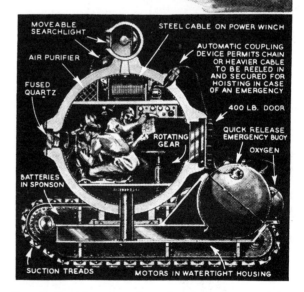

Cross-section of tractor-sphere shows arrangement of interior, location of motors, emergency buoy, and cable reel.

would carry the tractor-sphere to the selected location, lower it to the bottom, then release the chains to permit unhampered exploration. Short wave radio would then keep the explorers in constant communication with those aboard the ship, and the buoy released with completion of the work.

Will Monster Insects

Havoc that could be wrought by a monster longhorn beetle is graphically depicted in drawing.

Fantastic as it may sound, it is a scientific possibility that in some distant age man will disappear from the earth, his food supply ravaged by insect hordes who remain to dominate the world. Mr. Miller's article is a fascinating discussion of a subject which has been made increasingly important by the many existing crop-destroying pests.

A WORLD ruled by giant insects, with the last remnants of the human race as slaves is one of the favorite devices of one school of fiction writers.

Fantastic? Not at all. Thoughtful scientists recognize that as one of the possible endings for our civilization. In fact, all past history indicates that when, and if, the present civilization comes to an end, it will die because of an unsolved food problem, and that insects will be a contributing factor, and hence may be the survivors.

Gigantic animals once roamed the earth, and perished because of climatic changes and food shortage. It is equally probable that there will be another glacial era, upsetting all food and living arrangements, and that the human race will virtually perish. Because many species of insects have, next to man, the most highly developed social instincts, they would appear to be the logical successors.

Remove the competition of man and the higher forms of animal life in the food market, and there is a possibility that the present minute insect life might develop to gigantic proportions, until a recurring food problem again wiped them out.

RULE the WORLD?

by JAY EARLE MILLER

Six hundred years before the idea had occurred to philosophers in India, the Mayas invented zero. That doesn't appear so important, at first glance, but without it all mathematical calculations would be hopelessly involved. Instead of learning nine numbers, and then repeating them over and over, we would have to learn a different name for every number. To count to one million you would have to know one million different words, and what each of them stood for.

Yet, despite their advanced culture, city after city of the Mayas was abandoned because the inhabi-

The importance of the food cycle has become increasingly apparent as science delves into the past history of the world. The Maya civilization, the highest developed in pre-historic America and rivaling the best that Egypt produced, disappeared because of food shortage. At their height the Mayas knew more about astronomy than Egypt, Greece or ancient Rome. In architecture, sculpture and painting they were equals of the old world, save for the single exception that they never learned to build a true arch, and had to rely on the corbel.

The familiar spider and fly are fearsome creatures when enlarged.

tants, knowing nothing of cultivation and crop rotation, ate themselves out of house and home by exhausting the surrounding country.

117

Heat Evaporates "Milk" to Make Rubber

"Milk" for the new rubber manufacturing process is taken from crushed milk weed, a specimen of which is shown in this photograph. The new process promises to reduce costs of rubber making.

THE latest step in the search for processes whereby rubber may be made from plants has been taken by Arthur E. Bergquist, of Lindstrom, Minn., who has perfected a furnace which extracts rubber from milk-weed.

The apparatus employed in this new process consists of a pyramidal-shaped burner in which are arranged a series of baffle plates as illustrated in the accompanying drawing. The "milk" is fed onto a small wheel at the top and curds when struck by rising smoke. Solid matter from the "milk" sticks to the wheel, while the moisture passes off with the reduced heat. Chemicals are then applied to remove the residuum, from which rubber is made. The "milk" is obtained by crushing the milkweed and extracting the sap.

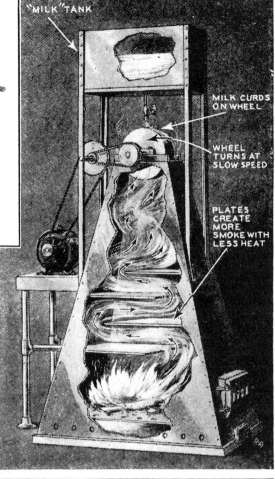

Moisture of "milk" is evaporated by smoke from which large portion of heat has been extracted by baffle plates, as shown in drawing of device above.

New York to Battle Gangsters with Armored Motorbikes and Shot Guns

The armored motorbike and sawed-off repeating shot gun with which N. Y. police fight gangsters.

NEW YORK'S most dramatic gesture in its recent declaration of war-to-the-last-ditch on gangsters is the adoption by the police force of the armored motorbike and the sawed-off repeating shotgun. Squadrons of these war-like motorbikes will patrol the streets to strike terror into the hearts of the criminals who have turned New York into a veritable No-man's land, raking the streets with submachine gun fire and cutting down everybody who happens to get in the way.

To expedite the capture of gangsters, New York police officials are planning to equip all squad cars and motorbikes with short-wave sending and receiving sets.

ELECTROCUTING WHALES

Here is an artist's conception of whale hunting with electricity, a heavy voltage being sent from a powerful generator through an insulated line to the harpoon to instantly electrocute the whale.

BIRGER HOLM-HANSEN, a Norwegian engineer, has invented a device for the instantaneous electrocution of whales. It consists of a small but powerful generator which is carried in the whaleboat, and a flexible, insulated line conveying a current of high voltage to the harpoon. At the instant the harpoon hits the whale the current is thrown on and the electric charge shot into the monster. The instrument has been tried out several times in the North Sea and in each instance the whale has been killed instantly. Many of the whale boats to be used this season have been equipped with the device. Heretofore, when a bull whale has been caught by a harpoon, he has towed the small boat containing the whale hunters for miles. In many cases whalers have been killed when they drew alongside apparently slain whales only to find the monsters capable of a few more tail blows. The electrocution of whales is expected to greatly diminish this loss of life and property. Wholesale destruction of sea lions is reported to be under way in Queen Charlotte Sound, British Columbia, the hunters wiping out the mammals with machine guns, because the sea lions feed on salmon.

Machine guns are being used, as shown above, to wipe out sea lions which prey on salmon.

Man Rolls Up Incline in a Ball

INCASED in a metal ball, a European performer lifts himself "by his own bootstraps" up a high spiral runway and then rolls down to thrill carnival crowds. Hand holds within the hollow sphere enable the skillful contortionist to shift his weight so as to climb the incline, in apparent defiance of the law of gravitation. When he reaches the top, he relaxes his strenuous efforts, and the ball and its human cargo come rolling down with gathering speed in a dizzy finale. Perforations in the globular shell and its "manhole" cover enable the occupant to breathe.

The ball nearing the end of its climb up the spiral ramp. At right, the performer is seen entering the perforated sphere, which he propels by shifting his weight

Pet Dog Makes Living Fur Piece

Jeanne Lorraine "pins" a corsage to her toy collie, Jiggs. Draped over her shoulders, as below, he passes as a fox skin

a residential hotel that barred pets, and Miss Lorraine has been using it ever since to take her dog through subways, past customs officers, on railroad coaches, and into other places where canine companions are not welcomed. To heighten the illusion, Jigg's mistress selects costumes in shades of brown that blend with her dog's coloring, and then attaches a "pinned" flower corsage to the dog's fur by means of an elastic band around his belly. The animal then promptly relaxes every muscle so that he can be draped

SIGNS reading "No Dogs Allowed" mean nothing to Miss Jeanne Lorraine, of New York City, since she taught her twelve-year-old pet toy collie, Jiggs, to drape himself around her neck and masquerade as a fur piece. The trick first worked on a clerk at gracefully around his owner's neck, like a fox, mink, or marten skin. For periods up to one hour at a stretch, Jiggs will hardly bat an eye, his only movement being an occasional tail wag, which his mistress covers up with a nonchalant stroke of her hand.

The Roadside Stand Goes "High Hat"

There is nothing like individuality to create lasting impressions. Here is a group of the once lowly roadside stands. Kinda ritzy, what?

It is easily seen that refreshment - seeking youngsters pick the place that catches the eye.

In "going modern," stand owners are overlooking nothing that will add distinctiveness to their business establishments. To the west goes the honor of pioneering in this movement.

Bizarre Eat Shops Built to Lure Trade

CONES!
An ice cream maker's specialty is cones. His shops throughout the city are shaped like inverted cones, thus advertising his wares and drawing attention.

ZEPPELIN LUNCH!
This unusual restaurant is housed within a model of a zeppelin. Note the mooring mast at left.

HOT DOGS
are purveyed by this eat shop, so the showman instincts of the proprietor have caused him to model the exterior of his stand after a puppy.

FLOWER POT TEAROOM is one of the unique attractions on the Pacific coast. Giant flowers rise realistically from the roof. Right — COFFEE POT specializes in quick lunches for passing tourists. Steam rises from the spout.

THE HAT,
copy of a brown derby, is popular among bizarre eating places. The restaurant is located within the crown of the hat, while the curved brim makes a very unusual veranda. The sign invites passersby to stop and "eat in the hat."

Scientist RESTORES LIFE of Dead Dog

BRINGING a dog back from death and keeping him alive for several weeks has been successfully accomplished by Dr. Robert Cornish of the University of California and his research assistants.

These men watched day and night over "Thirteen," the mongrel fox terrier used for the experiment, after putting him to death with nitrogen anaesthetic on April 13.

The miracle of restored life was brought about four minutes after death by injections of adrenalin, dog's blood, and heparin, together with special respiratory treatments. Less than half an hour after heart action was restored the dog barked feebly.

A terrific rate of heart action threatened to bring "Thirteen's" second life to an early end, but injections of gum arabic tided the dog over the crisis.

The animal displayed hunger and thirst, and raised his head when anyone entered the room, but his actions more resembled those of a creature neither dead nor alive. Dr. Cornish is certain some of the dog's brain cells have not completely recovered from the shock of death.

On the 17th day of his second life "Thirteen" caught a head cold which for a time doctors feared might complicate his condition.

New Plate Glass Supports Auto

New plate glass supported between steel cylinders holds up heavy touring car easily. It is ideal for automobile windows, since it is strong and practically shatterproof.

AN ENTIRELY new plate glass, developed in Europe and now being manufactured in this country, is believed to be the strongest glass ever made.

In tests one thickness of the glass supported a heavy touring car. The glass is practically shatterproof. Should a piece of it be broken by an exceedingly heavy blow, it crumbles into dust, leaving no sharp splinters to cause injury.

The new plate glass will be extensively used for automobiles and in other places where strength is required.

"Thirteen," the dog who was brought back to life after death by gas, was fed with a bottle until able to eat meat. Photo shows Dr. Cornish who conducted experiment.

Chops Wood With Steel Hands

DELICATE but powerful are the steel hands made by Andrew A. Gawley and his blind father. Though both arms were amputated thirty-two years ago in an accident, Gawley has learned to use his artificial arms to such an extent that today he earns his own living as a machinist.

He can dress himself, tie his shoe laces, use a knife and fork skillfully, and even break stones with his powerful hands. Wood chopping is easy for him, for his steel fingers grip tighter than human fingers.

Left: Andrew A. Gawley, known as "The man with the steel hands," ties own shoe laces with mechanical fingers. Right: Steel fingers grip ax firmly when chopping wood

MODERN
MECHANIX

AUG.

AND INVENTIONS

SEE PAGE

Saunders

DEPRESSION SPURS
LOST GOLD TREASURE HUNTS

MODERN MECHANIX AND INVENTIONS

NOV.

NOW 15¢

IN CANADA 20¢

SEE PAGE 32

HOW COMIC CARTOONS MAKE FORTUNES
World Celebrates The Airplane's 30th Birthday

MODERN MECHANIX AND INVENT

MAR.

NOW 15¢

IN CANADA 20¢

SEE PAGE 33

RADIO FLOATING SEADROME

RADIO STATION

ZXR

RADIO
OUTLAWS to
BROADCAST from
SUPER STATIONS
at SEA

August

MODERN MECHANIX

& INVENTIONS MAGAZINE

NOW
15¢
IN CANADA 20¢

NRA CODE

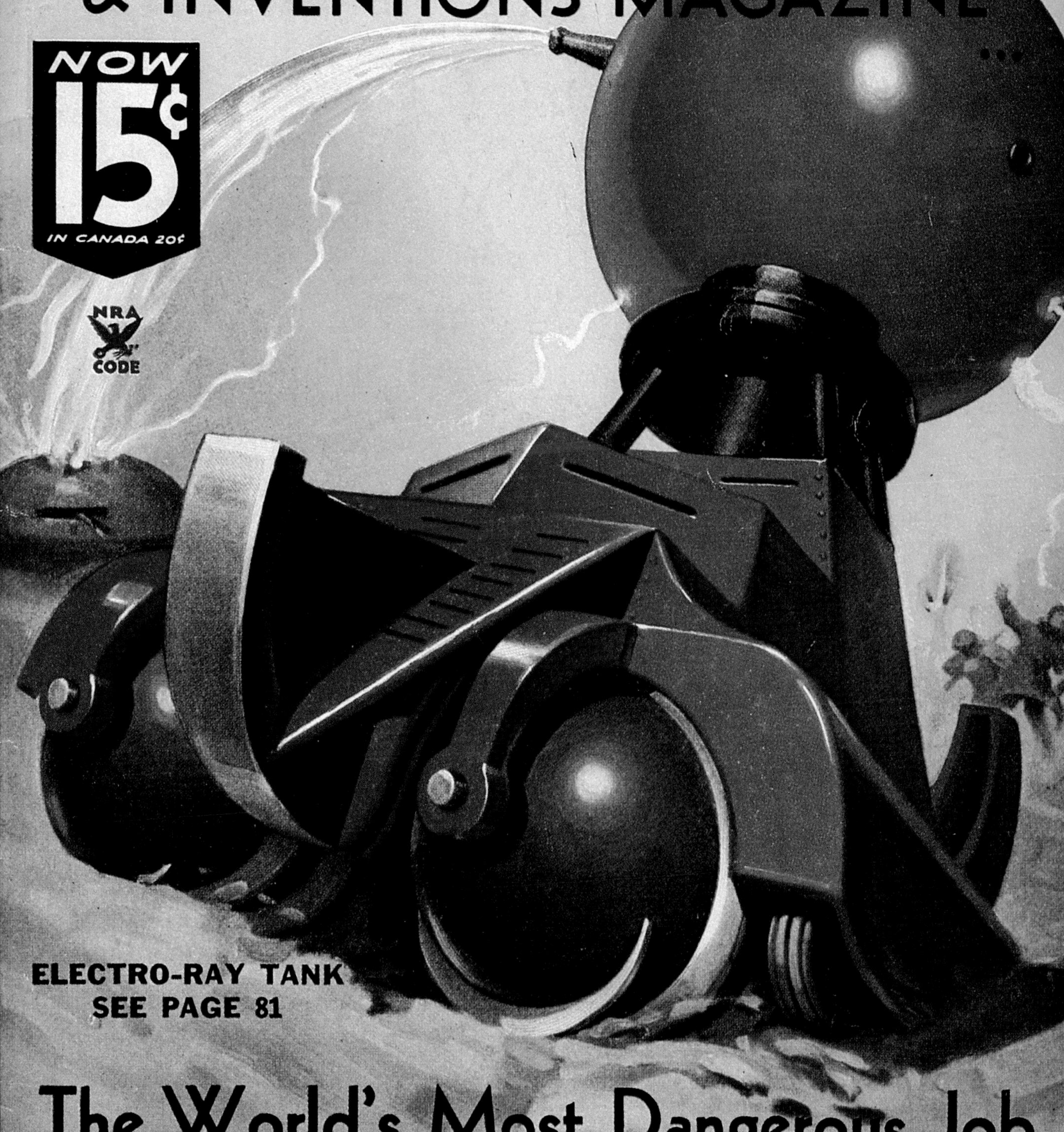

ELECTRO-RAY TANK
SEE PAGE 81

The World's Most Dangerous Job

Home Shop Plans—Furniture—Models—Kinks

JULY

MODERN MECHANIX

AND INVENTIONS

NOW
15¢
IN CANADA 20¢

SEE PAGE 72

SKYSCRAPERS DOOMED BY UNDERGROUND CITIES?

MODERN MECHANIX

July

& INVENTIONS MAGAZINE
...

NOW 5¢
CANADA 20¢

NRA CODE

RO-CAR
PAGE 87

rappling With Death Under the Sea

Debunking Poison Gas War Scares

MODERN MECHANIX

June

AND INVENTIONS
...

NOW 15¢
IN CANADA 20¢

NRA CODE

DYNO-WHEEL
MOTOR BUS
SEE PAGE 87

The World's Most Costly Blunders

POPULAR SCIENCE

JUNE
15 CENTS
20 CENTS IN CANADA

FOUNDED MONTHLY 1872

NOW 15¢

SEE PAGE 41

NEW INVENTIONS · MECHANICS · MONEY MAKING IDEAS
HOME WORKSHOP PLANS AND HINTS · 350 PICTURES

POPULAR SCIENCE

MONTHLY

NOVEMBER

15 CENTS

20 CENTS IN CANADA

NRA CODE

NOW 15¢

20 CENTS IN CANADA

See Page 43

NEW INVENTIONS · MECHANICS · MONEY MAKING IDEAS
HOME WORKSHOP PLANS AND HINTS · 350 PICTURES

MODERN MECHANIX

AND INVENTIONS

JUNE

NRA

NOW 15¢

IN CANADA 20¢

SEE PAGE 63

INSIDE UNCLE SAM'S NEW GOLD VAULT
BURIED ALIVE WITH THE TUNNEL BUILDERS

POPULAR SCIENCE

FOUNDED MONTHLY 1872

DECEMBER

15 CENTS

20 CENTS IN CANADA

NOW 5¢

SEE PAGE 49

INVENTIONS · MECHANICS · MONEY MAKING IDEAS
HOME WORKSHOP PLANS AND HINTS · 350 PICTURES

MODERN MECHANIX

AND INVENTIONS

May

NOW 15¢

IN CANADA 20¢

NRA CODE

SPINNING TOP
PLANE
SEE PAGE 83

Charles F. Kettering of General Motors Seeks

Secret of Hidden Power in Grass

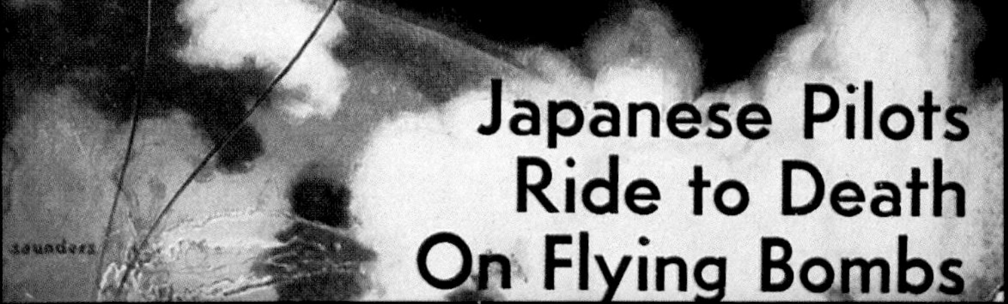
saunders
Japanese Pilots
Ride to Death
On Flying Bombs

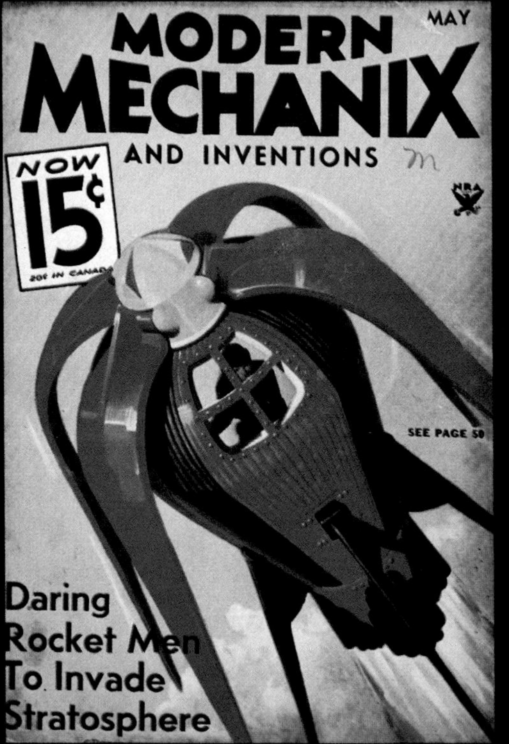
MAY
MODERN
MECHANIX
AND INVENTIONS
NOW
15¢
20¢ IN CANADA
NRA
SEE PAGE 50
Daring
Rocket Men
To Invade
Stratosphere

MODERN MECHANIX

JULY

AND INVENTIONS

NOW 15¢

IN CANADA 20c

SEE PAGE 32

saunders

DO WILD RADIO WAVES CAUSE AIR DISASTERS?
WORLD WAR CODE SECRETS — NEW SUMMER SPORT

January

MODERN MECHANIX

AND INVENTIONS

SEE PAGE

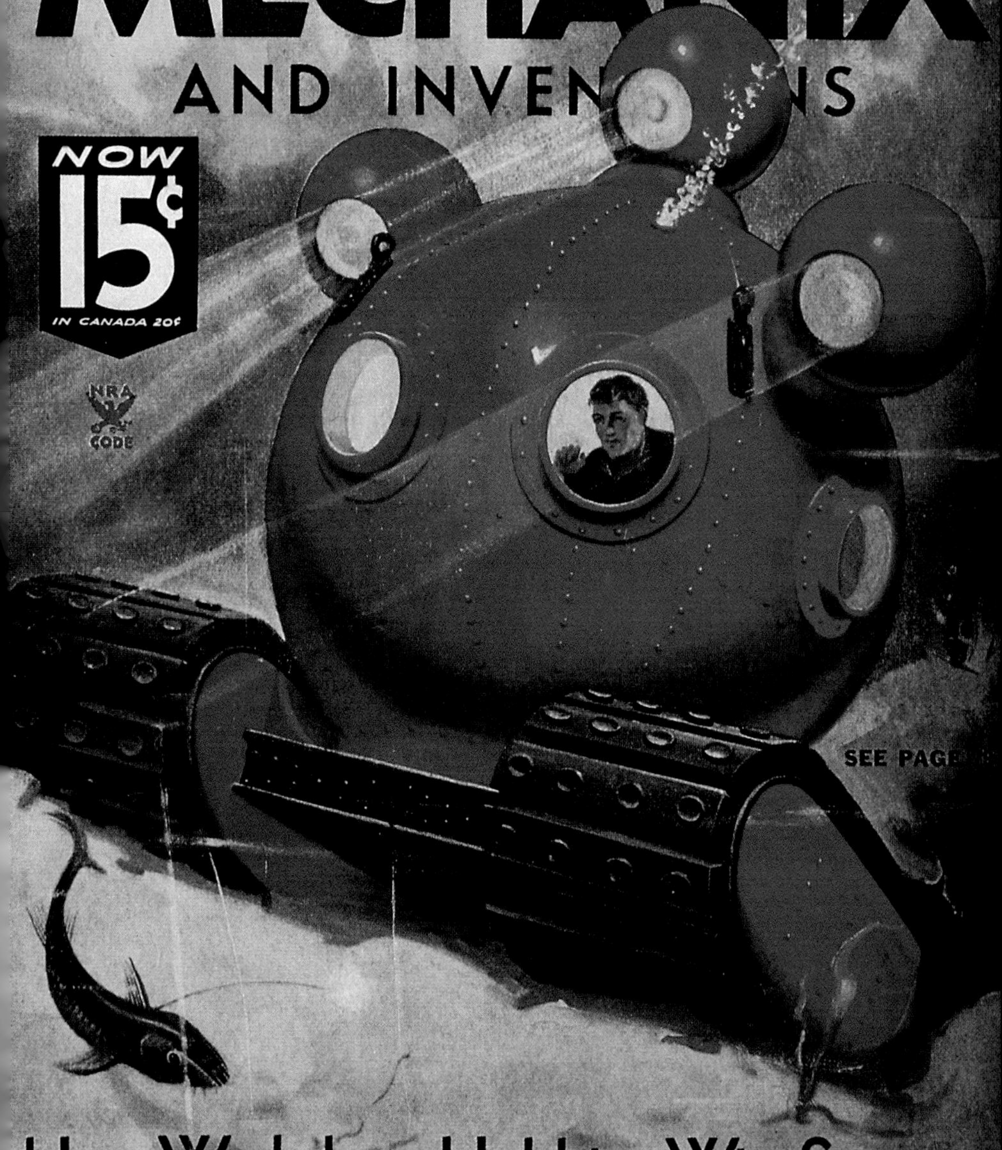

How Workshop Hobbies Win Success
By the President of Packard Motors

POPU AR
SCIENCE
FOUNDED MONTHLY 1872
APRIL
15 CENTS
20 CENTS IN CANADA
NOW
15¢
Making Movies in a Volcano
NEW INVENTIONS · MECHANICS · MONEY MAKING IDEAS

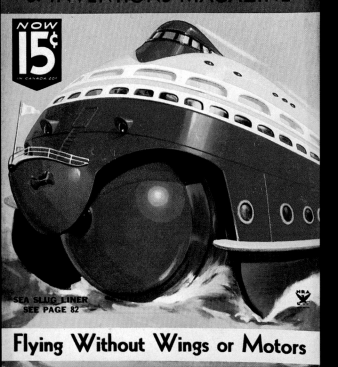

October

MODERN MECHANIX

& INVENTIONS MAGAZINE

NOW 15¢
IN CANADA 20¢

SEA SLUG LINER
SEE PAGE 82

Flying Without Wings or Motors

MODERN MECHANIX

& INVENTIONS MAGAZINE

NOW 15¢
IN CANADA 20¢

NRA

$1,750 CONTEST
More than 100
CASH PRIZES
See Page 42

Bernie Bierman's Football

MODERN MECHANIX
AND INVENTIONS

AUG.

RADIO TUBE TRAIN
SEE ___ E 68

POPULAR SCIENCE

FOUNDED MONTHLY 1872

MARCH
15 CENTS
20 CENTS IN CANADA

NOW
15¢

SEE PAGE 49

NEW INVENTIONS • MECHANICS • MONEY MAKING IDEAS
HOME WORKSHOP PLANS AND HINTS • 350 PICTURES

MODERN MECHANIX

AND INVENTIONS

December

NOW
15¢
IN CANADA 20¢

NRA
CODE

SEE PAGE 83

AMERICA'S
INDUSTRIAL
FUTURE
*An Interview
with*
**HENRY
FORD**

BIG CASH
PRIZE
CONTEST
DETAILS PAGE 46

LAST CHANCE TO WIN—$1000.00 CASH PRIZES

MODERN
MECHANIX

June
N.S.C

& INVENTIONS MAGAZINE

NOW
15¢

300 M.P.H. MOTORCYCLE
SEE PAGE 79

CAN SCIENCE MAKE US LIVE FOREVER?
Television—Our Next Industrial Boom

POPULAR SCIENCE

MONTHLY

APRIL

EXIT

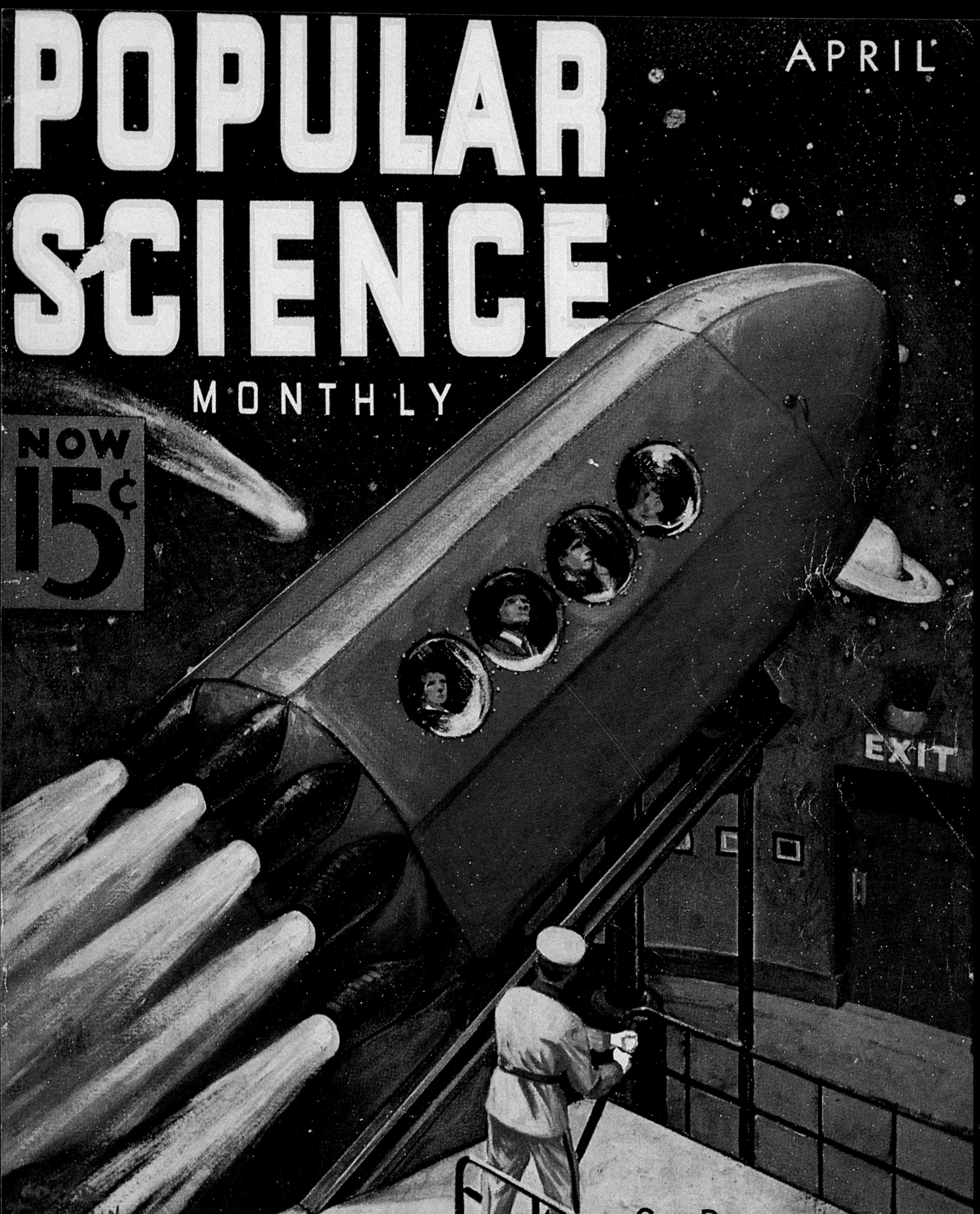

See Page 65

NEW INVENTIONS · MECHANICS · MONEY MAKING IDEAS
HOME WORKSHOP PLANS AND HINTS · 450 PICTURES

Healthful Sleep on Ultra-Violet Ray Bed

ULTRA VIOLET LIGHTS

In this new health bed, sleeper's body is bathed in ultra-violet rays during night, so that subject awakens in morning fresh and vigorous for work.

YOU grow healthy while you slumber and arise in the morning fresh and full of vitamines, if you sleep away the night in a special bed which has recently been devised by scientists.

What does the job of keeping the body of the sleeper fit is a battery of ultra-violet lights which bathe the flesh, as illustrated in the artist's drawing above. An opaque screen covers the bed, thus shutting out the view and providing the occupants with the utmost privacy.

With cities growing constantly larger and sunlight becoming more and more scarce, these ultra-violet beds may be called upon to furnish all health rays in the future.

Airman Builds Novel Runabout

SOMETHING distinctly unique in the way of vehicles has been designed by Sir A. V. Roe, noted English airplane designer and manufacturer. Shown below, it's a one passenger contrivance with one wheel forward and two aft.

Sir A. V. Roe, plane manufacturer, riding his runabout.

Home Remedies Best for Colds

THAT medical science knows, in reality, nothing much better for a cold than to stay home and let it get well is admitted by a recent editorial in the Journal of the American Medical Association.

Simple home remedies used for generations are about as good as anything to cure colds, the editorial stated. These remedies include going to bed, increasing perspiration by hot-water bottles and by hot drinks which are alkaline instead of acid, the careful use of simple drugs to reduce fever and pain, and especially watchful waiting for the appearance of any symptom of a more serious disease.

Midget Motor Has High Power

IDEAL for small power jobs where space is at a premium is a new fractional horsepower electric motor now available for commercial use. The motor operates on any voltage between 10 and 230 and on any A. C. frequency between 25 and 60 cycles. High starting torque is commendable feature of the midget motor.

High starting torque, small size make this new motor ideal for use in fans, heat regulators, etc. Any voltage between 10 and 230 may be used.

Seek Lost Gold City Under Los Angeles

Derrick structure at mouth of shaft engineers are sinking on hill overlooking downtown Los Angeles to reach lost city.

View of downtown Los Angeles, beneath which mining engineer Shufelt believes is lost city of gold dug 5,000 years ago by "lizard people." Special treasure finding instrument has located many tunnels of catacomb city.

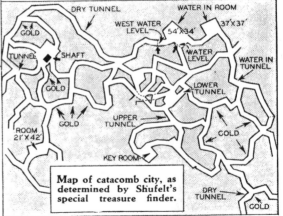

Map of catacomb city, as determined by Shufelt's special treasure finder.

THE lost city of the "lizard people," believed to be far beneath the streets of Los Angeles, has been located, G. Warren Shufelt, mining engineer, claims.

Using a treasure finding device of his own design, Shufelt has explored a large area of downtown Los Angeles.

"I knew I was over a pattern of tunnels," he declared, "and mapped out their course, the positions of the larger rooms, and the location of the deposits of gold."

He has secured financial backing for his underground explorations, and is now directing a group of men who are sinking a shaft in the heart of Los Angeles, just above what is thought to be the "key room" of the city of catacombs.

The shaft is already down to 250 feet. The group plan to go down to at least 1,000 feet before abandoning operations.

Legend has it that about 5,000 years ago three of these underground cities were burrowed out by a tribe of Indians after a great tongue of fire had "come out of the southwest destroying all life in its path." The labyrinths were dug to escape future fires.

The legend, as told Shufelt by an educated Hopi Indian, says the lost city was dug with powerful chemicals, without the need for removing either earth or rock.

The city was laid out in the shape of a lizard, this reptile being regarded as the symbol of long life.

According to the legend, all records were kept on gold tablets four feet long and 14 inches wide. Shufelt believes he has located thirty-seven of these tablets.

The apparatus used in locating the tunnels consists essentially of a plummet attached to a copper wire, and held by the hand inside a cylindrical glass case.

The plummet sways continually, its action depending upon the nature of the minerals or earth structure below.

Englishman Swallows Nose to Pull World's Ugliest Face

T. Cox, of Yarnton, England, the man with the India rubber face. He challenges the world to pull an uglier face.

Dog Is Mother to Baby Rabbits

BESSIE, a three-year-old purebred Alsatian dog in Orsett, England, had no puppies of her own, but longed for something on which to lavish her affections.

She adopted a baby rabbit, and was happy for a time. The rabbit died, however, and Bessie was so grief-stricken that her master bought her a tame rabbit.

Although rabbits generally have a deep fear of all dogs, they seem to sense the affection of Bessie, and are happy with her.

Bessie, a thoroughbred Alsatian, having no puppies of her own, plays mother to this tame rabbit bought for her.

THE man with the India rubber face is T. Cox, a farmer of Yarnton, England. He challenges anyone in the world to pull an uglier face than he can. So limber are his facial muscles that he can do just about everything but tie his cheeks into a knot.

Cox is able, by drawing up his lower jaw, puffing out his cheeks, and raising his lips up over his nose, to give the impression of having swallowed his nose.

No "bogeyman" is needed in this little town, for he can scare even the bravest of the little tots into eating their spinach.

Man of Future to Have One Eye

MAN'S eyes will come closer and closer together, the bridge of the nose will further diminish, and finally the two eyes will again become one—just one large, cyclopean eye in the center of the face—if the predictions of Dr. Thomas Shastid of Duluth, Minnesota, come true.

Dr. Shastid, eye specialist and editor of many optical magazines, bases his predic-

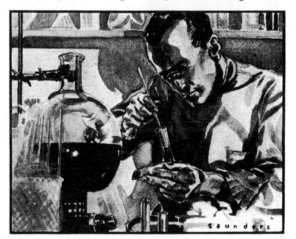

Artist's drawing of the face of the future, having one powerful eye in the center of the face. Left eye of today will gradually shrink away; right will be cyclopean.

tions upon his years of study of the eyes of humans, of animals, and of fish.

The left eye is being used less and less today—and soon will not be needed. The new eye will have two spots of sharpest vision in each eye, just as many birds have today, to obtain stereoscopic vision.

Although the field of view will then be narrower than now, the eye will be exceedingly acute for colors, for motion, and for form. It will probably be able to perceive as light many forms of energy which now produce in human eyes no sort of impression.

Dr. Shastid found that the eyes of birds are the best on earth, and are sometimes 100 times as good as those of man. They can not see blues or violets at all, but can see infra-red radiations.

Horses can see almost nothing above their heads because the lower part of their eyes are practically blind. The upper part gives off a bluish sparkle, however, which enables the horse to travel well in the dark.

Bed in Magnetic Field Gives Sound Sleep

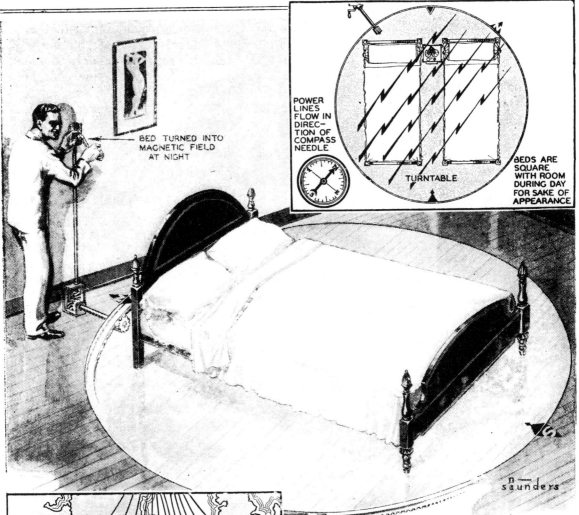

POWER LINES FLOW IN DIRECTION OF COMPASS NEEDLE

TURNTABLE

BEDS ARE SQUARE WITH ROOM DURING DAY FOR SAKE OF APPEARANCE

BED TURNED INTO MAGNETIC FIELD AT NIGHT

n. saunders

This drawing illustrates arrangement and operation of turntable which places sleeper's body in field of earth's magnetic lines of force. Insert above shows normal position of bed in daytime.

ACTING on the theory, deduced from extensive experiments, that human beings sleep most soundly when they lie parallel with the magnetic lines of force which encircle the earth from north to south, a German scientist has devised a special bed which permits a sleeper to get maximum benefits from the earth's magnetism.

For rooms where a bed would look awkward with its head toward the north and its foot toward the south, an ingenious turntable is employed. Each night before retiring time, the bed is turned to lie north and south by means of a crank which operates the turntable through a system of gears. Magnetic lines of force through the sleeper's body tend to bestow good health. Bed is turned to normal position in morning.

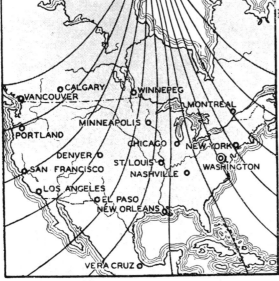

Most healthful sleep is to be had, a German scientist has discovered, when the body lies parallel to magnetic lines of force which pass from north to south over the earth's surface as illustrated in this map. Head of bed should be towards north, foot towards south.

The FREAK of the Month ~ No. 3

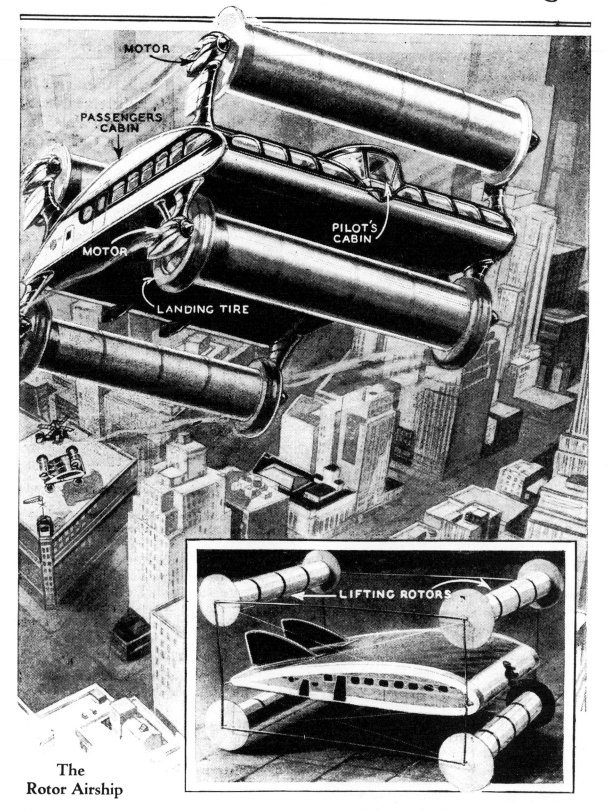

MOTOR

PASSENGER'S CABIN

MOTOR

LANDING TIRE

PILOT'S CABIN

LIFTING ROTORS

The Rotor Airship

The oddest contraption which has been brought to our attention this month is the rotor airplane designed by Ernst Zeuzem, of Frankfort-on-Main, Germany. The inventor's model is shown in the inset, while above is an artist's conception of how the full-size plane would appear in the air. Each of the four rotors will be driven by separate motors which need not be of exceptional power. The passengers will be carried in the wing section. In spite of its odd design, the principles of this plane are sound.

What will Your Next

Automobiles—
Yesterday and Tomorrow

The automobile industry is on the verge of a revolution in design which will make tomorrow's cars radically different from the present models. Amazing new trends in automotive engineering, affecting every American who owns a car, are fascinatingly set forth in this prophetic article.

THE automobile world—after eight or ten years of quiet and orderly development—is on the threshold of a period of radical change and improvement.

That, in a sentence, is the big news on the eve of the 1931 automobile shows.

Three things in the season of 1929-1930 forecast a new period of development. The first was the commercial introduction of the front wheel drive principle. The second—foretold by Fred Duesenberg in MODERN MECHANICS last April—was the appearance in early summer of free wheeling on cars of one make. And the third was the introduction by an American licensee of the British "Baby Austin," in size about midway between a perambulator and a flivver.

Reports from every automobile plant in the late summer showed feverish activity in the design department, and even more than the usual amount of secrecy. As late as the last of October one company which operates several subsidiary plants, each making a different car, was declaring it did not know

what it would show at the New York exhibition in January and the Chicago show the following month. Another company has developed a 16-cylinder car which will be shown at the shows for the first time. This makes two 16-cylinder cars on the American market.

And that statement probably was true. But the factories had several different cars built and was simply holding back to see what competitors might be doing.

From the maze of rumors floating around the auto industry it seems safe to predict that no less than six companies have built front wheel drive cars in the last year. One great auto group is said to be experimenting with no less than four different cars of this type.

Whether all, or any of them, will make their debut at the show, only time and tests can tell.

When Studebaker introduced free wheeling in the early summer it stole a march on the rest of the industry. At least two other

Car Look Like?

by JAY EARLE MILLER

companies had been testing free wheeling devices last winter and in the early spring, with equipment designed under other patents than those used by Studebaker. Free wheeling, as Fred Duesenberg, the famous auto designer, explained in MODERN MECHANICS of last April, is to the automobile what the coaster brake was to the bicycle.

In the early days of the bicycle the engine —represented by the rider's legs—pushed the machine up the hills and continued to operate on the down grades. When the coaster brake came along the human engine pushed the load up grade, and then rested and saved its energy while coasting down. The free wheeling device, which is built into the transmission behind the gear box, does just that. As soon as car momentum exceeds engine speed the car coasts, instead of turning the engine over against compression, in the same way that the first bicycles turned the rider's legs. Naturally there is a saving in gasoline and a saving in wear and tear. And—not the least important—it is as easy to shift from high down to second or first as it is to shift upward, and shifting can be done without the use of the clutch. In fact the clutch need only be used when starting.

With other patents available it is safe to say that the free wheeling principle will soon be extended to other

FUEL OIL TANK

DUAL DIESEL ENGINES

COMPARTMENT FOR LUGGAGE

SLIDING OR GLASS-TOPPED ROOF TO ADMIT SUNLIGHT

STREAMLINE BODY DESIGN ADDS 3 TO 5 MILES PER HOUR WITH SAME AMOUNT OF POWER

-N- SAUNDERS

FRAMELESS CHASSIS —TUBULAR DRIVE SHAFT SUPPORTS WEIGHT OF CAR

STREAMLINED HEADLIGHTS HIDDEN IN BODY

AUTOMATIC GEAR SHIFT

PILOT WHEEL TO AID STEERING

FRONT OF CHASSIS HIDDEN BY STREAMLINE BODY

Artist's conception of the automobile of tomorrow, embodying many seemingly radical ideas which, according to experts, are sure to come. Note particularly the streamline body, eliminating suction at the rear which slows down the speed of present cars. Side-frame members will be eliminated. Motors will more and more come to be mounted at the rear, driving either the front or rear wheels, or both. Automatic gear shifts are just around the corner on a number of new cars.

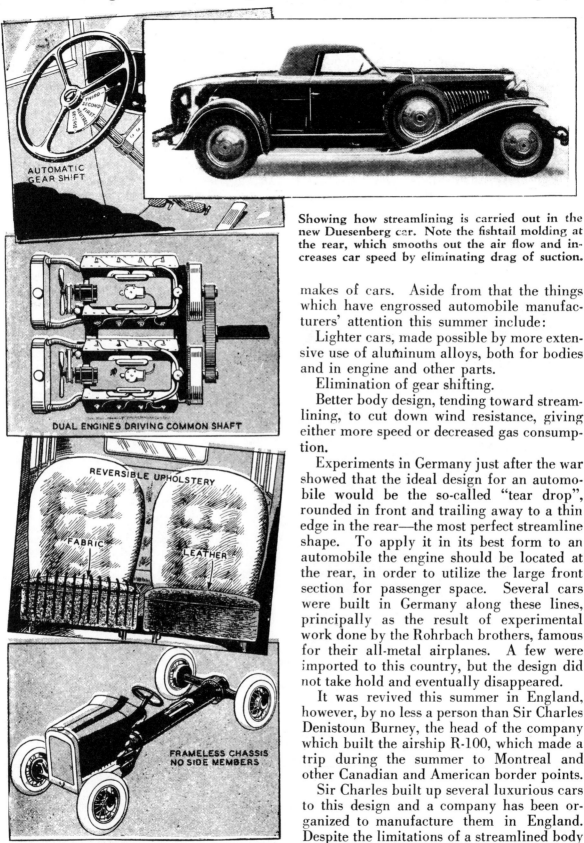

Showing how streamlining is carried out in the new Duesenberg car. Note the fishtail molding at the rear, which smooths out the air flow and increases car speed by eliminating drag of suction.

AUTOMATIC GEAR SHIFT

DUAL ENGINES DRIVING COMMON SHAFT

REVERSIBLE UPHOLSTERY

FABRIC

LEATHER

FRAMELESS CHASSIS NO SIDE MEMBERS

Trends in automotive design presented in graphic form. Automatic gear shifts are coming within a few months; dual engines driving a common shaft, rather than multiple-cylinder single motors, are being experimented with by European engineers.

makes of cars. Aside from that the things which have engrossed automobile manufacturers' attention this summer include:

Lighter cars, made possible by more extensive use of aluminum alloys, both for bodies and in engine and other parts.

Elimination of gear shifting.

Better body design, tending toward streamlining, to cut down wind resistance, giving either more speed or decreased gas consumption.

Experiments in Germany just after the war showed that the ideal design for an automobile would be the so-called "tear drop", rounded in front and trailing away to a thin edge in the rear—the most perfect streamline shape. To apply it in its best form to an automobile the engine should be located at the rear, in order to utilize the large front section for passenger space. Several cars were built in Germany along these lines, principally as the result of experimental work done by the Rohrbach brothers, famous for their all-metal airplanes. A few were imported to this country, but the design did not take hold and eventually disappeared.

It was revived this summer in England, however, by no less a person than Sir Charles Denistoun Burney, the head of the company which built the airship R-100, which made a trip during the summer to Montreal and other Canadian and American border points.

Sir Charles built up several luxurious cars to this design and a company has been organized to manufacture them in England. Despite the limitations of a streamlined body and their low overall height, they have ample room for seven passengers.

Aside from their tear drop lines they are chiefly notable for their clean exterior. The

The streamlined car built by Commander Burney, designer of the British dirigible R-100, in which the influence of aircraft practices can be plainly seen. Note the motor and radiator at the rear.

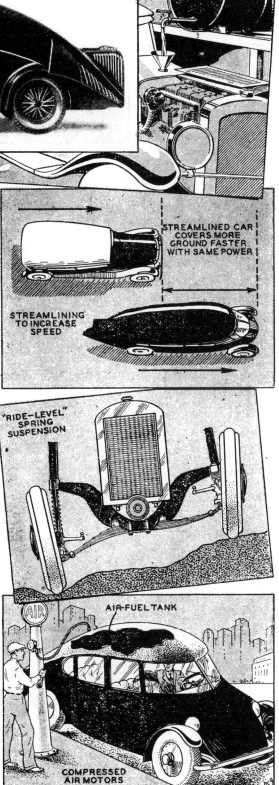

headlights are built into the body lines and the two spare wheels and tires are carried within the doors of the rear compartment, thus eliminating the wind resistance due to ordinary side wheel mounts.

The front fenders, instead of projecting from the body, are very small, attached to the wheels, and turn with them, so that the total wind resistance of the wheel and fender is but little more than that of the wheel alone. The rear fenders are practically all concealed within the body lines.

Because of the narrow front of the body, made possible by the absence of an engine, the front wheels can turn fifty degrees, enabling the car to turn in a very small radius.

Tests are said to show that the car can operate at a given speed with one-half the power required to move a car of ordinary design, and at a saving of 50 percent of the usual gas consumption.

The effect of wind resistance has not been given much consideration by automobile designers. Their method of increasing speed has been to increase the power, and therefore the cost of operation. Beyond speeds of 60 to 75 miles an hour, however, the rising curve of gas consumption has assumed such proportions as to become almost prohibitive for any but the very rich. A high powered American car which has a top speed of about 120 miles an hour gets but four miles to the gallon as it nears that speed.

Diesel engines have already been used in experimental cars, and will soon be commercially produced. Compressed air motors are being experimented with by a prominent American car builder.

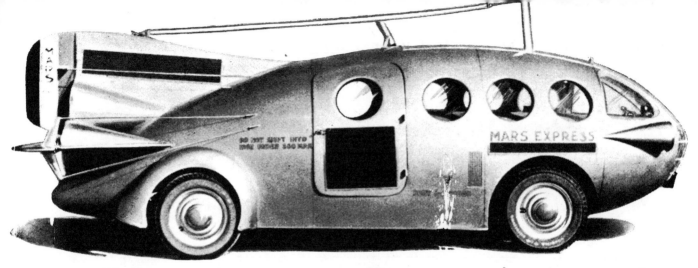

Rockets Boost Bullet Car's Speed

Nose-on view of the superstreamline car. Note the radio mast

CLOSELY resembling the fuselage of an airplane, a curious speed car designed by Peter Vacca, of Buffalo, N. Y., is powered by both a gasoline engine and a rocket motor. Fitted with a body made of aluminum, the streamline automobile measures twenty feet from the tip of its snub nose to the ends of the airplane-type rudders and stabilizers at its rear. Propelled by its gasoline power plant, an eight-cylinder V-type engine fitted with a supercharger, the radio-equipped bullet car will attain a speed of 115 miles an hour. At this speed, it is planned to bring the rocket vents into play to boost the car's speed to its maximum. The unique vehicle is said to have cost $16,000 to build.

Mounted at the rear are rocket vents which can be used to increase the car's speed above the 115 miles an hour made possible by its engine

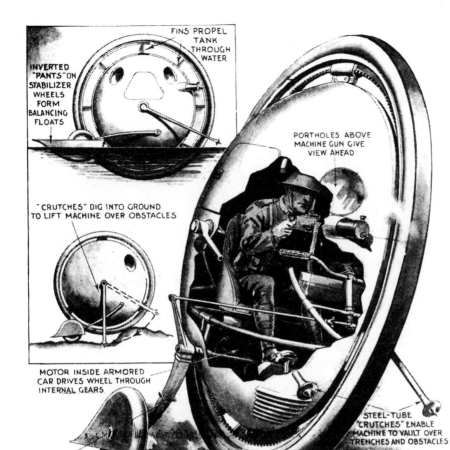

FINS PROPEL TANK THROUGH WATER

INVERTED "PANTS" ON STABILIZER WHEELS FORM BALANCING FLOATS

PORTHOLES ABOVE MACHINE GUN GIVE VIEW AHEAD

"CRUTCHES" DIG INTO GROUND TO LIFT MACHINE OVER OBSTACLES

STEEL-TUBE "CRUTCHES" ENABLE MACHINE TO VAULT OVER TRENCHES AND OBSTACLES

MOTOR INSIDE ARMORED CAR DRIVES WHEEL THROUGH INTERNAL GEARS

SPRING ARMS CARRY STABILIZER WHEELS

TURNING HANDLEBARS STEERS TANK BY LIFTING ONE STABILIZING WHEEL AND LOWERING OTHER TO SHIFT BALANCE OF MAIN WHEEL

This one-man war tank, propelled by a hidden motor, would roll into action as is shown above. The diagrams also give a clear idea of how the machine runs on land or water

War Tank

ON

One Wheel

OPERATED BY

ONE MAN

•

In England, an Italian inventor has just demonstrated a single-passenger unicycle in which he claims to have reached speeds of 100 miles an hour and to have made 280 miles on a gallon of gasoline. In the near future, he plans to bring the machine to the United States and demonstrate its adaptability to American highways. Perfected after more than ten years of experiment, this odd machine rests solely upon one huge pneumatic tire encircling the driver, and dispenses entirely with exterior steering apparatus. The metal rim within the tire supports the frame and driver's seat and is rotated by a motor of one and three-fourths horsepower. To guide the vehicle to left or right, a steering wheel tilts the central frame with respect to the wheel, shifting the driver's weight and thus steering the hoop. Models of various sizes are contemplated. the diameter of the hoop being suited to the height of the driver, so that a tall man, according to the inventor, would use a larger unicycle than a short man.

SUDDENLY, through the drifting smoke of a hard-fought battle, rush weird, one-man fighting tanks. They have the appearance of disk wheels and roll like hoops across the battlefield. Pouring out machine-gun fire, they leap over trenches, vaulting across on strange steel crutches to pursue the disorganized enemy.

Such is the startling vision foreseen by a New York inventor. He has just obtained a patent upon a unicycle-type tank which he believes will revolutionize battlefield tactics.

Housed inside the armored body, the operator will steer the single main wheel by means of two small auxiliary wheels at the rear. A turn of the handlebar lifts one stabilizing wheel and lowers the other. shifting the balance of the machine and turning it to one side or the other. An internal gear mechanism, operated by a motor inside the body, drives the wheel ahead at remarkable speed.

By a simple process of inverting the streamlined pants on the stabilizing wheels. so they form balancing floats. and attaching propelling fins to the main wheel. the tank can be turned into an amphibian

capable of plunging into a stream and rolling to the other side.

One of the oddest features of the revolutionary machine is formed by the steel-tube crutches that project ahead on either side like medieval lances. As the tank rushes upon a trench or obstruction, the operator will drop the tubes so they dig into the earth and the whole machine will vault through the air to the other side.

An open-type form of the vehicle, which is shown on our cover, has also been devised by the inventor. Without the armored body or the crutches. it is designed for highway use.

In various parts of the world, recently, engineers have been reviving the idea of the unicycle. Attracted by the economy and compactness of a one-wheeled vehicle, they have been attacking anew the problems of balance and propulsion which have been the stumbling blocks in the path of the inventors.

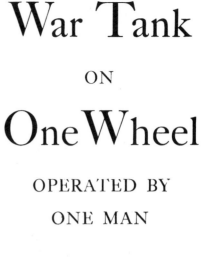

A new unicycle, credited with a 100-mile speed and 280 miles on one gallon of gas

Streamline Shell PEPS UP Motorcycle

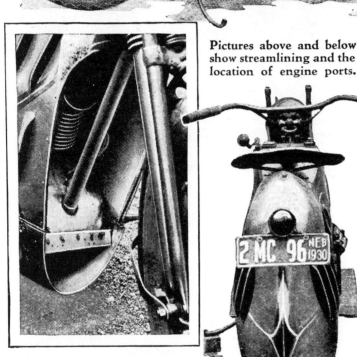

Pictures above and below show streamlining and the location of engine ports.

A front view of the shell, showing how the baffle plates deflect air upwards and around engine.

The snap door on the right permits easy access to the spark plugs. Two other ports are on the left side.

JOE SZAKACS, of Lincoln, Nebraska, has equipped his motorcycle with a 22 gauge aluminum shell which, besides improving the appearance of his machine, has increased the speed and reduced the weight by four pounds.

Only two pieces of strap steel, shaped to fit, were needed. Access to the engine is gained through three round snap-shut doors, each using a single hinge and a small arrangement comprising a steel coil spring which is connected to the door inside the shell. This spring rides in a rounded metal groove and prevents binding.

Most of the jointing was done with small rivets through a light strip of steel placed underneath and carrying a row of rivets through each adjoining aluminum edge. The front wheel was equipped with an aluminum disc to hide the spokes, while the rear wheel is not so equipped. Cranking the engine, shifting gears, and other details are as easy as before the shell was made. The paint job is a bright orange.

Brain Meter Tests Lawmakers' Intellect

Your Congressman's Brain

Based on partial survey of 89 senators and congressmen.

SENATORS' brain weights averaged 52 oz., congressmen, 50 oz. The greatest brain weight, 55 oz., was shown in members from Arkansas, Texas, Louisiana and Oklahoma.

The next highest brain weight, 53 oz., was found in members from Minnesota, Iowa, North Dakota, Nebraska and Kansas.

The lowest weight, 49 oz., was registered by members from California, Oregon and Washington.

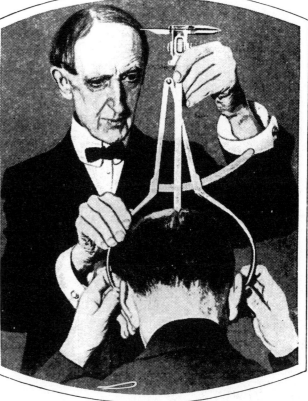

Dr. Arthur MacDonald, inventor of the brain meter, is shown with his new instrument, not unlike a pair of calipers, conducting one of his remarkable brain weight tests.

A scientist attached to the Smithsonian Institute displays fossilized brain specimens. In his right hand is that of an average person; in his left, that of a superior mentality.

PIONEERING in a new field of medical science, Dr. Arthur MacDonald, a prominent scientist of Washington, D. C., has perfected a new machine which weighs the brain in a living person—hitherto an impossible feat.

Recently Dr. MacDonald made a partial survey of the brain weights and body measurements of our national lawmakers as the first step in an experiment expected to lead to a study of the mental and physical equipment of legislative bodies throughout the world. Eighteen senators and seventy-one congressmen showed an average brain weight of 52 and 50 ounces respectively. The greatest brain weight—55 ounces—was shown by members from Arkansas, Louisiana, Oklahoma and Texas, who likewise possessed the greatest stature—70 inches—and the greatest head length—8 inches.

Legislators from California, Washington and Oregon registered the lowest average brain weight—49 ounces—and the smallest head length; yet, oddly enough, showed the strongest hand clasp, with an average of 203 pounds. Conversely, members from Kentucky, Tennessee, Alabama and Mississippi, although possessed of the greatest average body weight, scored lowest in the hand grasp test with grips of from 80 to 91 pounds. Lawmakers from Minnesota, Iowa, North Dakota, Missouri, Kansas and Nebraska revealed brain weights of 53 ounces and an average stature barely below 70 inches.

Aside from the novelty of these tests, groundwork is being laid for insuring an increase in the length of life of our national leaders. Comparative studies of these men who come from various sections of the country likewise offer an opportunity for scientists to establish data on the general physical and mental status of the nation.

An OCEAN LINER

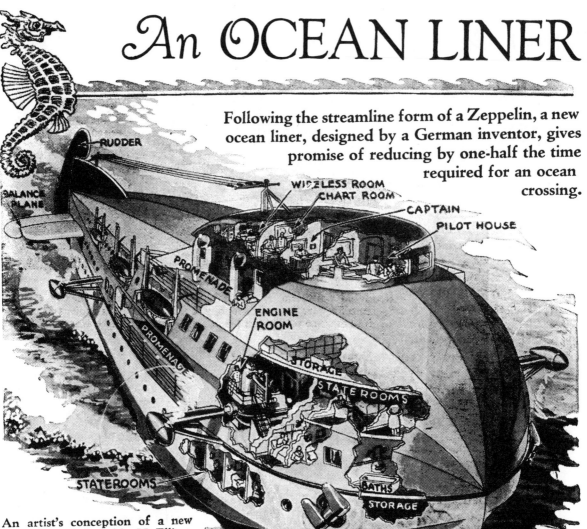

Following the streamline form of a Zeppelin, a new ocean liner, designed by a German inventor, gives promise of reducing by one-half the time required for an ocean crossing.

RUDDER

BALANCE PLANE

WIRELESS ROOM
CHART ROOM
CAPTAIN
PILOT HOUSE

PROMENADE

ENGINE ROOM

PROMENADE

STORAGE
STATE ROOMS

STATEROOMS

BATHS
STORAGE

An artist's conception of a new ocean liner designed by H. Ellinghausen. The streamline design adds to the ship's speed, and the broad beam provides much space for passengers and cargo.

WILL the ocean liner of the future take advantage of the lessons learned by airship engineers and pattern its design after the streamlined *Graf Zeppelin*, *Los Angeles*, *R-100*, and other famous lighter-than-air craft? That such is the present tendency is indicated by the contemplated ship shown in the artist's drawing above, and depicted on this month's cover of MODERN MECHANICS AND INVENTIONS. It is the invention of H. Ellinghausen, of Bremen, Germany, who in experiments with this type of design has developed speeds well in excess of 60 miles an hour.

Advantages of such a ship are obvious. Streamline design adds to the speed without requiring increase in power. The broad, rounded design of the ship allows interior accommodations to be laid out to the best advantage, without the necessity for cramped

An experimental streamlined boat used by the inventor in working out the design for the liner.

staterooms as on the ordinary vessel. Placing the air drive propellers outside the hull enables the motors to be taken care of in a comparatively small space.

There is no danger of such a ship rolling over in a heavy sea, owing to the broad V-bottom. Placing steps in the bottom, following the practice of speedboat designers, adds

Built Like a ZEPPELIN

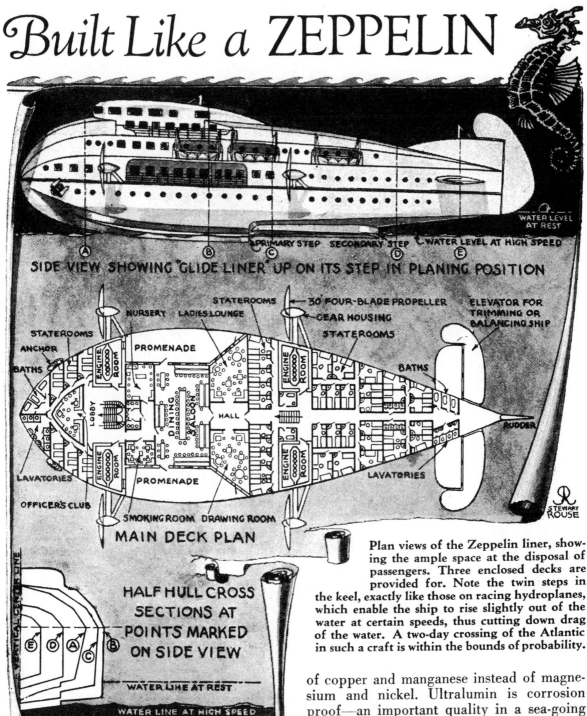

SIDE VIEW SHOWING "GLIDE LINER" UP ON ITS STEP IN PLANING POSITION

WATER LEVEL AT REST

PRIMARY STEP · SECONDARY STEP · WATER LEVEL AT HIGH SPEED

STATEROOMS · 30 FOUR-BLADE PROPELLER · ELEVATOR FOR TRIMMING OR BALANCING SHIP

NURSERY · LADIES LOUNGE · GEAR HOUSING · STATEROOMS

STATEROOMS · ANCHOR · BATHS · PROMENADE · ENGINE ROOM · ENGINE ROOM · BATHS

LOBBY · DINING SALOON · HALL · RUDDER

LAVATORIES · ENGINE ROOM · ENGINE ROOM · LAVATORIES

OFFICER'S CLUB · PROMENADE

SMOKING ROOM · DRAWING ROOM

STEWART ROUSE

MAIN DECK PLAN

HALF HULL CROSS SECTIONS AT POINTS MARKED ON SIDE VIEW

VERTICAL CENTER LINE

WATER LINE AT REST

WATER LINE AT HIGH SPEED

Plan views of the Zeppelin liner, showing the ample space at the disposal of passengers. Three enclosed decks are provided for. Note the twin steps in the keel, exactly like those on racing hydroplanes, which enable the ship to rise slightly out of the water at certain speeds, thus cutting down drag of the water. A two-day crossing of the Atlantic in such a craft is within the bounds of probability.

to the speed of the craft. Promenade decks are built into the side of the ship so that the wind created by the boat's own speed will not annoy the passengers. Tail controls similar to those on an airplane are used to keep the ship on its course, but an under-water rudder can also be added to get quicker response in emergencies.

A special light metal which is the invention of Mr. Ellinghausen will be used when the ship gets under construction. He calls this metal ultralumin, and it differs from the more familiar duralumin in that it is an alloy of copper and manganese instead of magnesium and nickel. Ultralumin is corrosion proof—an important quality in a sea-going craft—and it also has easier working qualities.

The record for an Atlantic crossing is now held by the German liner *Bremen*. It is notable that the *Bremen* is the first liner whose above-water parts have been consistently streamlined. Smokestacks, masts, and other exposed objects are streamlined to such good effect that it was almost inevitable she should capture the Atlantic speed record. Speed gained by streamlining is, as the saying goes, pure velvet. Adding more power to an existing design is an old way of increasing speed —at a considerable expense for fuel.

Iron Whale Swims Ocean Bottom Like Fish

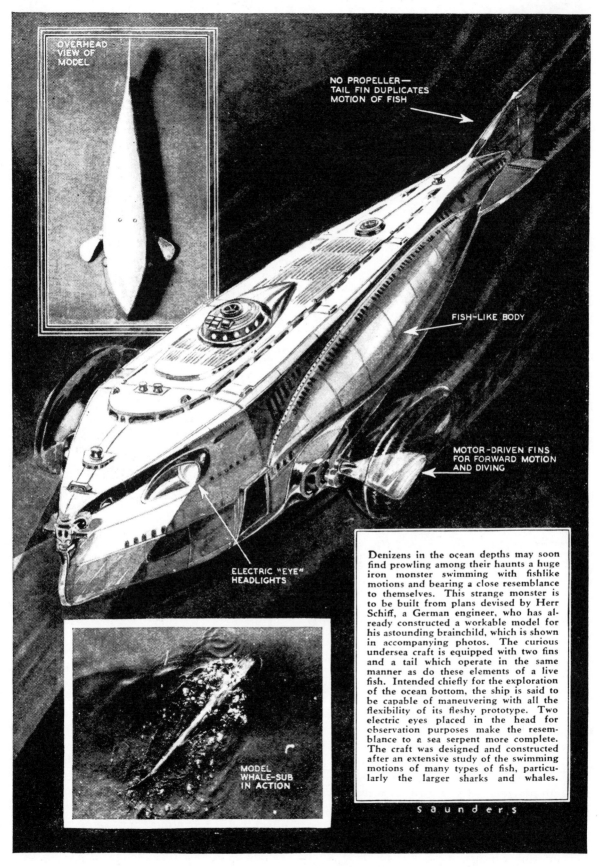

OVERHEAD VIEW OF MODEL

NO PROPELLER—
TAIL FIN DUPLICATES
MOTION OF FISH

FISH-LIKE BODY

MOTOR-DRIVEN FINS
FOR FORWARD MOTION
AND DIVING

ELECTRIC "EYE"
HEADLIGHTS

MODEL
WHALE-SUB
IN ACTION

Denizens in the ocean depths may soon find prowling among their haunts a huge iron monster swimming with fishlike motions and bearing a close resemblance to themselves. This strange monster is to be built from plans devised by Herr Schiff, a German engineer, who has already constructed a workable model for his astounding brainchild, which is shown in accompanying photos. The curious undersea craft is equipped with two fins and a tail which operate in the same manner as do these elements of a live fish. Intended chiefly for the exploration of the ocean bottom, the ship is said to be capable of maneuvering with all the flexibility of its fleshy prototype. Two electric eyes placed in the head for observation purposes make the resemblance to a sea serpent more complete. The craft was designed and constructed after an extensive study of the swimming motions of many types of fish, particularly the larger sharks and whales.

s a u n d e r s

At top is seen model of the iron whale ready for a test trip. Note the fish-like fins and the two electric eyes set in the head section of the body. At bottom may be seen the model preparing to submerge to prove the practicability of the plans.

Gar Wood Predicts Boats that Fly

Suggested lines of a speedboat which can fly as well as float are shown in this drawing of a double-purpose craft seen as a possibility of the future by **Gar Wood**, famous designer of racing boats.

MODERN speedboats show very little difference between the way they travel through the water and the way an airplane travels through the air. This is the observation of Gar Wood, noted designer of record-breaking speedboats, who recently remarked that he would not be greatly surprised to learn one of these days that boats are flying. A big thrill is in store for sportsmen when the time comes when one can own a boat and drive it about on the surface of the water, and then throw the engine into high, work the clutch on a propeller designed to get the craft into the air, and fly.

A speedboat, due to the step under the hull, is traveling almost in the air, or at least in a medium of spray and water that is largely bubbles. The veer or flare of a speedboat hull is in a measure a wing-like structure, helping to elevate the boat out of the water at high speeds. If the flare were exaggerated and broadened, as illustrated in the drawing above, it would be possible to lift the boat out of the water and maintain sustained flight in the air—provided, of course, that it was equipped with a propeller of sufficient size to provide forward movement.

What is now known as a "flying boat" is in reality an airplane that can float, not a boat that can fly. A real flying boat such as the one shown would be equipped with a water screw of special design so that it would fold up out of the way when the boat was flying, with a similar folding arrangement for the air propeller so that it would be out of the way when the boat was traveling on the water.

Windmill-Cycle Boat to CROSS Atlantic

COMBINING features of a windmill and bicycle, one of the most unique boats ever constructed has been designed by William H. Oldham of Sankey Bridges, Warrington, England, for a trip across the Atlantic ocean. If his attempt succeeds, he will hold the record for navigating the smallest craft between Europe and the United States. He is looking for a partner to accompany him on his adventurous trip.

The *Amy*, as Mr. Oldham has called his boat, is made entirely of steel and is only 12 feet long. In place of the sail usually employed by boats, a windmill with 16 vanes has been substituted. This is geared to the propeller through a transmission box, as shown in the drawing below, and is so arranged that it can be turned around to catch the wind coming from any direction.

If the wind fails, however, the *Amy* is in no danger of being becalmed. A bicycle arrangement attached to the screw permits one member of the crew of two to pedal the boat along in exactly the same way a cyclist travels on land. Steering is accomplished through ordinary handlebars, which are connected to the rudder. The entire arrangement is exceedingly compact, as may be gathered from the painting which is this month's cover of MODERN MECHANICS AND INVENTIONS. So tiny is the boat that only one man can sleep at a time, the other being constantly required to steer or pedal the ship. Compass and other essential navigation instruments are carried, together with provisions for a 40-day trip.

Perilous as an Atlantic crossing in this unique boat would seem to be, Mr. Oldham does not regard it as foolhardy, since he claims that the boat is so designed that it is practically impossible for it to overturn. Its solid steel construction, too, renders it immune to damage in case of collision with derelicts or floating wreckage. The *Amy*, though not a comfortable craft to ride in because of her small proportions, is nevertheless reasonably safe.

If you have a leaning toward sea adventure and would like to be Mr. Oldham's partner on his trip, he'll be glad to hear from you. His address is 158 Liverpool Road, Sankey Bridges, Warrington, England.

Details of the windmill-cycle boat shown on this month's cover are presented in this drawing by Stewart Rouse. When wind fails, boat can be pedaled like bicycle.

WINDMILL ROTOR

BEVEL GEARS IN MILL HEAD

TURNTABLE MOUNT FOR FACING MILL INTO WIND

CLUTCH LEVER

COMPASS

WORM GEAR FOR TURNING MILL TO FACE WIND

HAND WHEEL REMOTE CONTROL FOR MILL

STEWART ROUSE

RUDDER OPERATED BY HANDLE BARS

SCREW PROPELLER

AMY

FRONT PART OF BOAT FOR PROVISIONS

BICYCLE TYPE CHAIN FROM LARGE SPROCKET

FOOT POWER SPROCKET AND BEVEL GEARS

CLUTCH RELEASING MILL FROM PROPELLER DRIVE SO FOOT POWER CAN BE USED

CONTROL ROD FROM CLUTCH LEVER

BEVEL GEARS

Turbo Wheel Liners to Speed Across Seas

AVIATION'S rapid strides are revolutionizing all other modes of transportation. Railroads are meeting the demand for greater speed with streamlined trains. Automobiles are following the most modern trends in streamlining.

On the seas, however, even a streamlined ship will not be able to meet the competition of regular airplane schedules touching airports anchored in the ocean. Resistance from wind is great, but the sea itself slows down an ocean liner much more.

To overcome this an inventor has conceived the Turbo Wheel liner, which is expected to reach a speed of 100 miles an hour. At this speed the rapidly revolving wheels of the liner will lift the hull out of the water. The ship will ride on the outer rim of the wheels only.

A lifting tail of airplane type holds the hull parallel to the line of travel. Normal airplane rudder and tail flaps control steering at high speeds.

At low speeds a revolving tail float is lowered to support the rear end of the hull and provide steering. Powerful Diesel type engines slung low within the rotor wheels drive each wheel independently through gearing. The Turbo Liners are expected to be capable of a speed of 100 miles per hour.

This radical design for an ocean liner would revolutionize sea travel. The ship could travel 100 miles an hour.

EFFECT OF HIGH SEAS ON TURBO-WHEEL SHIP COMPARED WITH VESSEL OF ORDINARY TYPE

40 FT.

DRIVING BLADES

CONTROL ROOM

DRIVE GEAR

FIXED HUB

CABINS

PORT POWER PLANT

AIRPLANE TYPE TAIL SURFACES

SEAWORTHY HULL RESTS ON WATER WHEN NOT IN MOTION

TAIL FLOAT LOWERS TO SUPPORT REAR END OF HULL WHEN FORWARD SPEED IS REDUCED AND TAIL BEGINS TO DROP

Cutaway drawing above shows location of power plant and gear drive to revolve wheels. Huge fluted wheels propel the liner at 100 miles per hour. At rest the huge cabin hull would float on the ocean as shown in the right background.

Aero-Drive Desert BUS Replaces Camels

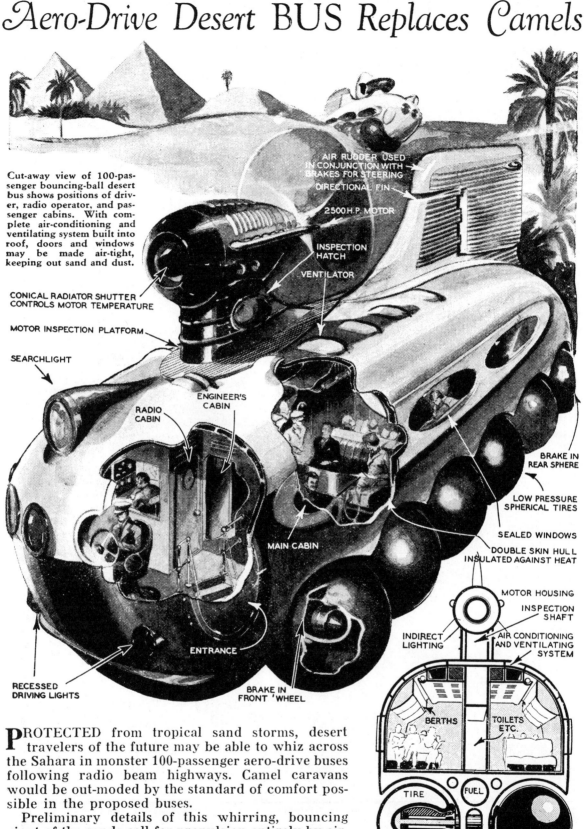

Cut-away view of 100-passenger bouncing-ball desert bus shows positions of driver, radio operator, and passenger cabins. With complete air-conditioning and ventilating system built into roof, doors and windows may be made air-tight, keeping out sand and dust.

AIR RUDDER USED IN CONJUNCTION WITH BRAKES FOR STEERING

DIRECTIONAL FIN

2500 H.P. MOTOR

INSPECTION HATCH

VENTILATOR

CONICAL RADIATOR SHUTTER CONTROLS MOTOR TEMPERATURE

MOTOR INSPECTION PLATFORM

SEARCHLIGHT

ENGINEER'S CABIN

RADIO CABIN

BRAKE IN REAR SPHERE

LOW PRESSURE SPHERICAL TIRES

SEALED WINDOWS

DOUBLE SKIN HULL INSULATED AGAINST HEAT

MAIN CABIN

MOTOR HOUSING

INSPECTION SHAFT

INDIRECT LIGHTING

AIR CONDITIONING AND VENTILATING SYSTEM

ENTRANCE

RECESSED DRIVING LIGHTS

BRAKE IN FRONT WHEEL

BERTHS

TOILETS ETC.

TIRE

FUEL

HUB

FIXED SHAFT

PROTECTED from tropical sand storms, desert travelers of the future may be able to whiz across the Sahara in monster 100-passenger aero-drive buses following radio beam highways. Camel caravans would be out-moded by the standard of comfort possible in the proposed buses.

Preliminary details of this whirring, bouncing giant of the sands call for propulsion entirely by air, with a 2500 h.p. aviation engine and pusher propeller mounted atop the roof. Most unusual feature of the desert bus is a series of spherical tires on each side which would provide good traction over the shifting sands. Directly back of the propeller is a steering fin which controls the direction of the ship.

Cross-section of new desert travel ship, showing construction of inflated spherical rubber tires and mounting of motor. Brakes on front and rear wheels are independently controlled, permitting their use in steering the huge bus.

Revolving Paddles Lift Odd-Style Plane

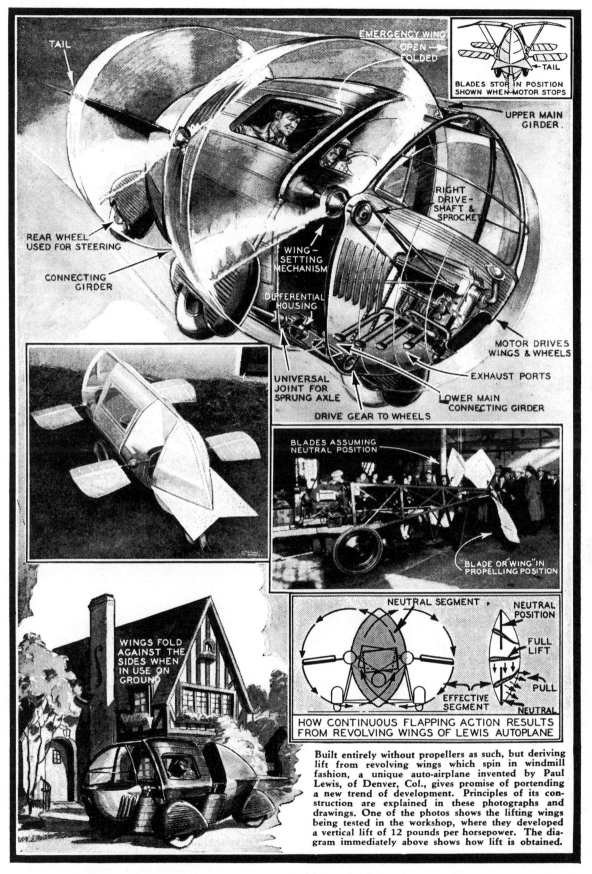

EMERGENCY WING
OPEN →
FOLDED
BLADES STOP IN POSITION SHOWN WHEN MOTOR STOPS
TAIL

TAIL

UPPER MAIN GIRDER

RIGHT DRIVE-SHAFT & SPROCKET

REAR WHEEL USED FOR STEERING

CONNECTING GIRDER

WING-SETTING MECHANISM

DIFFERENTIAL HOUSING

MOTOR DRIVES WINGS & WHEELS

EXHAUST PORTS

UNIVERSAL JOINT FOR SPRUNG AXLE

LOWER MAIN CONNECTING GIRDER

DRIVE GEAR TO WHEELS

BLADES ASSUMING NEUTRAL POSITION

BLADE OR "WING" IN PROPELLING POSITION

WINGS FOLD AGAINST THE SIDES WHEN IN USE ON GROUND

NEUTRAL SEGMENT

NEUTRAL POSITION

FULL LIFT

PULL

EFFECTIVE SEGMENT

NEUTRAL

HOW CONTINUOUS FLAPPING ACTION RESULTS FROM REVOLVING WINGS OF LEWIS AUTOPLANE

Built entirely without propellers as such, but deriving lift from revolving wings which spin in windmill fashion, a unique auto-airplane invented by Paul Lewis, of Denver, Col., gives promise of portending a new trend of development. Principles of its construction are explained in these photographs and drawings. One of the photos shows the lifting wings being tested in the workshop, where they developed a vertical lift of 12 pounds per horsepower. The diagram immediately above shows how lift is obtained.

Clever folding design of the wings makes it possible to use the autoplane as a three-wheeled car on the ground.

Six Hours to Europe in Stratosphere Liner

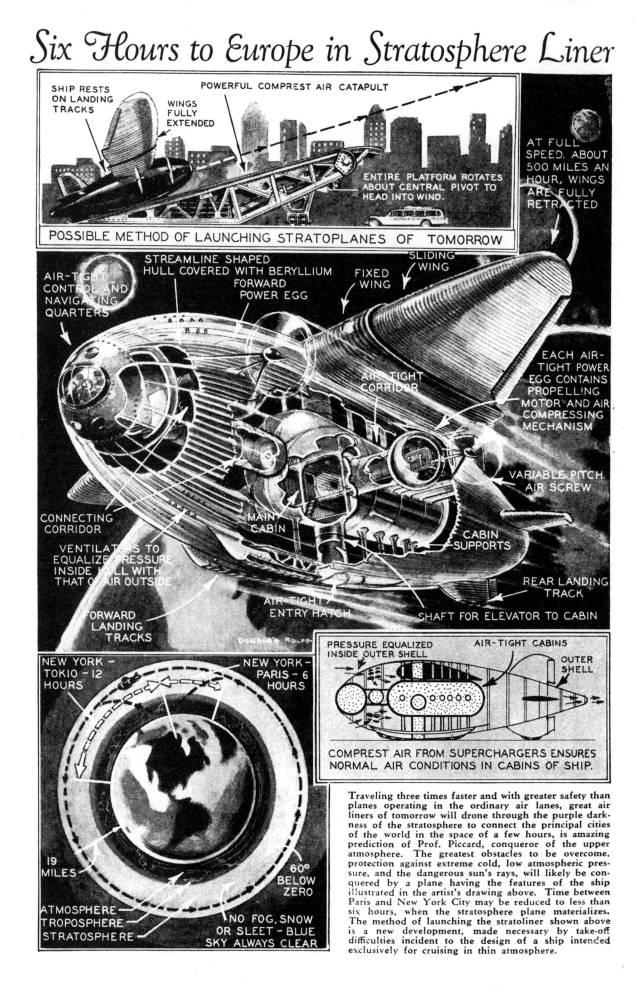

SHIP RESTS ON LANDING TRACKS

POWERFUL COMPREST AIR CATAPULT

WINGS FULLY EXTENDED

ENTIRE PLATFORM ROTATES ABOUT CENTRAL PIVOT TO HEAD INTO WIND.

AT FULL SPEED, ABOUT 500 MILES AN HOUR, WINGS ARE FULLY RETRACTED

POSSIBLE METHOD OF LAUNCHING STRATOPLANES OF TOMORROW

AIR-TIGHT CONTROL AND NAVIGATING QUARTERS

STREAMLINE SHAPED HULL COVERED WITH BERYLLIUM FORWARD POWER EGG

FIXED WING

SLIDING WING

AIR-TIGHT CORRIDOR

EACH AIR-TIGHT POWER EGG CONTAINS PROPELLING MOTOR AND AIR COMPRESSING MECHANISM

VARIABLE PITCH AIR SCREW

CONNECTING CORRIDOR

MAIN CABIN

CABIN SUPPORTS

VENTILATORS TO EQUALIZE PRESSURE INSIDE HULL WITH THAT OF AIR OUTSIDE

REAR LANDING TRACK

FORWARD LANDING TRACKS

AIR-TIGHT ENTRY HATCH

SHAFT FOR ELEVATOR TO CABIN

NEW YORK - TOKIO - 12 HOURS

NEW YORK - PARIS - 6 HOURS

PRESSURE EQUALIZED INSIDE OUTER SHELL

AIR-TIGHT CABINS

OUTER SHELL

19 MILES

60° BELOW ZERO

ATMOSPHERE
TROPOSPHERE
STRATOSPHERE

NO FOG, SNOW OR SLEET - BLUE SKY ALWAYS CLEAR

COMPREST AIR FROM SUPERCHARGERS ENSURES NORMAL AIR CONDITIONS IN CABINS OF SHIP.

Traveling three times faster and with greater safety than planes operating in the ordinary air lanes, great air liners of tomorrow will drone through the purple darkness of the stratosphere to connect the principal cities of the world in the space of a few hours, is amazing prediction of Prof. Piccard, conqueror of the upper atmosphere. The greatest obstacles to be overcome, protection against extreme cold, low atmospheric pressure, and the dangerous sun's rays, will likely be conquered by a plane having the features of the ship illustrated in the artist's drawing above. Time between Paris and New York City may be reduced to less than six hours, when the stratosphere plane materializes. The method of launching the stratoliner shown above is a new development, made necessary by take-off difficulties incident to the design of a ship intended exclusively for cruising in thin atmosphere.

Motorcycles of the Air

TOOL BOX AND BATTERY COMPARTMENT

GAS AND OIL TANKS

BRACING WIRE

WING-TIP AILERONS

LANDING WIRE

DRAG WIRE

BRACING (FLYING) WIRE

SIDE RESTS ARE LOWERED TO FORM SUPPORT FOR SHIP WHEN AT REST

AIRWHEEL

ULTRA-LIGHT TWO CYLINDER AIR COOLED MOTOR

SINGLE SPAR WING BRACED FORE AND AFT

CONTROL CABLE

CENTRALLY PIVOTED CRUCIFORM TAIL

AILERON HORN

CONTROL CABLES TO ELEVATOR AND AILERONS

AILERON

RUDDER

FIN

INVERTED CONTROL STICK

STABILIZER

SUPPORTING HARNESS

SLOW SPEED HIGH LIFT TYPE BIPLANE WINGS

The above drawing shows details of an aerocycle plane as conceived and drawn by Douglas Rolfe, airplane expert. Ships of this type, though not yet commercially produced, have been made possible by recent development of new materials such as extremely strong but light metal alloys and light weight motors. "Flying scooters" like the one illustrated on this month's cover would not be practical for long-distance flying, but would be ideal for sports use. With the cost at a moderate figure, these aerocycles would very likely displace gliders in popularity. There are no novel departures from accepted airplane practice in these designs.

This ski-glider, developed by Halvor Garos and Carl Messolt, of New York City, shows close adherence to accepted principles of airplane design. The clever control system permits perfect handling when the glider takes off as the skier slides down the hill.

Strange Lifting Force

Looking like an immense Zeppelin hangar floating in the sky, the gyro-airship, with an immense load-carrying capacity and tremendous speed, bids fair to put railroads out of business as freight-carriers if the hopes of its inventor are justified.

How does this airship keep aloft with neither propellers nor lifting gas? It's the strangest craft yet designed to cruise the skies and represents as far a departure from conventional types of aircraft as can be imagined. You'll find this description of the ship fascinating.

WHAT is certainly the most unique airship in the world is now under construction in the form of an experimental model in the factory of its inventor in Denver, Colorado. As depicted on these pages, the extraordinary ship will use neither propellers nor gas to keep it in the air, but will depend on a mechanism which its inventor, Edgar R. Holmes, calls the "gyradoscope".

Each horsepower of gyradoscope is expected to lift 1,000 pounds vertically in mid-air and sustain the load at any desired elevation by regulating the speed, and the inventor expects a machine weighing 2,000 pounds to lift 500 tons.

Briefly, the gyradoscope combines gyroscopic action with centrifugal force. As described in the prospectus of the company, the gyradoscope consists of two wheels rotating in opposite directions in the same plane. Each wheel has several weights, the arms of which are connected to eccentrics on each wheel, which propel the weights in opposite directions in such a way that a lifting effect is exerted when the weights are at the top point of travel.

The exact mechanism by which this effect is produced is somewhat obscure, but a model of the device already built has been bolted to the floor of a freight elevator, it is claimed, and succeeded in raising and lowering it with ease. In this test a 20-horsepower gasoline engine furnished power.

Lifting force exerted by the gyradoscope is likened to that of a ball thrown on the end of a string. The weight of the ball at the moment it draws the string taut exerts a lifting effect on a pencil or other object to which the bottom of the string may be tied. In the gyradoscope the moving weights on the wheels are analogous to the thrown ball. To a casual scrutiny the whole idea seems very much like lifting one's self by one's boot straps, but the success attained with models indicates that the inventor may be successful in developing an entirely new type of aircraft.

Forward motion is to be supplied by a gyradoscope in horizontal plane, and steering will be accomplished by a similar mechanism. In case of accident to the lifting gyros, which would result in the ship's dropping

Used in Novel Airship

like a plummet, auxiliary machines are provided which are kept running at idling speed ready to be called upon in an emergency. Four hydraulic landing feet, one on each corner of the ship, absorb the shock of landing, which is expected to be insignificant since rate of descent is controlled by speed of the gyradoscope. Mr. Holmes, inventor of the gyro-ship, also has the invention of a popular front wheel drive for autos to his credit, as well as a four wheel drive and a caloric steam engine.

This latter machine would supply the power for the airship. As developed by Mr. Holmes, waste heat from oil combustion is used in the caloric engine to convert water into steam, which drives a turbine, and is then condensed to be used over again.

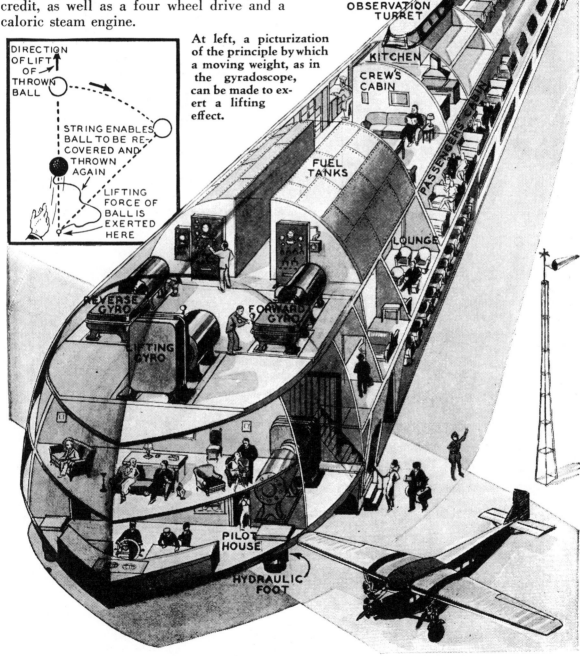

DIRECTION OF LIFT OF THROWN BALL

STRING ENABLES BALL TO BE RECOVERED AND THROWN AGAIN

LIFTING FORCE OF BALL IS EXERTED HERE

At left, a picturization of the principle by which a moving weight, as in the gyradoscope, can be made to exert a lifting effect.

DINING ROOM

OBSERVATION TURRET

KITCHEN

CREW'S CABIN

PASSENGER'S CABIN

FUEL TANKS

LOUNGE

REVERSE GYRO

FORWARD GYRO

LIFTING GYRO

PILOT HOUSE

HYDRAULIC FOOT

Above is a phantom view of gyro-airship, planned for production, showing arrangement of parts.

Mysterious New Aircraft Powered by Reaction Motor

IMAGINE a heavier-than-air flying craft devoid of any visible means of propulsion, which rises from the earth and travels through the air in apparent defiance of the law of gravity. Lifting itself by its own bootstraps, by slinging weights about its interior, it could navigate at will in the stratosphere or even in the unknown reaches of outer space. Such a craft is brought within the realm of speculation by pioneer experiments of Harry W. Bull, of Syracuse, N. Y., with an entirely new form of propulsion that he terms the reaction motor.

Suspended from a pair of light, flexible wires, in his laboratory, hangs a cylindrical tube about a foot long. At the touch of an electric switch, it becomes alive and leaps forward, as if drawn by some invisible magnet. Actually the power plant, a curious system of reciprocating weights, is contained within the tube itself.

This elementary form of reaction motor operates on a principle that has long been neglected by engineers, but which Bull believes can be applied in aircraft and other vehicles. It depends upon the difference in effectiveness of two ways of transmitting energy, which can be termed impact and impulse. If a weight is thrown against a solid wall, it is stopped by impact, and much of its energy is wasted in distorting the weight and wall and in producing heat. However, if the weight is thrown against a spring fastened to the wall, it is stopped by impulse, the spring conserving the energy of the moving weight and transmitting the resulting force, with little loss, to the wall. Tests have shown a weight will yield three times more force by impulse than by impact.

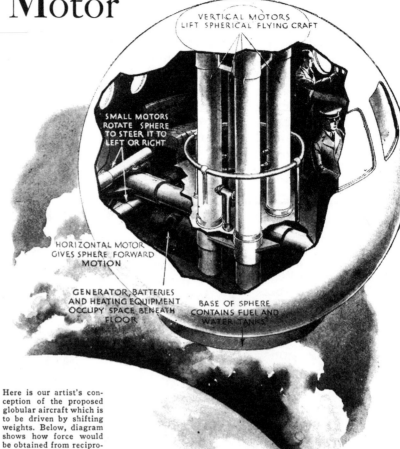

Here is our artist's conception of the proposed globular aircraft which is to be driven by shifting weights. Below, diagram shows how force would be obtained from reciprocating weights striking against the springs

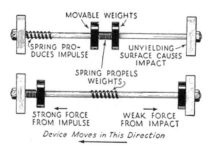

Device Moves in This Direction

Applying this principle in the manner shown in the accompanying diagram, he mounts two movable weights in a cylinder and starts them simultaneously in opposite directions. One is stopped by a flat steel plate, and the other by a spring. The difference in the effectiveness of the two blows, as explained above, is sufficient to kick the cylinder forcibly in the direction of the spring. The weights may be returned to their original positions by any standard mechanical means, and the cycle repeated continuously, providing a steady and self-contained driving force without recourse to propellers, rocket jets, or any other familiar means of propulsion.

From the present experimental model to a reaction motor powerful enough to lift aircraft seems a long step. Achieving a practical reaction motor, Bull points out, depends to a large extent, paradoxically, upon how inefficient it can be made. The more force that can be wasted in impact, the greater force will be left to push ahead, a new problem for engineers, who have spent years trying to conserve energy rather than dissipate it. Likewise, much experimentation remains to be done upon the impulse side of the apparatus, which is still far from efficient.

Supposing these difficulties overcome, what would an airship, driven by a reaction motor, look like? Bull visualizes a globular craft with a motor in the form of an upright cylinder containing two pistons operating in opposite directions, one delivering an impulse and the other an impact. A carburetor adapted for mixing vaporized oxygen and gasoline would supply an explosive mixture to drive the pistons. Several cylinder units could be used to obtain a steady lifting force. Others placed horizontally would provide forward motion. A similar impulse-impact cylinder of reduced size, operated electrically and mounted near the outer shell of the ship, would rotate the craft for steering. An airship driven by this new method could travel at high speed and could be used at either high or low altitudes.

Harry W. Bull, Syracuse, N. Y., inventor, exhibits an experimental model of his reaction motor with which he hopes to power an aircraft that will, apparently, defy gravity. When the power is shut off the two pointers, above, coincide. Weights in the device are operated by electromagnets

The AUTOGIRO--How and Why It Flies

Marvel of modern aviation, the autogiro can take off in 15 to 30 feet, fly safely at 15 m.p.h., descend vertically, stop in mid-air without danger and land in the average back yard. It cannot stall, spin, or crash from motor failure and has no ailerons, rudder or lifting surfaces other than the rotating vanes.

FIG. I.

Senor Juan de la Cierva, inventor of the autogiro. The stalling tendency of early planes prompted the idea of rotors, or freely revolving wings.

BLADES ATTAIN TAKE OFF SPEED · CABLE DROPS · AS MACHINE GATHERS WAY DRUM SPINS ROTOR VANES · CABLE · DRUM ON ROTOR SPINDLE · ANCHORED CABLE

FIG. 2 FIRST ATTEMPT TO MECHANIZE ROTOR STARTING

Early attempts to fly the autogiro were not successful. Gyroscopic action set up by the whirling rotor capsized the ships before they got into the air. Cierva finally articulated the rotor blades and overcame this difficulty. In the drawing above one of the first crude but successful ships is shown in flight. On the ground is an unsuccessful four-bladed model with fixed vanes. Absence of ailerons on latter indicates Cierva's early belief in principle of direct control, used in autogiros today.

DUAL TAIL · FIG. 3 · SLIPSTREAM FROM AIR-SCREW DEFLECTED UPWARDS AND FORWARDS

Drawings above and to the left show early methods of setting rotor blades in motion. Fig. 1—Taxiing around field to pick up required speed. Fig. 2—Speeding up rotors by cable and drum. Fig. 3—Deflecting the propeller slipstream to rotor blades from surface known as a "starting tail."

The 1929 ship at left shows position of blades when not in motion. Note also starting tail shown in Fig. 3. Blades are hinged and free to move up, down and a limited distance in direction of travel to avoid breakage.

PATH OF AIRPLANE THRU BUMPY AIR · PATH OF AUTOGIRO THRU BUMPY AIR · RIGID WINGS · FLEXIBLE WINGS · UNSPRUNG CAR · WELL SPRUNG CAR

DIAGRAM SHOWING HOW RIGID WINGS AND FLEXIBLE BLADES COMPARE IN ROUGH WEATHER

Diagram above shows action of plane in bumpy air. Left, a cutaway view of the latest type blade showing construction details and how balance is effected.

STEEL TUBE SPAR · BALANCE WEIGHT · WOOD RIB · FABRIC · WOODEN END PIECE

2-BLADED ROTOR - EACH BLADE 14 FT LONG

FRICTION DAMPENERS · ROTOR STARTER DRIVE GEAR · STARTER SHAFT · SUPPORT STRUTS · VERTICAL HINGE · LATERAL HINGE · LATERAL AXIS · ROTOR BRAKE · LONGITUDINAL AXIS · SOCKET FOR DUAL CONTROL · CONTROL COLUMN

50 H.P. 2-CYL. MOTOR

Tilting the rotor forms the sole means of controlling an autogiro and necessitates the complicated hub shown at the left. No other rigging is employed to support the blades. Right—A one-place autogiro now in production, equipped with a two-bladed rotor. This ships weighs 610 pounds with a full load and will fly at about 95 m. p. h.

AT LAST—a Convertible

A STARTLING new vehicle which may be used in the air as a fast, sturdy airplane, and on the ground as a speedy, comfortable two-passenger coupe car, will shortly be available to aviation enthusiasts. The craft is really a streamlined mid-wing monoplane of 30-foot wing span, propelled by a 125-horsepower air cooled motor of regulation aircraft type. For ground use the ship may be quickly converted into a streamline car, simply by removing the wings and the rear end of the fuselage, leaving the closed cabin body resting on its three wheels, ready to drive through the streets. This transformation occupies about 20 minutes, by means of quickly detachable joints.

The development of the "Ascender," as the new ship is called, has taken many months of painstaking work in the selfsame Engineering Department which produced the fastest airplane in the world, Doolittle's "Flying Silo" which set a new world's record of 296 m.p.h. at the Cleveland air races last fall. The first Ascender has already been built and flown enough to prove itself a most unusual craft both in the air and on the ground.

Control of this craft, in the air and on the ground, is by an automobile type steering wheel, a foot accelerator, and hand and foot operated brakes which act on all three wheels. While on the ground the ship rests on a three wheel landing gear, each wheel of which is equipped with internal brake and hydraulic shock absorber, as well as a large airwheel tire. The front wheel is steerable with the rudder of the ship, so that when the pilot moves the steering wheel to right or left, either on the ground or in the air, he guides the direction of his craft as he would a motor car.

On the takeoff there is no necessity of getting the tail up and balancing on two wheels while steering the ship down the runway by means of a rudder bar, as one is obliged to do in piloting the ordinary airplane. In this new craft, one merely sits behind the wheel, opens the throttle, and drives the ship down the field or runway as one would a car, with no possibility of "nosing over" even if brakes are applied suddenly, or from obstructions such as bumps, ditches, or soft spots. When sufficient speed has been attained the driver has merely to pull the wheel slightly toward him, whereupon the front wheel leaves the ground and the ship "takes the air."

Landing the Ascender is a simpler task than in the ordinary airplane. It is no longer necessary for the pilot to judge his speed and distance so that the ship will stop flying directly over the spot in the field where he wishes to land. With this craft, he need merely throttle the engine, point the nose down until the ship assumes a normal glide toward the field and set the ship onto the ground at a speed much greater than is safely possible in the ordinary airplane. As soon as the two rear wheels touch the ground, the front one is forced down, and brakes may be immediately applied to bring the ship to a smooth stop.

The convertible airplane-auto has been designed by the makers of this famous Gee-Bee type sportplane which won the Cleveland air races last summer at 296 mph.

Motor Ring acts as propeller guard

← Visibility angle 270°

Brakes on all wheels— individually sprung

The airplane is made ready for street use in 20 minutes by removing the wings and tail unit, easily detachable. Note the location of motor where it serves equally well for ground or air use. Angle of visibility is exceptionally broad.

AUTO-PLANE

by THEODORE A. HODGDON

Rudder and front wheel synchronized

Detachable wings and tail

Two views of the "Ascender," showing appearance in flight, and method of converting into an automobile. On the ground, a wire screen is usually employed around the propeller as a safeguard, though the arc of the blade is well within the confines of the car.

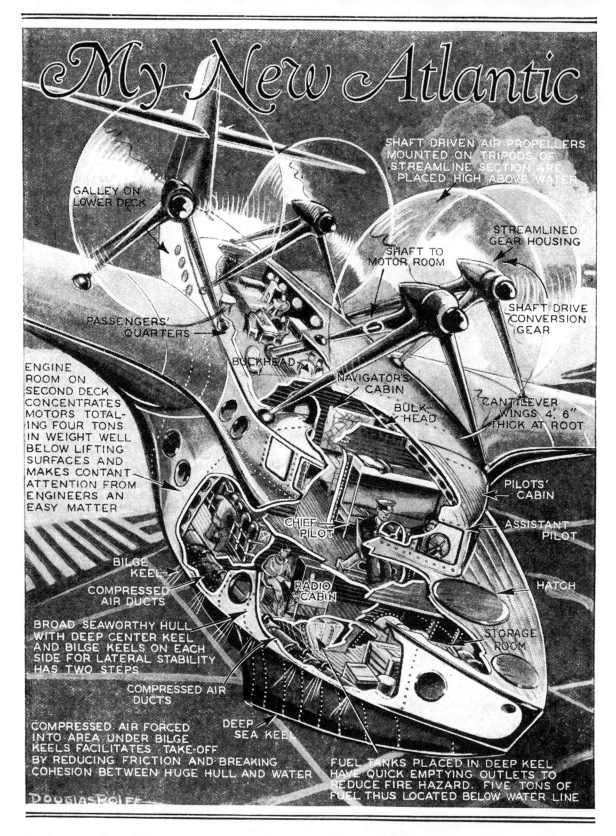

My New Atlantic

SHAFT DRIVEN AIR PROPELLERS MOUNTED ON TRIPODS OF STREAMLINE SECTION ARE PLACED HIGH ABOVE WATER

GALLEY ON LOWER DECK

STREAMLINED GEAR HOUSING

SHAFT TO MOTOR ROOM

SHAFT DRIVE CONVERSION GEAR

PASSENGERS' QUARTERS

BULKHEAD

NAVIGATOR'S CABIN

BULK-HEAD

CANTILEVER WINGS 4', 6" THICK AT ROOT

ENGINE ROOM ON SECOND DECK CONCENTRATES MOTORS TOTALING FOUR TONS IN WEIGHT WELL BELOW LIFTING SURFACES AND MAKES CONTANT ATTENTION FROM ENGINEERS AN EASY MATTER

PILOTS' CABIN

CHIEF PILOT

ASSISTANT PILOT

BILGE KEEL

COMPRESSED AIR DUCTS

RADIO CABIN

HATCH

BROAD SEAWORTHY HULL WITH DEEP CENTER KEEL AND BILGE KEELS ON EACH SIDE FOR LATERAL STABILITY HAS TWO STEPS

STORAGE ROOM

COMPRESSED AIR DUCTS

COMPRESSED AIR FORCED INTO AREA UNDER BILGE KEELS FACILITATES TAKE-OFF BY REDUCING FRICTION AND BREAKING COHESION BETWEEN HUGE HULL AND WATER

DEEP SEA KEEL

FUEL TANKS PLACED IN DEEP KEEL HAVE QUICK EMPTYING OUTLETS TO REDUCE FIRE HAZARD. FIVE TONS OF FUEL THUS LOCATED BELOW WATER LINE

DouglasRolfe

A phantom view of Hans Rohrbach's projected Atlantic air liner, drawn from plans, models, and a description by the author. The most unusual feature of this huge flying boat will be the central engine room, with the propellers connected to the motors by shafts run through streamlined struts. The main advantage of this method of power transmission will be the keeping of weight below the center of lift, making for easy riding both in the air and on the water. This advantage will be accentuated by placing the gasoline tanks at the bottom of the hull, well below the water line in case the ship is forced to descend while at sea. The flying boat will also be provided with a water propeller and a deep sea keel, making fairly rapid progress possible, even if forced to descend in a heavy sea.

Air Liner

by HANS ROHRBACH
Famous German Seaplane Designer

WATER PROPELLER

The beautiful streamlining of the huge craft is shown in this picture.

The name of Rohrbach is well known in the aviation world because of the giant planes which he has designed. He built 5,500 airplanes for the German army during the World War, including four giant bombers with eight engines each. Since then he has designed most of the large European transport planes used on passenger lines.

A portrait of the author, Hans Rohrbach, the well-known German designer of airplanes, automobiles and many types of gasoline and heavy oil engines.

THE conquest of the Atlantic by air, both from America to Europe and Europe to America, has become almost a commonplace since Col. Lindbergh's great flight. But, as a recent article in MODERN MECHANICS pointed out, there is no airplane built today capable of flying the ocean non-stop while carrying a sufficient payload of passengers and freight to make the trip financially worth while.

For a non-stop trans-ocean air line a flying boat is needed, one so built that it can land at sea, ride out bad weather, and, in event of damage to the wings or tail surfaces, navigate to shore under the power of a marine propeller. It must have speed sufficient to make the crossing in a reasonable number of hours, excess fuel capacity to give a wide safety margin, and sufficient load capacity to accommodate enough passengers so that the fees received will pay expenses and profits.

I have designed such a ship, a thirty passenger flying boat that is radically different from anything yet built, but based, as I will demonstrate, on sound technical facts.

As designer to the German government during the war, when some 5,500 airplanes were built under royalty rights from me, and as chief engineer of the Rohrbach all-metal airplane factory, which produced the Roland, Rocco and Romar ships—the latter a giant three engines flying boat—I have had considerable experience with this type of craft.

Comfort, Speed Provided by

PRIVATE automobiles, buses and trucks have in recent years taken away so much passenger and freight traffic from the railroads that profits of many of the largest railways have shrunk alarmingly This situation has awakened executives to the realization that the modern railroad is, in many respects, not modern at all. Gigantic new locomotives have been built; passenger cars are now constructed of steel instead of wood—but except for a few technical improvements of this sort, today's railway train is little different from its sister of fifty years ago.

What the railroads need to bring back business, in the opinion of forward-looking engineers, is a complete re-designing of trains to take advantage of recent mechanical and scientific progress. That the railroads themselves are alive to this need is evident from the fact that the Westinghouse Electric Co. has been experimenting with designs for a streamlined locomotive, that a rubber tired wheel for rail cars has been perfected, that Germany has developed a railway car designed along the lines of a Zeppelin, driven by a propeller—and by a score of similar indications.

The drawing on this page shows a train which at first glance may seem exceedingly novel. But a moment's study will serve to show that there is nothing really radical about it. None of the improvements shown are visionary or impractical. Let's take them up one by one, if you are skeptical.

To begin with, steam locomotives in present use are mere refinements of Stevenson's *Rocket*. Cinders and smoke add nothing to passenger comfort, so tomorrow's train will use either oil-burning Diesel engines, hooked up to generators which furnish an electric drive, or if steam boilers are used methods will be perfected for discharging smoke at the rear of the train, where it will not annoy passengers. Whatever the type of locomotive used, it will be streamlined for greater efficiency, since speed—around 120 miles an hour—will give the railroads an advantage which auto buses cannot duplicate. The engineer will sit in the nose of the car, his line of vision directed

INDIVIDUAL ELECTRIC LIGHTS

OIL TANKS

RADIO OPERATOR

DIESEL ENGINES

PERISCOPE GIVES ENGINEER REAR VIEW OF TRAIN

RUBBER TIRED WHEELS

WEATHER CONDITIONER

LOW CENTER OF GRAVITY

STREAMLINED NOSE

A brief study of these features of a re-designed railway train will show that there is nothing fantastic or impractical in the ideas. Passenger comfort, speed and safety are the ends achieved by this design, which is a composite of the ideas of several prominent railway men who are convinced that present-day trains are out of date. A train such as this could attain speeds of 120 m. p. h. easily, due to streamline design and light-weight construction.

Coming TRAIN Design

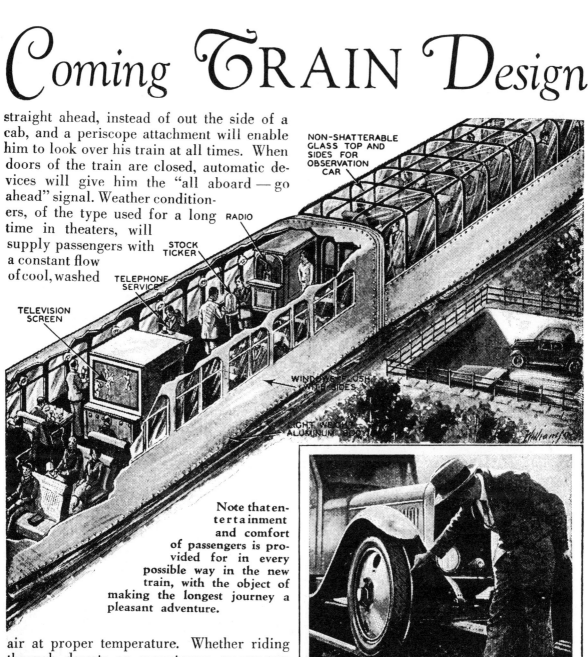

NON-SHATTERABLE GLASS TOP AND SIDES FOR OBSERVATION CAR

RADIO

STOCK TICKER

TELEPHONE SERVICE

TELEVISION SCREEN

WINDOWS FLUSH WITH SIDES

LIGHT WEIGHT ALUMINUM ROOF

Note that entertainment and comfort of passengers is provided for in every possible way in the new train, with the object of making the longest journey a pleasant adventure.

straight ahead, instead of out the side of a cab, and a periscope attachment will enable him to look over his train at all times. When doors of the train are closed, automatic devices will give him the "all aboard — go ahead" signal. Weather conditioners, of the type used for a long time in theaters, will supply passengers with a constant flow of cool, washed air at proper temperature. Whether riding through deserts or snowstorms, passengers will be perfectly comfortable. Entertainment devices, such as television screens and radio sets, can easily be installed in trains. Stock ticker service will appeal to business men travelers, who also will appreciate the advantages of having a radio operator on board to send emergency messages. Individual lights at each seat will supplant ceiling lamps.

Rubber-cushioned wheels for trains are now in an experimental stage, and they promise to add immeasurably to the silence of train travel. These wheels do not have rubber rims, but the cushion is placed inside, at the hub. To gain greater speed, alloys of aluminum, light and strong, are beginning to replace steel in car construction. The saving in weight not only speeds up the train, but

A new competitor for railroads is the motor bus fitted with flanges along its wheels for rail travel.

reduces the amount of fuel required and helps to lower the center of gravity of the car, which in turn makes operation safer.

Shatter-proof glass tops and sides for observation cars will be provided, so that in passing through scenic mountain country passengers will be able to gain an unobstructed view. Windows will be built flush with the sides of the cars to offer as little wind resistance as possible. Chairs in the cars, too, will be the latest word in comfort, with deep upholstery replacing the old-time red plush.

Gyroscope Monorail Car to

This German monorail will revolutionize rail transportation. At 300 miles per hour it will meet the challenge of the air transport lines.

The monorail car above has just been developed in England to provide fast transportation as a substitute for street car systems. Driven by propellers fore and aft this monorail developed a speed of 100 miles an hour in a demonstration near Glasgow. Guide rail prevents side sway.

KEEP RIGHT →

Engineer Buchardt's improvement over the English monorail is shown above. For street transport systems large steel structures would be unnecessary. Gyroscopes would eliminate a guide rail to stop side sway. Greater speed is possible.

RAILROADS may challenge the increased popularity of air travel by developing a superspeed monorail car. Balanced by gyroscope and controlled by radio, the gyroscope monorail would be capable of more than 300 miles an hour, its inventor claims.

The gyroscope, not a modern invention, has only recently been applied to transportation. It steadies ships in storm tossed seas. It aids in the automatic control of airplanes in flight.

Applied to rail transportation, the gyroscope will permit much greater speed without sacrificing safety. In fact, Raymond C. Buchardt, engineer of the Telefunken company, of Germany, who designed the gyroscope monorail, claims his superspeed car provides greater safety than is now possible.

Car Stands Upright on Monorail

Buchardt's monorail has all the latest developments in streamlining and makes use of airplane features to guide the car on its single rail. The gyroscope monorail stands upright on its single rail, while present monorails are suspended from the rail.

The gyroscopes are used to balance the car on this single rail. They do away with the side sway that would be present were great speeds attempted with the suspended monorail.

Radio Will Replace Block Signals

"Because of the terrific speed of more than 300 miles an hour, the ordinary block signal will be impossible for the trans-continental monorail," said Mr. Buchardt. "Signals would not be visible and in fog, rain or smoke the vision of the pilot would be entirely obscured.

"To meet this difficulty I propose to use the radio to transmit signals and orders to the pilot just as transport planes are now controlled. Radio messages from a dispatcher's office would tell the pilot when to slow up and would warn him of any dangers ahead."

The enormous air pressure created by the great speed would throw an ordinary car from the rail. Buchardt has solved this problem by designing a long, sloping curve

Travel 300 Miles an Hour

Above is a cross section of the cross country high speed gyroscope monorail designed by Buchardt.

The 300-mile-an-hour gyroscope monorail is shown in the artist's drawing above. The long forward sloping planes hold the car to the rail. Radio signals would guide pilot.

This latest railroad car design follows the streamlining used on the gyroscope monorail. This English rail car attained a maximum speed of 60 miles per hour.

on either side of the car, which he calls a "wind catcher." The air pressing against this "wind catcher" would hold the car on the rail.

In his experiments with his invention, Buchardt found that the monorail would have trouble taking curves. The car took the curve perfectly, but the centrifugal force nearly threw it off the rail after completing the curve.

For that reason stabilizing fins were placed at the front and rear of the car along with a large rudder. The forward fin also houses the radio antenna.

The gyroscope car is driven by two large propellers at either side of the rear end of the car. One gyroscope would be housed in

the forward end of the car and the other in a rear compartment. Power would be supplied by Diesel engines.

The rail used would be round and the wheels curved in such a way as to form a ball link.

The traction system type of monorail would be much smaller than the car used in cross country runs. The latter would be a double-decked car with the pilot housed in a third deck forward.

The trans-continental type would carry approximately 100 passengers.

Proposed Rotary "Aero-Zep" Uses Novel Screw Vanes

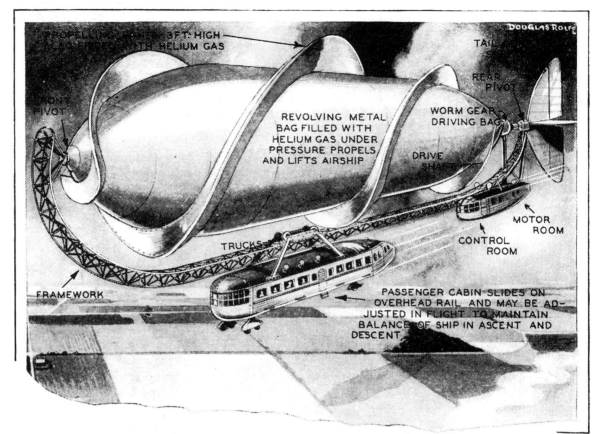

Revolving spiral vanes on the gas container of this novel dirigible are designed to propel it forward through the air. The entire gas-shell revolves around the stationary track framework of aluminum.

A MOST unusual type of dirigible involving wide departures from established principles has recently been patented by two South Dakota inventors. They call it the "Rotary Aero-Zep," and aside from the fact that the entire craft is designed to be constructed of aluminum, the most novel feature of the invention is the metal gas bag which is designed to revolve around the frame trackway carrying the passenger car, screwing the airship forward in the air through the action of spiral vanes mounted on the side of the bag.

These vanes, three feet in height, are V-shaped and hollow, and are themselves filled with helium separately from the gas bag. The passenger cabin is suspended from a track running beneath the ship, being mounted on trucks which are free to move along the track to keep the weight of the ship balanced as the angle of ascent or descent varies. The track framework, curving upward at either end, supports pivots on which the bag turns freely. To call the gas container a bag is somewhat of a misnomer, since it is to be of corrugated aluminum.

A motor cabin, mounted permanently at the rear of the trackway, contains engines which will drive the revolving bag. Tail control surfaces are of conventional design, except that each of the four sections is separately controllable—that is, the right half of the elevators can be controlled independently of the left, and the top section of the rudder independently of the bottom, in contrast with usual practice in which both sections of rudder or elevator are operated together.

Seven hundred miles an hour is the rather incredible speed anticipated from the craft by its inventors, Rev. Carl H. Loock and Lorrin L. Hansen of Rapid City, South Dakota. The bag itself, through its novel drive, will revolve comparatively slowly even when the ship is traveling at top speed, the inventors believe. A safety valve at the end of the body is provided in case gas pressures are built up to a dangerous degree. As yet this amazing new idea in aeronautics has not progressed beyond the model stage, and it is not at present known when a full size ship will be built.

OUTGOING RAIL CAR

INCOMING RAIL CAR

SPACE BETWEEN TRACKS SERVES AS EXPRESS HIGHWAY

PILOT AND CONTROLS OCCUPY FORWARD COMPARTMENT

THICK WINGS OF "HIGH-LIFT" TYPE

DOUBLE-DECK PASSENGER QUARTERS

STANDARD FLANGED WHEELS

ROLLERS

RETAINING CHANNELS KEEP CAR CLOSE TO TRACK

STANDARD RAIL

Broad motor highways fill the area between the tracks. The rail cars, as indicated at the left, are double-decked

Winged Rail Car Rides on Air

• •

WINGS LIFT FORWARD END OF CAR FROM RAILS

At high speeds, the front wheels leave the rails, reducing friction

CAPTIVE airplanes with clipped wings would hurtle across country at more than six miles a minute, in a "flying-railway" system proposed by a European engineer. His scheme calls for a giant new type of streamline passenger car, having stubby wing surfaces and a body like the fuselage of an airplane. At low speeds, as in starting and stopping, the vehicle rolls along standard rails on flanged wheels at front and rear. Under full throttle, however, the whole front of the car rises from the track and, lifted by the wings, rides on air, so reducing friction that speeds up to 400 miles an hour may be attained. Retaining channels and rollers prevent the forward or "flying" end of the car from zooming dangerously high. Meanwhile the rear wheels, remaining in contact with the rails, continue to supply propulsive force from the vehicle's Diesel power plant. Passenger seats are arranged in pairs on the double decks of the curious train, while the engineer-pilot sits high in the front of the vehicle in a special cockpit resembling that of a modern transport plane. The space required between tracks, to allow clearance for cars traveling in opposite directions, would be used as an express automobile highway.

Fast Electric Air Trolleys Planned by French Inventor

SUSPENDED MONORAIL OR WIRE

FIN-LIKE WINGS SUPPORT MOST OF CAR'S WEIGHT WHEN IN MOTION

TOP SPEED 150 M.P.H.

ELECTRIC MOTOR DERIVES CURRENT FROM TROLLEY

TRAVELLERS OPERATE CAR BY PUSH-BUTTON CONTROL

A UNIQUE air-trolley propelled over a monorail by an electric motor at a speed of 150 m.p.h. has been designed by Joseph Archer, a French engineer, who expects to demonstrate his unique invention in Paris shortly. The drawing above illustrates the essential features of Archer's design. The car is streamlined and when in motion most of its weight is supported by fin-like wings projecting from its sides. By reversing the propeller passengers can bring the car to a stop within 100 yards.

New Rail Car Runs on Air-Electric Perpetual Drive

25 ton air electric rail engine ready for tests. Battery drives electric motor running, starting air compressors to get 400 lb. pressure in air tanks; air engine drives car; wheels drive main compressor to refill tanks, and battery charging generator.

FROM coast to coast by rail in 24 hours, traveling literally on air—that is what W. E. Boyette of Atlanta, Georgia, claims for his invention, a railroad engine that runs almost entirely on air.

Air for fuel—speeds of up to 125 miles an hour on rails—low transportation costs —these are possibilities conjured by Boyette's air electric car. After being started by batteries, the car needs only air to keep it running—a close approach to perpetual motion.

Inventor Boyette claims his invention is quite simple, even though it is contrary to all principles of engineering.

Large tanks on the sides of the car are pumped with compressed air by a starting air compressor which is driven by an auxiliary electric motor and 4800 pound storage battery set. Compressed air then operates the air engine connected to the driving wheels, bringing the car up to speed.

As the car moves, a large air compressor directly connected to the front wheels pumps air back into the tanks. An electric generator connected to the farthest rear pair of wheels is continually charging the batteries. Thus the movement of the car refills the air tanks and partly recharges the batteries.

With the engine pulling two passenger coaches over a 250 mile rail run, it is said that about $2.50 worth of electricity for fully charging the batteries at the end of the run will be the only fuel expense.

"Wingless" Autogyro Is Successful

A WINGLESS type of autogyro plane, designed and constructed by Juan de la Cierva, inventor of this type of aircraft, rose from the ground after a run of but 10 yards in its first test at Hanworth Airport.

The flying "windmill," absolutely without wings, is supported in the air by the tremendous wing-spread of the horizontal propellers, and driven forward by the customary perpendicular airplane propellers.

Wingless autogyro designed by Juan de la Cierva takes off for its first test at Hanworth Airport. Horizontal propellers replace wings, enabling take-off in 30 feet.

ROCKETING *to the*

Prof. R. H. Goddard

FOR YEARS scientists have been forced to study the moon through its reflection in the observatory mirror. Since the moon refused to come closer to the earth than 220,000 miles, however, man may find it possible to exercise the alternative of Mahomet and go to the moon, in the opinion of a distinguished man of science. He is Dr. Robert Hutchings Goddard, for six years professor of physics at Princeton University, director of research for the U. S. signal corps at Worcester Polytechnic Institute and Mt. Wilson (California) Observatory during the world war, fellow of the American Geographical Society, member of the American Physical Society, American Meteorological Society and the American Institute of Social Sciences, and for the past ten years professor of physics and director of the physical laboratories of Clark University, at Worcester, Mass.

IS IT possible to transport a human being to the moon? To answer that question in the affirmative is to bring smiles to the faces of skeptics without number. And in fact had this suggestion been made before I began the extensive researches upon the rocket method of reaching extreme altitudes, to which I have devoted many years of labor, I must confess that I should have dismissed the thought of reaching the moon as merely another figment of the mind of Jules Verne. Now, however, I am of the firm opinion that it is possible with the use of a rocket of the type I first patented in 1914 and which I have been improving ever since, to reach the moon's surface. And what may be of

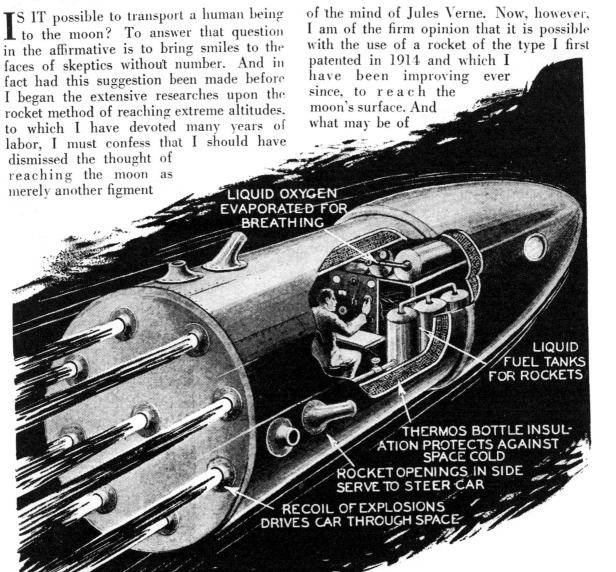

LIQUID OXYGEN EVAPORATED FOR BREATHING

LIQUID FUEL TANKS FOR ROCKETS

THERMOS BOTTLE INSULATION PROTECTS AGAINST SPACE COLD

ROCKET OPENINGS IN SIDE SERVE TO STEER CAR

RECOIL OF EXPLOSIONS DRIVES CAR THROUGH SPACE

An artist's conception of a rocket equipped for a trip to the moon after the manner described by Prof. Goddard in his article. Note the provisions for breathing and insulation against extreme cold.

Moon

by **Prof. R. H. GODDARD, B.Sc., A.M., Ph.D.**
as told to William Robertson

This photo of the full moon, taken from the Mt. Wilson observatory, shows the numerous craters and mountains which pit the surface of the satellite. A rocket landing on the moon would, Prof. Goddard believes, find sufficient chemical elements to recharge its fuel tanks, and therefore would not have to carry a sufficient supply of fuel for the return trip.

particular interest to anyone who might contemplate making a journey thither in this new form of conveyance, I believe it would be possible for him to return to the earth in safety and report to the world the results of the first journey to one of our celestial neighbors.

Contrary to popular impression, I am not at present engaged in an attempt to perfect a rocket which will carry a human being to the moon. That will come later, but it should be understood that what I am now developing is a comparatively small affair and is not intended for reaching heights

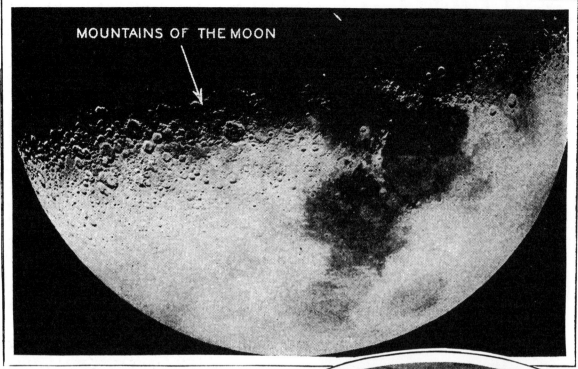

MOUNTAINS OF THE MOON

A view of the moon in its first quarter. The latest theory of scientists is that the surface of the moon, with its mysterious dark "lakes," is made up of volcanic dust which is never blown about because of the absence of an atmosphere.

much greater than just outside the atmospheric envelope of the earth. There are two reasons for this:

First, the expense and time for the development are much reduced if the work is carried out on a small scale.

Second, the uses of such a rocket, even in exploring the atmosphere, are so important that the development seems to stand a good chance of being continued. And furthermore, if anything is designed for the purpose of passing through the earth's atmosphere, it is well to have a knowledge of the earth's atmosphere first.

Although I have been engaged in rocket work since 1914 when I was granted my first patents, the public evinced no particular curiosity regarding the possibilities my investigations might open up and the recent interest displayed came in the nature of a surprise.

At this moment I am engaged in the highly important problem of stabilization, and feel that it would be premature to give out data upon the results before this matter has been settled, and the work may be called complete. Nevertheless, the tests I have made, including that of July 17th

Prof. Goddard holding one of his experimental rockets which attained a speed of 8,000 feet per second, one fourth the speed necessary for it to leave the earth forever.

when my experimental rocket was fired several thousand feet, have demonstrated clearly that the method of propelling it is operative and practical.

This new method involves the use of liquid propellants and makes possible a rocket with most of its weight consisting of propellant material of high energy value. This is the new feature. And it is one that is quite vital if a rocket is to be used for reaching extreme heights. Although all of the basic principles involved in the high altitude rockets were patented by me in 1914, a few of the ideas I advanced at that time have been used abroad but only with black powder rockets.

The liquid propellant I am using is as far ahead of black powder as the automobile is ahead of the horse and buggy. Yet with the use of three black powder rockets, Fritz von Opel, a German, recently succeeded in launching an airplane 75 feet in the air and circling half of a German airport at a high speed before he lost control of the machine.

But the rockets I have been testing for the past nine years, are, so far as I know, the only ones actually constructed that have embodied any considerable number of my original principles.

Before launching a man-carrying rocket to the moon, Prof. Goddard proposes to send a camera-carrying rocket around the satellite, directing its course by means of light-sensitive photo-electric cells.

The first use of the rocket will be to send up instruments which will permit the study of the atmosphere at great heights. Another practical step beyond that, in all probability, will be to send a camera round, and close to, the moon, having it guided throughout the journey by photo electric cells. With the knowledge thus obtained, a trip to the moon may well be planned.

The idea of such a history-making trip appeals most vividly to the imagination and is one to which I have given considerable study.

To the layman, undoubtedly the first thought is:

"Who is going to make that first solo flight into the unknown?"

Much risk is to be involved, undoubtedly, but not nearly so much as would seem at first blush were I free to make public the result of my investigations to date. When the time comes to attempt a flight into space

the dangers ahead will be proportionately less grave in the light of scientific knowledge than those which seemed apparent when Columbus started west with his caravels over the uncharted seas only to find that the troubles predicted for him were largely imaginary.

And many with the hardihood and the scientific knowledge necessary for this, the most thrilling of all adventures in human experience, will be willing and eager to shove off into the vast unknown.

The great rocket, with a compartment large enough to hold a passenger comfortably with all of the equipment necessary for his task, will not need to carry propellants for the return trip. The chemical elements necessary for refueling exist on the moon to the most careful astronomical observations, and it will be possible for the passenger to take off without any outside assistance for the return journey.

That of itself removes one of the greatest

A close-up of the mysterious moon craters which may yield their secrets to the intrepid adventurer who first lands on the moon's surface via rocket. The c r a t e r s shown average 50 miles across. Shadows are cast by the sun's rays.

difficulties by restricting the weight of the space cruiser. Successive explosions are necessary to propel the rocket and the speed will be governed according to their frequency. This may be regulated automatically or by the passenger himself, from a control board within his cabin.

"Is it possible to acquire the amazing speed necessary for the purpose in mind?" has been asked.

To answer that I will point to the experiment I made last summer with the rocket I am shown holding in my hand in the accompanying photograph.

The gases shot from that small rocket at a speed of 8,000 feet (more than 1½ miles) per second.

That is more than 90 miles per minute— enough to send the gases away from the moon forever if fired straight up from her surface. The earth, however, has four times the gravitation force of the moon, and the velocity of the rocket launched into space from our world will have to be four times that great, or 360 miles a minute. That speed may be easily attained by a larger rocket. And thus it can be readily seen that the time required to leave the earth and penetrate into space will be brief indeed.

But how will it be possible for one to live inside this projectile?

First, I have demonstrated that the rocket can be started without a jar sufficient to endanger life within it. Neither need there be any when the rocket lands. For it will be so equipped that it may be guided to earth as easily and safely as an airplane.

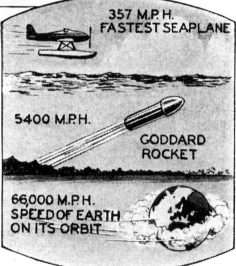

357 M.P.H. FASTEST SEAPLANE

5400 M.P.H.

GODDARD ROCKET

66,000 M.P.H. SPEED OF EARTH ON ITS ORBIT

Comparative speeds of "fastest" objects are graphically shown above. Prof. Goddard's experimental rocket has already traveled at a speed which would carry it into outer space if launched from the moon.

Of course, the passenger must breathe. The simplest plan of supplying oxygen is by evaporating a supply of liquid oxygen carried along. The cold of space would make the t r a n s p o r t a t i o n of liquid oxygen a comparatively easy matter. Insulation from the cold of space would be by the ordinary "thermos bottle" principle which we know works well down to a temperature nearly that of outer space.

The danger developing from friction would be nil, as no noticeable heat would be generated because the speed through the dense part of the atmosphere would not exceed 2,000 feet per second and the great increase in speed necessary to leave the earth would occur from 20 to 700 miles above terra firma.

According to my calculations, the trip to the moon can be made in 48 hours or an average speed of 4,750 m.p.h., an astonishing rate when compared with the swiftest methods of present-day transportation.

Radio Tube Train Gets Power from Air

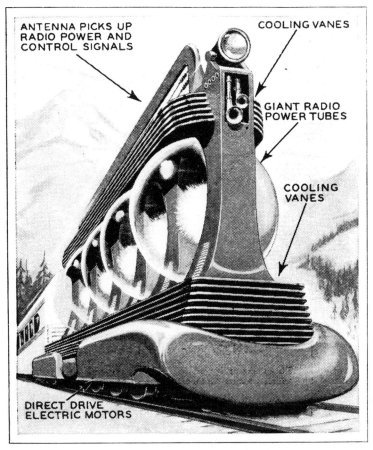

ANTENNA PICKS UP
RADIO POWER AND
CONTROL SIGNALS

COOLING VANES

GIANT RADIO
POWER TUBES

COOLING
VANES

DIRECT DRIVE
ELECTRIC MOTORS

This design for a radio powered train was suggested by
an electrical engineer. Radio impulses would supply power and control train eliminating necessity of a pilot.

TRANSMISSION of power by
radio will result in some radical changes in industry, especially in the field of transportation.

Recent experiments with railroad handcars run by radio suggested the design for a radio tube
locomotive shown on the left.
The electrical engineer who conceived the unusual power plant
claims that such a locomotive
could be controlled without a
pilot.

The body of the locomotive
would be surmounted by a series
of huge radio rectifier and receiving tubes. The gigantic tubes
could be built of unbreakable
glass. Vanes running the full
length of the car above and below the tubes will radiate excess
heat and prevent the red hot
electrodes from melting.

Electrical power impulses
from a hydro-electric generating plant would be picked up by
the antenna, rectified, and transmitted to the motors. Radio impulses could also control the
train.

Aerial Ferry Carries Automobiles

SPANNING the Colorado River near
Searchlight, Nev., is the only aerial ferry
in the world for transporting automobiles.
Forty miles down river from Boulder Dam,
the ferry completes a short cut between
Kingman, Ariz., and Boulder City. A 25 h.p.
gasoline engine is mounted on the upper
deck where the operator rides. The ferry
carries three tons and makes the 640-foot
trip across the river in 2½ minutes.

Eight cables above and two below support this aerial automobile ferry. A gas engine on upper deck operates it.

Outboard Bike Used in Water Polo

This water steed develops 18 to 25 miles an hour and is
controlled by one hand. It was designed for water polo.

A SEA-GOING mount has been designed
for the exciting sport of water polo.
The boat is controlled by the player's left
hand so that the right is free to swing the
mallet.

The rider sits comfortably in a motorcycle saddle and controls the speed and
direction with a special motorcycle hand
grip on the steering bar. The boat has a
speed of 18 to 25 miles an hour. The hull
is a watertight pontoon, with a rubber
bumper all around it. The boat is propelled
by an outboard motor.

Most Scientific Fiction

A rocket designed by Ludvig Ocenasek, Czecho-Slovakian inventor, blew itself to pieces when tested, as shown above. The inventor hopes to evolve a rocket which will reach the moon under its own power.

by WILLIAM J. HARRIS

You've probably read scores of so-called scientific fiction stories, but the chances are you don't know why most of these tales can't possibly come true. Mr. Harris sets forth here the scientific objections to fantastic projects such as transporting a human being by radio and rocketing to Mars.

ONE of the leading lights of the pseudo-scientific fiction writing school recently produced a story in which his characters used a marvelous German-built airship to reach an imaginary world in the imaginary hollow center of the earth. The airship was unusual because it contained a vacuum instead of gas, and was built of a mysterious metal so strong it could withstand the enormous air pressure on the outside.

Another entertaining writer of the same ilk followed with a yarn in which people were reduced to radio energy, transported through space by wireless, and instantaneously reassembled at the other end, minus metal fillings of their teeth and any other metal they might have had on their persons.

The writer who transported his characters through the air by radio ignored the power factor, for he had his villain using a portable outfit run by a small gasoline driven generator.

The reduction of a human body to electrical energy and a wireless wave presents a pretty problem. Presumably the body would turn into a wide variety of metals and gases before it could be converted into electrical energy, and at the other end would have to go through a similar process to be reassembled. The hypothesis stated by Prout in 1815 that all elements are aggregates of hydrogen is abundantly borne out by the modern atomic theory, which holds that the atom of any element is a positively charged

CAN'T COME TRUE

This scene from a UFA film, "The Girl in the Moon," depicts a space-traveling rocket landed on the mountainous surface of the moon.

Scientific fictioneers like to write of human beings reduced to electrical energy and transported to other planets by radio. They ignore the very important factor of power required.

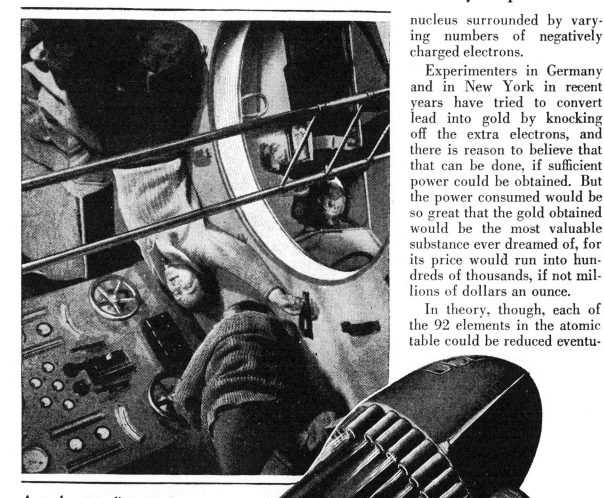

nucleus surrounded by varying numbers of negatively charged electrons.

Experimenters in Germany and in New York in recent years have tried to convert lead into gold by knocking off the extra electrons, and there is reason to believe that that can be done, if sufficient power could be obtained. But the power consumed would be so great that the gold obtained would be the most valuable substance ever dreamed of, for its price would run into hundreds of thousands, if not millions of dollars an ounce.

In theory, though, each of the 92 elements in the atomic table could be reduced eventu-

A rocket traveling to the moon would reach a point in space where gravity was nullified, and consequently occupants would cling to ceilings or hang suspended in the middle of the rocket until their space ship reached a point where gravity began to be exerted again.

Movie producers like scientific fiction as well as magazine publishers. This space rocket was used in the movie, "Just Imagine." Assuming the ability to generate tremendous quantities of power, such rockets would have to be built with enormously thick walls to withstand air pressure from within.

Characters in the German moon rocket film, "The Girl in the Moon," examine the elaborate space ship which carries them to the moon in the story—although there is no air on the satellite. Photo courtesy of UFA films.

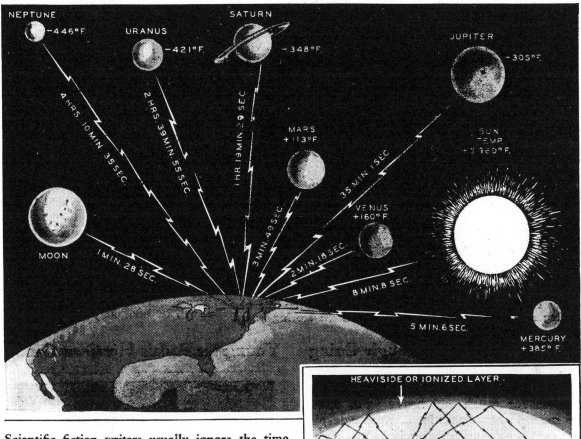

Scientific fiction writers usually ignore the time required to send a radio signal to the planets. The above chart portrays the time element graphically, and also gives the mean temperatures—far above or below those which the human body can endure —that exist on practically all of the planets.

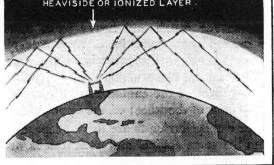

Science has proved the existence of an ionized strata of air (the so-called Heaviside layer, named after the mathematician who predicted its existence) which deflects radio waves back to the earth, and thus makes it impossible for a weak radio signal from earth to penetrate through space.

ally to hydrogen, the lightest of all, by successively changing the atomic structure through removing the excess atoms, and, going a step further, it might be possible to reduce the basic hydrogen atom to electrical energy by dissolving the hold which its nucleus has on its surrounding electrons.

But if such a process were possible and the power to accomplish it were available, then the carbon in one's body, for example, would first turn into boron, and then successively to beryllium, lithium, helium and hydrogen, while the trace of iodine in the human frame, being No. 53 in the atomic table, would have to go through that many steps before it was reduced to the common denominator. And in the process it would become in turn many rare and wonderful things, including krypton, antimony, argon, arsenic, cadmium, gallium, manganese, molybdenum, rhodium, and even silver.

Fortunately the writing of tales of imaginary science doesn't require that the adept stick even to plausible facts, but sometimes the writers in this school of entertainment go to unnecessary pains in inventing startling ideas that are but little better than ordinary truth.

The wonderful vacuum airship, for example, would be so little better than an ordinary gas-filled fabric-covered zeppelin that if the metal hull weighed but 20,000 pounds more than a fabric bag the two would have equal lift—assuming both ships to be of approximately 2,000,000 cubic foot capacity.

Daring Rocket Men to Invade

Experimenting with giant rockets, dauntless scientists are planning fresh invasions of the ether. Here is a complete story of their latest projects.

Success of the rocket-driven auto, left, paved the way for conquest of the ether.

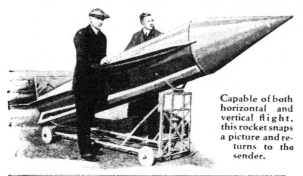

Capable of both horizontal and vertical flight, this rocket snaps a picture and returns to the sender.

The late Herr Tilling, German rocket builder, explains novel features of his wing rocket.

Penetration of the stratosphere to a depth of fifteen miles is planned by the Cleveland Rocket Society, here shown conducting a successful test of a new rocket motor. The model motor consists only of a combustion chamber. A highly volatile gas combination is fed through two tubes in the nose. Oxygen is poured through one inlet and gasoline under 250 pounds pressure through the other.

THE rocket-shooters are going to pitch in again this coming summer. Undaunted by reverses and tragedies during the past year's experiments, the rocketeers are tackling their work with renewed vigor and ambition, plus improved apparatus and chemicals.

Ernst Loebell, famous German engineer and rocket designer, promises to bring the rocket engines to their greatest point of achievement next summer. He is now in this country and is an active worker in the Cleveland Rocket Society.

Loebell has been carrying on his preliminary experiments on the big Hanna estate in a suburb of Cleveland. In their operations the Cleveland group has been making use of the lessons taught by the experiments of Loebell's countryman, the late Reinhold Tilling, a noted radio engineer and rocket builder.

Prior to his death, Tilling had been experimenting with rockets and rocket planes for months. The success of a rocket which reached a height of 6,000 feet in 1931 spurred him on to the construction of a rocket with glider wings which unfolded when the fuel was exhausted and brought the projectile gently to earth. This feat was hailed as one of the first practical steps toward the development of mail and passenger carrying rockets.

The Tilling rockets were set in motion by telignition from a distance of 100 yards. They attained a speed of 700 miles an hour and landed five miles from the starting point, in accordance with calculations. Herr Tilling was working on a system designed to manipulate his rockets by radio control when he and a female assistant were killed in the explosion of a rocket which they were charging.

Such information as emanated from the secrecy surrounding Tilling's operations at Osnarbrueck, Germany, has since been in the possession of the Cleveland Rocket

the STRATOSPHERE ~ by ALFRED ALBELLI

HIGHEST ATTAINED BY FREE BALLOON 61,237 FT.

ROTOR BLADES ABOUT TO UNFOLD

BLADES OPEN FOR DESCENT

An artist's conception of the man carrying rocket of the future. Note autogyro vanes which float the rocket back to earth when power is spent, allowing it to settle gently on landing fins.

Society's guiding geniuses. They plan to adopt the Tilling heritage and carry his work to further perfection.

Ernst Loebell and his assistant, Ted Hanna, have also investigated another secret German rocket—that of the famous Fischer brothers, details of which have also been closely guarded. The Fischers have achieved the biggest advance thus far in the field of passenger rocket flying.

The Fischers pursued their experiments on the island of Rugen in the Baltic Sea under the auspices of the German War Ministry. Otto Fischer, brother of Bruno, who designed the rocket, was shot up 32,-000 feet, more than six miles, into the air in a 24-foot steel projectile.

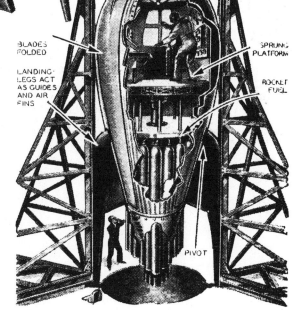

BLADES FOLDED

LANDING LEGS ACT AS GUIDES AND AIR FINS

SPRUNG PLATFORM

ROCKET FUEL

PIVOT

Balloon-Rocket to Soar 43 Miles

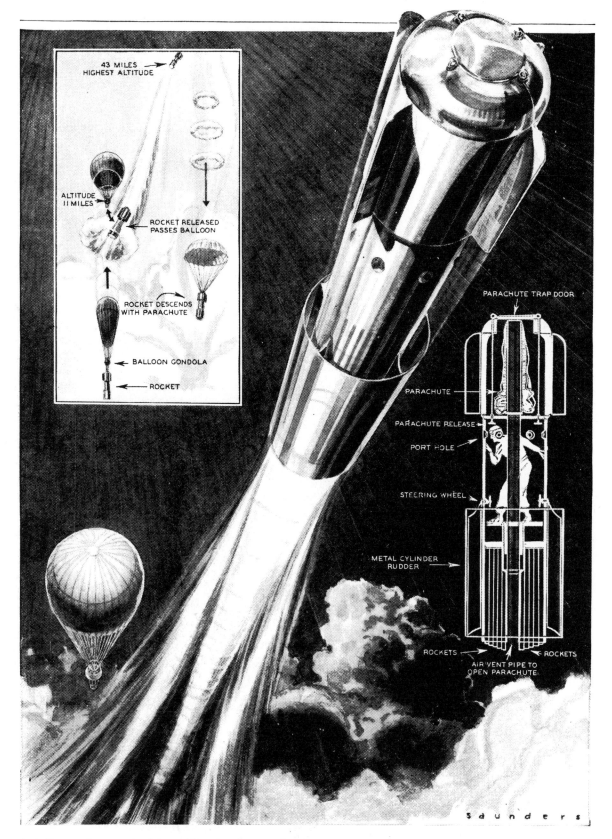

A balloon-rocket conceived by a Wyoming inventor is expected to roar 43 miles into the stratosphere. Carried 11 miles by the balloon, the operator cuts loose, ignites two opposed rockets and soars 33 miles higher. One mile is lost cutting away from the balloon. When the rocket power is expended, an air vent is opened, filling a parachute which floats the tube to earth. Inserts show release of rocket and details of the operating mechanism of the cylinder.

MM'S Cover from Painting to Magazine

Three photo negatives are made of 21"x30" oil painting (below). At same time screen of 133 dots to inch is placed between plate and lens. On one negative all but blue color is filtered out, second all but red, and third yellow. Proof of type for the cover is photographed. Type on negative is masked for drawing (above).

George Rozen, MM's cover artist, makes an outline of this month's cover from a sketch supplied by the editor. He makes a small color rough to get tone values, then completes oil painting.

REGISTER MARKS

REGISTER MARKS

REGISTER MARKS

BLUE   RED   YELLOW

Three color plates (left) each of which makes a separate color impression on finished cover are needed. Photo print is made on copper plate of type, over which red negative is superimposed for red plate. Plate is etched, acid eating metal where there is little or no red. Shading is obtained by varying size of screen dots. Use magnifying glass on cover to see these. Black is obtained by piling three colors on top of each other. Register marks line up plates for proofs. Electrotypes for presses are then made from lead mold of copper plates for the actual printing.

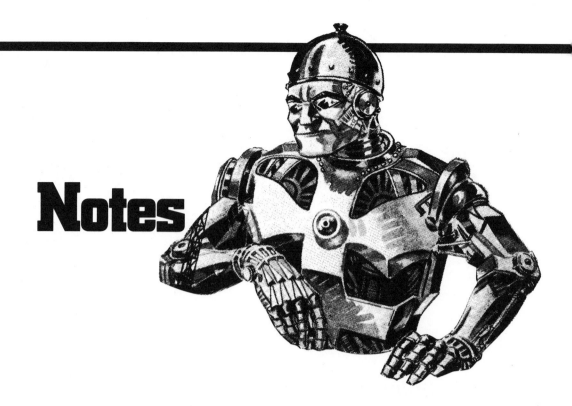

Notes

Is Man Doomed by the Machine Age? (*pages 18–23*)

This alarming piece sounds inspired by Technocracy, though the proposals mentioned are not nearly as radical. It seems to express the consternation that must have been felt as technology began its advance while millions were jobless and the economy had collapsed.

The illustration at the top of the first two pages is a featured piece of artwork used in *The Technocrats' Magazine,* which is mentioned in the introduction to this book.

Compare this piece with the tone of the next one.

Wanted—Ten Billion Dollar Inventions (*pages 24–27*)

The inconsistency in the illustration on the first page of this piece is that electromagnetic lifting is not feasible for altitudes such as those depicted. A similar principle, though, has been proposed in conjunction with linear-induction transportation systems. Generating an electromagnetic field to lift a vehicle a short distance from its track requires the application of a technology known as superconductivity.

Direct conversion of sunlight to electricity, shown on the second page, is an ongoing project. The yield of the "silver selenide" cells depicted here, however, is far from the 14 percent theoretical quantum efficiency that is considered the break-even point in direct conversion. With new technology, it has become possible to manufacture solar cells from single-crystal silicon, and this has increased the efficiency of these cells. There still remain problems of per-unit cost and the mass storage of the generated energy.

Harnessing the Power of the Sun (*pages 28–31*)

The power plant on the first two pages of this article is a heat-exchange system that relies on relatively small temperature differences to generate power. A similar system has been proposed by Clarence Zener, the physicist credited with the creation of the electronic diode that bears his name.

Geothermal power, described on the third page of this piece, is being commercially generated on a limited basis in northern California. As the article describes, there have also been attempts to synthesize the geothermal process by pumping cold water into hot rock beneath the surface of the earth.

This is one of the few energy-related articles to appear in these magazines during the 1930s. Today this topic is very popular with the same magazines and their readers.

Coal Costs Cut by Water-Pipe Shipment (*page 32*)

This idea is back again and is being proposed by a number of sources. During the 1930s, a strong, efficient, and low-cost rail system existed, so the proposal was ignored.

Pulling Power from the Skies (*pages 34–35*)

The Volf Windmill (illustrated on the first page of the article) presages the current interest in wind generation of electricity. Though highly imaginative, it is far too complicated in design and is described by one physicist as "typically Germanic" in concept. Today's windmill research, new airfoil techniques, and in particular, the windmill configuration known as the "vertical spool," are all simpler and more efficient. Wind generation, like direct conversion of sunlight, still has the problem of energy storage to contend with.

The power plant on the opposite page is another heat-exchange unit, this time on a tethered balloon. The power cable/tether would need to be extremely light, so that the balloon could lift it the prescribed ten or fifteen miles.

Endless Belt Subway to Expedite Traffic (*pages 38–39*)

A perennial idea that, in this form, bears a certain similarity to the Synchroveyer system designed by Larry Bell of the University of Illinois Department of Industrial Design, a transportation specialist who received a 1970 National Design Award for the system. Details of the Synchroveyer, and other Bell projects, can be found in the June 1978 issue of the *Futurist*.

Marvelous Movie Miniatures Portray Cities of the Future (*pages 42–43*)

Researchers in the area of past futures should note the film for which these miniature sets were built. *Just Imagine* (Fox, 1930) is a science fiction musical comedy, set in the year 1980! The plot has comedian El Brendel ("Yumpin' Yiminy!") dying in 1930 and being revived fifty years later, only to discover that he can't cope with the changes that have occurred in technology, social life, etc. Sound familiar? It is also the plot of a Woody Allen film, *Sleeper*.

Just Imagine also contains a dumb romantic subplot and about a dozen songs. The depiction of the 1980 metropolis (an art deco nightmare) was designed by art directors Stephen Gooson and Ralph Hammeraf.

Big Cities to Have Cooled Sidewalks (*page 46*)

Aside from the relative inefficiency of a system like this, there is no mention made of what to do with the hot air generated by the mammoth air-conditioning plants.

Modern Science Predicts Made-to-Order Weather (*pages 48–49*)

Direct and reliable control of the weather has not advanced much since this piece was penned. There have long been rumors that weather control has been achieved for military purposes, but there is little or no evidence to support these claims. Cloud seeding, the most popular technique experimented with, only increases the *chances* for precipitation by a relatively small percentage.

Skyscraper Fires of the Near Future Will Likely Be Fought from the Air (*page 51*)

There is still no proved way to handle an out-of-control skyscraper or high-rise blaze, but airborne control of forest fires is practical, with the use of chemicals.

The inconsistency in this illustration is that, even if these novel little one-man helicopters were employed, their chemical-holding tanks would be large enough to furnish only a single, inconsequential squirt.

Giant Air Tower to Guard Paris (*page 55*)

This plan, like the proposal calling for a midcity airport for the city of London (page 54), would have been a prime target during World War II. The size of this tower looks more realistic than it would have been, as the illustration is completely out of scale.

Up or Down by Belt (*page 58*)

Conveyances like these were actually built in Great Britain, and a few exist today. They were given the nickname Pater Noster because the passenger would literally "get on and pray."

Freak of the Month (*pages 62, 110, 129*)

Freak No. 1 (62) ignores the fact that the airfoil is less efficient than the hydrofoil at speeds a vehicle like this could attain.

Freak No. 2 (110) seems cursed by the absurdly inefficient "air screw" in the front of the craft.

Freak No. 3 (129), with its "lifting rotor" principle, is inexplicable.

Ergometer Checks Pensioners (*left, page 64*)

This German idea—to determine mechanically a person's capability for physical labor—epitomizes the fears of the antitechnologists. It is absurd, naturally, to consider only one's capacity for exertion and not other potentially complicating physical impairments. It is not known whether this system was ever practically employed.

"I Can Whip Any Mechanical Robot" (*pages 68–69*)

For the record, robots received their name in Karel and Josef Capek's Czech play, *R.U.R.* (*Rossum's Universal Robots*), written in 1921, and robot fantasies are as popular today as they ever have been.

Dempsey's claim was probably accurate when this article was written. Any fighter wishing to make the same statement today, however, should see the current experiments in robotics connected with Stanford's artificial intelligence project. It is reported that one of Stanford's multidegree "arms" can pick up an egg without breaking its shell, yet hurl a beer can with remarkable force and accuracy.

Great Wall of China to be Motor Highway (*pages 70–71*)

This proposal, and the one to erect an amusement park ride atop the pyramids (next page), are the two best examples of sheer folly to be found in this type of magazine. Needless to say, the "government approval," which both plans were awaiting, never came.

Radio Power Will Revolutionize the World (*pages 74–79*)

Over thirty-five years after his death, a Nikola Tesla cult has formed among some of today's scientists. Tesla was a remarkable man—a "pure" scientist who was both an aesthete (he memorized the plays of Goethe) as well as a discoverer of some of the basic principles of modern electricity.

Tesla's brilliance, though, was tarnished by his eccentricity. He arrived in New York in 1884 from his native Croatia (via Budapest and Paris), with a broad knowledge of languages, a bankroll of four cents, a book of poetry, and an introduction to Thomas A. Edison. Seven years later, he became an international celebrity, concerned that his concepts of alternating and high-frequency currents should benefit the masses. He predicted wireless communication before Marconi and later produced synthetic lightning in a way that has never been duplicated.

In 1892, Tesla stated that he had received radio signals from other planets, later convinced J. P. Morgan to fund his experiments in transmitting energy, and around the time of this article, announced that he had invented a "death ray." He seldom profited from his inventions and theories (some of which were sold to George Westinghouse) and continued to invent without seeking patents. Before his death in 1943 (at the age of eighty-two), Tesla became a virtual recluse, living in various New York City hotel rooms.

Television Now Gives Radio Eyes and Ears (*pages 80–82*)

Before you go looking for the "scanning motor" inside the living room TV set, be reminded that scanning was one of the last major problems of television transmission and reception and was solved later in the decade with the introduction of the cathode-ray tube. Scanning is accomplished electromagnetically in the tube.

This article neglects to mention that it is John Logie Baird, a Scotsman, who is generally credited with the invention of the medium.

Home Movies from Phonograph Records (*page 84*)

Another idea that has refused to die. This proposal, utilizing pre-cathode-ray tube technology, was way off in its simplicity and failed to take the bandwidth of a television signal into account. A videodisc playback device, based on the principle of breaking the picture down into audio signals, was marketed for a short time in the early 1960s, but was limited to displaying still pictures.

Present videodiscs spin at enormous speeds, from 600 to 1,800 rpm, and the most practical of the systems, so far, seems to be the Philips/MCA system, using a tiny laser to read its discs, rather than a mechanical stylus.

Like a report in one of these magazines, the modern videodiscs have been announced many times, yet have been slow to reach the market.

Television Shown in Theaters (*page 85*)

Large-screen television, now reserved for exhibiting heavyweight boxing championships and for home use by affluent media freaks, was once thought to be a competitor for motion pictures.

The system described here would work, but was superseded by the Schmidt optical system, which is reflective rather than refractive.

Giant Receiver Gives Radio to Whole City (*pages 86–87*)

This was a tremendously prophetic idea, except that it used radio instead of television. That's just what this is—cable radio, complete with the concept of "head ends" for distributing the signal in widely separated areas. Even the programming concepts are typical of those found on today's cable TV systems.

One point of interest is mentioned on the first page, as the proprietor of the system is described preparing to rebroadcast a baseball game. During the 1930s, rebroadcasting did not mean replaying a transcription; rather, it meant *recreating* a program (complete with sound effects) for listeners. Prior to economical and reliable long-wire transmission, baseball, boxing, and other sporting events were often broadcast in this way, sometimes from Western Union wire reports.

Television in Three Dimensions (*page 88*)

It is impossible to tell whether this system used its red and green neon tubes in the way early 3-D films used the two colors or whether it used them to simulate color. In either case, it doesn't look as if this one would have worked.

For the last decade or so there has been talk of holographic television, but the limitations of both media seem to preclude this.

Build Yourself a Wristwatch Radio (*page 89*)

Obviously inspired by Chester Gould's *Dick Tracy* comic strip, this little radio was small and light, but only without the other components necessary for its operation.

Your Newspaper by Radio! (*pages 92–93*)

Facsimile transmission was proposed many times in these magazines and may yet see mass popularity. Currently, there are three electronic newspaper experiments ongoing in Great Britain. "Ceefax" and "Oracle," owned by the BBC and the Independent Television Authority, broadcast their signals. The third system, "Viewdata," operated by the British Post Office, is a two-way system sent via phone lines. All three systems display text and illustrations on a standard television set, using an adapter to decode the messages.

Television Programs Sent on Light Beams (*page 95*)

This idea was sound in theory, though coherent light and lasers (which made it practical) were not part of the technology of the decade. As the economy and availability of laser technology increase, the amount of information sent via fiber optics (which contain the light) will increase.

Shooting the Rapids—Thrill of Grand Canyon Scenic Ride (*pages 100–101*)

Disney must have seen this one. It forecasts the mammoth "environmental" thrill rides in his parks and the theme parks that followed. Its predecessors were world's fair attractions like Thompson and Dundy's "A Trip to the Moon" (1901) and Roltair's "Creation" (1904)—both spectacular theatrical "dark rides."

Projector Makes Living Movies (*page 107*)

Any possible need for this room-sized opaque projector was eliminated when television cathode-ray tubes became available later in the decade. In order to produce a satisfactorily bright viewing image, the light source for this device would need to be strong enough to generate abundant heat and would probably fry the subject's facial features.

An adaptation of this idea was depicted in 1939's *The Wizard of Oz.*

Movie Slot Machine Shows Pictures of Latest News Events (*page 109*)

This type of machine actually existed and met with limited acceptance. It selected a reel of film, threaded the projector, played the film, and then returned the reel to its original location. By its nature, it was extremely complex. Most of the applications for these devices were as "movie juke-boxes," known as Soundies, during the 1940s. In the 1960s, a similar French import known as Scopitone appeared very briefly, and the idea may be revived with the arrival of videodiscs.

The Roadside Stand Goes High Hat (*page 22*)

This page and the following one offer examples of novelty architecture. The best remaining example is, of course, Los Angeles's Brown Derby restaurant. Designer Norman Bel Geddes called the style "Coney Island" architecture, and there is a brief discussion of it in his book, *Horizons*. It is interesting that Bel Geddes seemed to enjoy this style of design, though it differed greatly from his own. He called it an expression of the 1930's new "liveliness." Only a few examples remain today, outside of amusement and theme parks.

Airman Builds Novel Runabout (*bottom left, page 125*)

These unusual little three-wheeled vehicles were actually built in Great Britain. The several thousand that were made were known simply as Roes, after the inventor.

Seek Lost City Under Los Angeles (*page 126*)

It is surprising that these magazines did not carry more treasure-hunting features during the Depression. The time was certainly right.

This scheme is reminiscent of the ongoing fascination with the mystery of Oak Island, near Halifax, Nova Scotia. The island is the site of a labyrinth of man-made tunnels. Speculation about what is hidden in the tunnels ranges from the traditional pirate treasure to the lost manuscripts of William Shakespeare.

What Will Your Next Car Look Like? (*pages 130–133*)

The auto on the first page of this article, as well as the Rocket Car on page 134, are reminiscent of R. Buckminster Fuller's Dymaxion Car. This piece acknowledges the growing popularity of the tear-drop shape, the basis of the streamline style.

Other similar designs from this period include Norman Bel Geddes' plans for both private and public transportation (1931–1934) and Raymond Lowey's exquisite designs for autos, taxicabs, and buses. This design movement was preceded, in 1914, by a special Alfa-Romeo designed by Italian coach builder Castagna. Vehicles actually built in this style include the Burney Streamliner (shown at the top of the fourth page) and the Stout Scarab.

The offbeat concept illustrated at the bottom of the fourth page—a compressed-air-powered auto—is not just impractical and inefficient, but most likely dangerous as well. The air tank (on the roof) would probably rupture in an accident. As for economy, the plan ignores the energy expended in running the air compressors to fuel such an auto.

Brain Meter Tests Lawmakers' Intellect (*page 137*)

Ah, if this were only so! Unfortunately, the debate regarding the correlation between brain mass and intelligence has only shown that there is none. Moreover, measuring the outside dimensions of the skull with calipers is absurd.

Iron Whale Swims Ocean Bottom Like Fish (*page 140*)

This design goes right back to Jules Verne for its appearance. There have been several mechanical emulations of animals, another of which was the "ornithopter"—the flying machine that flapped its wings like a bird.

Windmill-Cycle Boat to Cross Atlantic (*page 142*)

Briton William Oldham, who proposed this journey, claimed that the craft pictured here would be stable. As anyone can see, the center of gravity of the craft is so high that the reverse would be true, unless there were a few hundred pounds of ballast in the boat's skimpy keel. The idea of having a windmill drive the propeller is imaginative, but impractical. The system would need to be geared so low that nothing short of a gale could turn the blades rapidly enough to move the propeller at a reasonable speed.

Turbo-Wheel Liners Speed Across Seas (*page 143*)

This fanciful, unattributed, and unsigned article may have been the creation of Weston Farmer, a major influence on *Modern Mechanix* and occasionally described in the magazine's masthead as a "naval architect and designer of light planes." Farmer is characterized by a former staffer as "the brains of the outfit," who possessed a vivid imagination.

Aero-Drive Desert Bus Replaces Camels (*page 144*)

The inconsistencies in this plan are that the forces necessary to move the bus would be tremendous and the prop wash would produce huge clouds of sand in its wake.

Mysterious New Aircraft Powered by Reaction Motor (*page 150*)

The most mysterious thing about this aircraft (and the one on the following page) is that it was taken seriously for a second. Both ignore an elementary law of physics that states that the center of a mass cannot be moved in an isolated system—the force must come from outside. Therefore, no matter how many weights of any size were shuttled about inside either one of these, no forward or upward motion would result. The idea did, however, provide a few pages of fairly intriguing copy.

The Autogiro—How and Why It Flies (*page 151*)

The autogiro (or autogyro) was the darling of popular aviation during the 1930s. Despite the unusual appearance, the rotary wing (the blades) was quite effective, and the autogyro's claims were indeed valid. This type of craft lost out to the helicopter in the end, and the predictions of an autogyro in every garage were soon forgotten.

At Last—A Convertible Auto-Plane (*pages 152–153*)

The safety of a propeller-driven auto on busy streets is debatable. One thing that is more certain is that the Flying Silo—the Gee Bee air racer pictured on the first page—was a notoriously dangerous and difficult aircraft to fly. Doolittle, as legend goes, was fortunate to live to tell about his Cleveland air race victory.

New Rail Car Runs on Air-Electric Perpetual Drive (*page 163*)

Fortunately, this article admits that the invention is "contrary to all principles of engineering." Perpetual motion schemes never seem to go away. Most of them have involved elliptically shaped wheels with swinging counterweights that supposedly neutralize the effect of gravity. No perpetual motion device has ever proved workable, and this one goes one step further by proposing a simplistic and inefficient approach to the problem, while confounding the reader with its complexity.

Rocketing to the Moon (*pages 164–168*)

Goddard, of course, was the developer of the liquid propellant rocket, the basis of missile and space travel technology as we know it. Looking backward, the energetics of a moon voyage are *comparatively* simple. Goddard's miscalculation of the forty-eight hours necessary for the trip can only be attributed to a bad guess.

Most Scientific Fiction Can't Come True (*pages 170–173*)

This is one of the few instances where *negative* predictions were put forth in these magazines. Rocket development is scoffed at, and a moon voyage is ruled out because of the lack of air in the moon's atmosphere. The statement about gravity, in the caption on page 3 of the article is, of course, totally inaccurate.

It is puzzling why this piece was published because other predictions in the same magazine were far more radical than these.

MM's Cover from Painting to Magazine (*page 177*)

This page is included as credit to the creator of many of the remarkable *Modern Mechanix* covers included in this book, George Rozen. Rozen and his twin brother, Jerome, possessed nearly identical painting styles, both marked by a bold compositional sense and vivid use of color. Their drafting styles were strongly realistic, and both brothers later contributed heavily to pulp magazines. George produced dozens of covers for *The Shadow* series, and Jerome worked on *Nick Carter* covers. These, however, represent only a few of dozens of titles the brothers worked on.